Z –

If you haven't yet, you should
get to the top of Pedernal –
Just be careful,

Daddo

WHERE
WITH
ALL

Roman Ramsey

Acknowledgements

Thanks to Geraint Smith for the generous use of his exquisite photograph gracing the cover.

To Cate, for her continued support, keen eye and song:

"Long Gone Man" by Cate McDonald 2020.

Dedication

To those, like our heroes inside, who engage in the elusive pursuit of "truth" and "knowing," not only in their personal relationships but a larger, overreaching sense, especially in these times when information is cheap, sources are dubious and the intent to deceive is rampant.

And to Kim, as honest as they come, for keeping me laughing during a pandemic.

1

June 1973

Davis Takes His Lumps

Once Davis was sure he knew the eventual track of his bullet, HIS path became clear. He would report back to his unit and take his lumps. Yes, he had shot his M-1 into a crowd of unarmed students on American soil and, yes, four of those students had died, with another nine injured, but he knew now, beyond any shadow of a doubt, his lone round had not found human flesh.

From what he had heard, charges were being brought but depending on whose account you listened to, either the shooters were totally justified and those ne'er-do-well protestors had it coming to them—or this was the greatest tragedy in American history.

It didn't matter to him. He knew.

Granted, his "evidence" wasn't going to hold up in a court of law: his position on the hill, his line of sight and the hole in the tree where someone had fished the slug out. What was questionable was how he came about that information—passed along by his former girlfriend based on intel she had gotten from an evil entity in an attempt to get her to come over to the Dark Side. That part of his knowledge he might just keep to himself. What mattered to him was he knew he hadn't shot anyone. Besides, there was the matter of his intent—he certainly didn't MEAN to hurt anyone; his gun had fired inadvertently.

Sure, he had flipped off the safety after a protestor had beaned him in the helmet with a chunk of concrete, and yes, he had taken aim at the back of that tie-dyed target as he ran in fear, but he hadn't pulled the trigger there. The involuntary contraction of his finger would come later.

Armed with that information, Davis turned himself in to the National Guard authorities, exactly 1,126 days after not reporting for duty.

He would accept responsibility for going AWOL, he would go through whatever legal machinations were in store for him, but he would do it unburdened with guilt.

He KNEW.

He knew that and a whole lot more since that fateful day at Kent State. What he didn't know was what trajectory his life would follow after.

Not that he had before. The last three plus years had been lived with no regard for the future, taking what each new day offered and making the best of it. By making this decision—to turn himself in—he was leaving his "new" identity behind and putting himself at the mercy of the authorities. Whereas before, every day had been a new blank canvas—sometimes literally—now he would succumb daily to the whims of others, and he was OK with that.

What Davis did find about his life on the lam was the consequences of turning himself in were not nearly as heinous as he had made it out to be. Any member of active-duty military, that is, in this case, regular Army, who fails to report when and where they are expected is considered absent without leave (AWOL). Even if you're just a few minutes late to a drill, you could be considered AWOL, and subject to penalty. The Reserves, however, handle AWOL a bit differently than their active-duty counterparts. And in this case, there were a whole lot of extenuating circumstances surrounding Davis's status, not the least of which was he was one of the accused shooters.

Technically, Davis was considered an "unsatisfactory participant" for missing his monthly obligations and punishment was going to be relegated to whatever sanctions local brass felt was appropriate, which again, fell into the camp of it-depends-who-you-ask. Public opinion, and even opinion amongst his cohorts was divided. The gun-nuts, the military gung-ho were spouting "You're damn right they shot." The pacifists were placing the Guardsmen in an untenable position of following an order that may or may not have been given. Davis was willing to surrender to whatever the court decided, which would end up putting his future in limbo for years to come.

Acceptance back into the ranks was another issue. He was shunned by the hard-core while achieving almost hero status by those soldiers whose participation on that day in May of 1970 had been reluctant. Davis didn't care; he had grown used to solitude in his time sequestering himself in New Mexico, although more recently, his reunion with Becca in New Mexico was going to make staying in Ohio that much harder.

Except for Mary, that is.

2

July 1973

Curious Mary

Mary had discovered Davis sobbing at the site of the shooting, granted, a thousand plus days later, but still... suffering a breakdown of sorts at having discovered his bullet had not injured or killed anyone. She had been walking across campus and came upon him curled up in a fetal position at the base of a tree. Not one to let a fellow human suffer alone, she had embraced him, just letting him weep.

Gradually, she was able to get some of his story out of him—that he had been a Guardsman on that fatal day. Everyone even remotely associated with that university lived and breathed the event even years later. Mary's first impulse had been one of compassion for another's suffering. When she was finally able to cajole Davis's story out of him, it just made it that much more... interesting.

She took Davis home to her apartment, just off campus in an area where many of the support staff of the university lived. She had attended Kent State and graduated eleven years earlier, having stayed on after graduation and now had worked her way up to an assistant director of Human Resources.

She fixed Davis up on her couch for the night. Emotionally exhausted, he had fallen into a deep, untroubled sleep. While his future was uncertain, he knew the general direction he was headed, which was back into the system.

Davis woke to the smell of coffee brewing and bacon frying. That smell always took him back to the first day at Woodstock, when he and his friends had pulled together their bacon-and-eggs feast on a tiny camp stove. Thoughts of Woodstock always included Becca and he thought back to the somewhat cryptic phone call he had very recently made. He had not communicated all he had been experiencing; at that time, it wasn't especially clear even to him.

And now, here they were: apart again.

Slightly disoriented, he recollected the events of the previous day and the life-changing revelation about his role in the shootings. Guilt over the possibility of killing or injuring one of those protestors on the Kent State campus had colored everything he had done over the last almost forty months.

Interestingly, in some ways, it had DEcolored them—in his new incarnation as a painter, his work had gotten somber, dark. He looked down at his fingers, stained from constant contact with his medium, since he didn't use brushes. It gave the skin on his hands a greyish cast—dead, devoid of life.

He felt lighter now, but lighter with a heavy task facing him—turning himself in to the Guard to face the music around being a part of something he hadn't signed on for. At the same time, he knew it was the right thing to do.

He also knew the other "right" thing to do was to call Becca back and tell her his plans, which included staying in Ohio. There were still questions: stay where? Ask Becca to come? What would he do for work? Would he continue to paint?

Those questions buzzed around his head like so many no-see-ums until they were interrupted by Mary presenting him with a plateful of breakfast. The works: scrambled eggs, bacon, toast, orange slices and hash browns.

"I hope you're hungry," she said.

Davis inhaled and let the scent of the food chain bombard him. He hadn't paid much attention to sustenance over the last couple of days, feeding his obsession instead.

"Starving, actually. Thank you."

Mary's plate was every bit as full as Davis's and they dug in, silently. After the first few mouthfuls, Mary said, "So, something tells me there is a story behind your emotional..." and here she hesitated, looking for the right word.

Davis filled in her silence despite half a mouthful of food. "Display? Breakdown? Expulsion?"

The last word was accompanied by a few fragments of scrambled eggs spewing from his mouth, the symbolism not being lost on either of them. Davis started laughing, trying hard to keep the rest of his mouthful intact. He put the napkin Mary had supplied over his mouth and managed to keep the rest of the food inside but it sent the two of them into a fit of laughter. When he was finally able to swallow, his eyes tearing from the laughter, he said, "Oh, it feels good to laugh again."

"Yeah, laughter is good for what ails ya," she replied. "So is confession. I know you don't know me, but sometimes a stranger is the best kind of person to unload on. It's Saturday, and I've only got a few errands to run. My ears are yours if you want to talk."

Davis looked over at her. She was about his age, maybe a little older. He recalled weeping into her long blond hair and her softness as she had embraced him in his despair. He remembered her smelling faintly of cinnamon, or was he confusing that part with breakfast?

"I don't want to burden you. Without getting overly dramatic, this is my cross to bear." In the back of his mind, Davis went to the image of the cross on the hill back in New Mexico he had painted.

Mary debated whether to push or just let him be. Having finished her meal, she rose and started clearing dishes, fully intent on letting it go.

But she couldn't.

As she was shuffling back and forth to the kitchenette, her curiosity got the better of her. "You mentioned you were one of the Guardsmen there that day."

She let the statement hang, but it was really more of a question.

Davis was still finishing up his breakfast and he had been lost in thought about what he had left behind in New Mexico.

"Uh, yeah, I was there."

"That must have been, what? Scary? Confusing?"

She came to the table to fetch his now empty plate and laid her left hand on his shoulder. Pausing, holding the plate in her right hand, her eyes settled into his. While he hadn't wanted to get into the details of what had happened, his instinct was this was a safe place, he wasn't going to be harshly judged.

Gently wresting the plate from Mary's hand, he set it back on the table, without breaking their eye contact.

"Pull up a chair," he said.

Mary did, close enough she could lightly rest a hand on his knee, with her elbow on the table (manners be damned!) propping up her head. Over the next half hour, Davis proceeded to tell his story: how his rifle had accidently gone off, the chaos, the horror of realizing people had been hit, the 67 shots in thirteen seconds, and then finding out later four people had died and another nine had been injured.

He hadn't practiced his story. Indeed, this was the first time he had told it as it had played out, but in the back of his mind, he was aware it wasn't the whole story. While details were spilling out at a rate that surprised him, he realized he was censoring somewhat as he went along, deleting one main aspect of the tale.

Becca.

Davis had Mary's full attention while the egg scraps crusted and bacon grease congealed on the plates. He told her the part about going AWOL and his road trip across the country and how the specter of the shooting had hung over him, compelling him to come back and get the answers he needed.

"So, did you?" she asked.

"Did I what?"

"Get the answers you needed?"

Davis hesitated, not sure he wanted to open the can of worms that ultimately led to his surety.

"Yeah," he answered, but his reply came out so softly it was almost a whisper.

"And?"

"And I know my round didn't hit anyone. It actually went through the sculpture and hit a tree."

Mary's sympathetic nature was at the forefront, but her critical mind was wanting to ask the question, Are you sure? It slipped out. "You know that?"

"Yeah, I know it." He let his mind wrap around all the "evidence" he had to support that claim and reasserted his answer, "I KNOW it."

Absent in his declaration was his relationship with Becca, her vision and encounter around his experience and their insights that led him to his discovery. It was a huge gaping hole in the story but one that very few were going to accept at face value. Hell, he wasn't sure HE could accept it at face value; one had to suspend certain ideas about normality.

"Well, that must be a relief," Mary said.

"Yes. Yes, it is." Davis leaned back in the chair, breaking the bubble that had surrounded them while he had told his story. Mary removed her hand from his knee. It left a damp, sweaty mark there.

"So," and here Mary hesitated, her empathetic side telling her to stop and her curiosity poking her to push for more information. Her curiosity won. "Did they do ballistics testing? Is that how you knew?"

Davis drew back. "Are you an attorney for the defense or the prosecution?"

"I'm sorry; I shouldn't have said anything else." Mary stood and hurriedly started clearing the table of the congealing dishes.

Davis sat in his chair, looking into the distance, imagining himself sitting in a witness box, having to answer questions like these. When he went through the possible scenarios, he had come around to absolutely telling the truth: "Yes, I fired," and "No, I did not intend to shoot anyone." Where he ran into a problem was the answer to possible incriminating questions: "Did you aim at anyone?" (He had, but that was not when he shot), and "How did your rifle discharge if you didn't intend to shoot?" He was not proud of the fact his weapon had fired accidently. He even imagined a tough prosecutor asking him, almost sarcastically, "Oh, you had a gun that fired by itself?"

And his answer had to be, "No, I fired the gun, but I didn't hit anyone."

He imagined the follow-up question would then be, "Which is it? If you fired accidently, how can you know where your bullet ended up? But if you know where your bullet ended up, you must have aimed there." And then telling the court he knew where his bullet went because his girlfriend had a vision with a dark entity who told her Davis couldn't hit the broad side of a barn and cryptically where his bullet did indeed land. It just didn't sound to him like credible testimony.

All this whirled through his head while Mary busied herself in the kitchen. He got up from the table and approached her.

"I don't know if they have done ballistics testing or not. But I know my bullet didn't hit anyone. There are some things you just KNOW."

Also missing from the explanation was the experience of certainty that Davis had with Becca over their inside world as a result of their grafting:

exchanging small sections of their flesh in an ancient ritual Becca had been exposed to and actually participated in during her time serving with the Peace Corps in Africa. While they didn't always know everything the other was thinking or feeling, most of the time, no additional information was necessary. Having been reunited with Becca (again) and now being separated (again) was serving as a constant reminder of the bond they had.

And how much he was missing her.

Mary put the plate she was washing into the dishrack and put her soapy hand gently on Davis's forearm (yeah, she was a toucher). "Just so you know, I believe you. But if we are keeping score, I'd have to put that testimony in the prosecutor's column."

"That may be. But it doesn't matter what conclusions they come up with. I don't have any control over that. I'm turning myself in and I will accept their verdicts. Regardless of how I say it: "my rifle discharged," "it went off accidently," I didn't mean to shoot"—I fired my weapon and I am going to take responsibility for that. If you're going to carry a gun for any reason, you've got to be prepared for consequences."

"Huh. So, you are going to do the stand-up thing."

Davis looked at her, not having considered that value assessment of his decision. "Yeah. It's the right thing to do. I should not have fired my rifle, but I did. And I am willing to accept whatever penalties might come as a result."

3

Freedom's Just Another Word for

"Nothin' Left to Lose"

Davis liked the sound and the subsequent feel of Mary's assessment: "stand-up." His life over the last couple of years—on the lam (in his eyes anyway), had a fair amount of anxiety attached to it. Having people know him by his middle name, "Miles," was part of that. He was afraid the military was always around the corner, waiting to throw him in the brig for insubordination. Next on his list of 'right' things to do was to call Becca and let her know what his plans were.

It had been just a day since he had talked to her, right after the revelation about his bullet. He had not been thinking clearly at all and didn't have an accurate recollection of the conversation—only he hadn't told her much and now here they were. Separated again.

"Hi Bec. It's Davis."

"Davis! Where are you? Are you OK?"

"Yeah, I'm fine. I'm still in Ohio."

"Oh. OK."

A silence hung on the line, neither of them sure what to say next.

In the short silence, Becca cycled through the emotions she had experienced since Davis's phone call: relief, frustration, anger, sadness, loss, resignation. She realized the relief did not cancel out the smorgasbord of other shit that went along with it.

Davis spoke first. "I... I'm sorry, Becca. I guess my call could be viewed as having been somewhat incomplete."

"OK. I'll grant you that. What else ya got?"

"You sound mad."

"That's very perceptive of you. But really, Davis, that only goes a very short way in describing everything I'm feeling..." And with that, Becca launched into a five-minute tirade about how she REALLY felt. Davis sat on the other end of the line, the receiver held away from his ear, knowing he fully had this harangue coming, determined to sit through it and take his medicine for what he himself deemed bad behavior.

"...and so now what do you suggest we do?"

Davis gave the ensuing silence a few seconds to land, then moved the receiver back to his ear, realizing Becca had left him with the world's most open-ended question and he didn't have a clue as to how to answer it. He opened his mouth to speak and the beginning of an "I" tumbled out, unfully formed, a guttural utterance, unlike any semblance of language.

Becca pounced. "That's it?! That's all you've got?"

Davis realized that, despite all the time he had spent procrastinating about this call, he had not prepared what he wanted to say. Becca pushed again and he interrupted her, "Becca, Becca, Becca..."

She stopped talking.

"The good news is we were found to be not at fault. The Attorney General, John Mitchell, stepped in and basically said we were off the hook. But for me, as you well know, that's not the whole story. I shot and then, once it started looking like the shit was gonna hit the fan, I ran. I took the coward's way out. That is not who I am. That is not who I want to be. I want to take whatever punishment the Guard is going to mete out for deserting and then move on. I don't want to spend the rest of my life looking over my shoulder. This could be a lot worse; I could be on trial for murder, but I think the politics of this were in my favor. But I need to deal with how I handled this."

Now it was Becca's turn to be silenced. She spent a moment "checking in" with her intuition she had come to trust so well and it helped her to shift her perspective.

"OK. I get it. I just feel like we had gotten to a place of balance, where we could just BE. And now we are apart again. Obviously, you are going to need to stay in Ohio. Do you want me to come there?"

Davis had considered this possibility but had not come up with an answer, and now here he was, faced with having to make another decision.

"I can't ask you to do that; there is so much uncertainty. Why don't we wait and see what's going to happen? At the very least, I have the rest of my obligation to the Guard. This is a different reality than what I had in New Mexico."

Becca paused to consider not only what Davis had left behind—his burgeoning career as an artist—but also the pastoral quality of her life, including some of the new developments that had occurred since his departure. Without consciously thinking about it, Becca found herself surrounded in song, melody, music. It was a presence that followed her constantly and she was convinced it was a result of having grafted with Davis; somehow adopting his music gene. She let the music fade into the background and returned to the conversation.

"I have to say I am torn about us being together. You know—I KNOW you know—about how good we can be together. And yet, there always seems to be some force that drives us apart, whether it's internal or external. There's a part of me that doesn't want to ever be apart from you and another part that doesn't want to have to resist the things that keep us apart. I just wish it could be easy."

"Easy," Davis repeated, and let that concept surround him for a brief moment. "Yeah, I like the easy part, too." He immediately felt himself stir, sexually. But he also knew it wasn't just about the sex; it was their connection; they were bound.

"So, now what?" Becca asked.

"Stay there. Let's let the situation here unfold. We can stay in touch and just play it by ear, if I may be allowed a musical metaphor."

"Ok, I can do that. And speaking of music..." Becca went on to tell him about her experience in the shower, where she had "discovered" her voice, literally. How, all of a sudden, she could sing. Davis let her gush about the new sounds she could make, and how she understood the sounds musicians made: how she "got" music, as a construct. He let her go on, understanding the concept completely, having grown up around it, but never wanting to fully adopt it himself.

He knew it was from their graft; there was no doubt in his mind, and while a part of him wished he had had it, he was thrilled to have passed it on to her. "I guess some things skip a generation," he said. "Hey, sing something for me!"

"Over the phone?"

"Sure, why not? You'll never have a more supportive audience."

Becca gathered herself and reversed the phone receiver in her hand, wrapped the cord around it a few times so the mouthpiece presented itself as a microphone and launched into a version of "Me and Bobby McGee," the Kristofferson song made famous by Janis Joplin.

The fidelity on Davis's end was terrible: tinny, flat, one-dimensional. But that's not what he heard. What made its way through to him was not only pitch-perfect, but rich and soulful. He imagined Becca rising up on her toes, singing with her whole body, eyes closed, bringing the song to life with a hint of a smile on her lips and felt a warmth go through his body. Tears welled up in his eyes; this was what music done right was supposed to do—move you.

Yep, he thought, she's got it.

4

September 1973

A Prayer for Davis

Becca had been surprised, but not, by Davis's decision. They were both vagabond spirits. Gypsies. Wanderers. And it seemed like the rest of the world was doing the same thing. People were not staying in one place anymore. She was the perfect example, at 24 years old she had been to Africa with the Peace Corps then came back and traveled through 21 states.

And Davis's situation had serious ethical and moral components to it. Still, as she hung up the phone, she felt a sense of loss. This was going to be one of those periods she referred to as 'without.' One of her favorite phrases, though, was 'nature abhors a vacuum.' As much as she missed Davis, she was not prone to pining. Now she had music, and once she had engaged, she realized what a wide world she was stepping into. It was like learning a new language, and she immersed herself in it. In a way, not having a "significant other," (that new term tickled her) freed up a lot of time.

She sang constantly. It was fall of 1973. The previous ten years had provided the music world with an explosion of creativity, although now it seemed like there was going to be another shift. The rock world had lost three of its most influential innovators: Hendrix, Joplin and Jim Morrison, all to supposed drug overdoses. After Morrison's death in 1971, which came after Hendrix' and Joplin's, Becca thought back to the music "vision" she had had years ago about the death of what was popular at the time during the heyday of the hippie movement. She wondered if it was a

17

foreshadowing of what was to come: a mechanized, canned pablum for the masses.

Yes, disco was right around the corner.

That was never going to be Becca's cup of tea and while that would flourish it would afford her the chance to hone her musicianship, her voice and her attitude for the musical revolution that was to spring up in reaction to the cookie-cutter world of disco.

She bought a used Yamaha acoustic guitar, and in her solitude, practiced chords and solo runs over and over. It came easy to her. But while most of her hippie brethren in Taos were stuck in the rock music that defined their generation, Becca sought out all kinds of music: classical, country, jazz, folk, soul, even 40's Big Band and crooners like Sinatra. When she would hear something new and obscure, she would soak it in like a sponge.

To her, anything with a melody was a joyful noise and it would all go into what would much later be described as a data base, but for then, it was simply memory and all she had to do was to hear something once and she could replicate it.

She tackled piano, and that came easy also. There was an old upright at one of the communes and she would lay her fingers on those keys every chance she got.

She became a regular on the plaza in Taos, setting up her guitar case and playing for the tourists; it wasn't long before she had gotten a regular gig at The Taos Inn. She was a natural in front of crowds, having found her stage presence early on with all of her rabble-rousing on college campuses. Not being classically trained in music theory, she was not a musician who played music around a construct, but rather an innate understanding. When Kiki Dee released "I Got the Music in Me" in 1974, for Becca, nothing could have summed up her relationship with music any more succinctly. She quickly outgrew the music scene in Taos and would venture down to Santa Fe and Albuquerque to find more of an audience and also more collaboration, because, while creating music on her own was satisfying, the synergy she felt when creating it with others amplified it tenfold.

She kept in touch with Davis periodically. They would talk on the phone once a month or so. Sometimes he would call, sometimes her; they still had their psychic connection, even separated by miles. Very often, the phone would ring and when one of them would answer, the first thing either would say would be, "I was just thinking about you."

It was spring of 1974 and Davis had called. Becca could tell instantlysomething was wrong.

"What's going on?" she asked.

"The new Attorney General has reopened the case against the National Guard. The whole thing is going to start over again. It's kind of weird though; what we're being charged with is depriving the protestors of their constitutional rights."

"Well, that doesn't sound so serious."

"It could be. They're felony charges. I don't know what's going to come next. There are very passionate arguments on both sides about the fate of the shooters. Mine will be in the hands of prosecutors and ultimately a jury of my peers and I have no idea how long it's going to take. One thing I know is everyone that had a rifle that day signed it out on a log and all the rifles got turned back in and because of that they should know which ones were fired. The rifle I signed out was fired. Period. One rumor I heard, though, was the log that had all of our rifle sign-outs has disappeared, so there is no evidence of who fired what."

"That's in your favor, right?"

"Yes, but I'm not confident about what the judge or jury will find. You and I both KNOW my bullet didn't hit anyone, but the prosecution is going to try their best to hang this on someone. There are people out there who want their pound of flesh."

"Yeah, I get that. At the end of the day, something happened that shouldn't have, and it's natural to want to lay blame."

"What scares me is there are some people who feel like the protestors got what was coming to them, and in their heart of hearts, this is what happens. What also scares me is that's the kind of thinking that could keep me out of jail. And there's something about that just isn't right."

"Be careful, Davis. You're starting to sound like a martyr."

"I know. At this point, I have surrendered myself over to the system. Before, I ran, not trusting I wouldn't get punished for something I didn't intend. I don't know if we will be asked to take the stand, I don't know if I will have a voice in this, I don't know anything else right now."

"Is there anything I can do?"

"This is going to sound strange coming from me, but... pray for me."

Becca was a little taken aback. "Pray?"

"I know, I know... where's that coming from, right?"

In the time they had spent together, organized religion and the trappings around it were not a part of either of their spiritual leanings.

"Yes," Becca hesitated, "and no. I know you want the right outcome in this. You made a mistake and you hope to not have to pay a price for it. So, yes: I'll pray for you, Davis."

"Thanks, Becca."

While Becca's spiritual path did not include "prayer" in the sense most people would think of it, she knew what it was that Davis needed, and whether it was called "support" or "intent" or "sending good vibes his way," she was certainly willing to provide that.

Once she had some time alone and was able to go "inside," she considered what might be the best outcome for Davis, and that did not exist without imagining how that dovetailed with her own life. She knew him, she knew he was innocent—well, yes, he did shoot his gun toward a crowd of American citizens—but it had been accidental. She knew it was not his intent to harm anyone. The best outcome of the trial would be for him to be found not guilty.

She thought too of the families that had lost loved ones and those who got injured and the scars they would take forward. Was there justice in a "not guilty" verdict? Were all of the Guardsmen going to be tried together? Did some of the others intend to cause harm? She didn't have answers to these questions and felt herself looping around in circles.

Becca hiked to one of her favorite places up in the mountains, a grove of nothing but aspens. The leaves had started to turn and created a golden glow about her. She was all alone and sincerely wanted to send Davis her support, so she knelt into the soft earth. Some of the leaves had already fallen and created a soft cushion beneath her. She bowed her head, feeling the sun on her bare neck. She debated about what to do with her hands—Do I place them flat against each other or interlock my fingers? She alternated between the two before deciding the interlocked finger approach felt more appropriate.

She stopped herself. Just pray, she admonished herself. Pray? I don't know how to do that. Like, get on my knees and fold my hands?

A voice answered, indeterminate, genderless, almost mocking, "Sure, why not? Millions of people do it all the time. It's not going to kill you. Really, don't worry; there won't be any lightning bolts."

But I don't believe in God, she responded, without actually voicing it.

"A minor detail. We'll just set that aside for now."

"Dear God..."

"No, no, no," the voice whispered at her. "This isn't about any god, especially if you're not a believer. You're making this harder than it has to be. You already know how to pray. You did it in Africa with Embartu. You do it every time you do a reading for someone, you do it when you meditate. Just open up your heart and send out your best resolve around what Davis is going through. Not an outcome, not a solution, just what's just."

Becca realized the "voice" she was "hearing" was her own thoughts, coming from another part of her, a part outside of her, but inside at the same time. She settled in and became a part of the aspen forest. The breeze rustled the leaves slightly, just enough for them to deserve their "quaking" nickname. The temperature was neither too hot nor cold.

While there were times Becca felt like she had premonitions about the future, she didn't experience any of that, nor did she try to impose what should come of Davis's legal proceedings, only that it would somehow end not only in his favor but for everyone involved. The analytical part of her knew on some level that wasn't possible, but she didn't allow that criticism to impose.

She didn't know how long she stayed that way, but eventually became aware of her hands starting to lose circulation. She slowly unclasped them and repositioned her legs so her ass and feet were on the ground. She lifted her head to the sky, taking into the azure blue of the New Mexico fall framed by the tallest aspen branches. She breathed the damp air, slightly moldy as the leaves had already begun to decay. The earth was getting ready to rest. Winter would be coming soon and she felt a sense of the ebb and flow of the seasons.

She realized she had not considered any of how whatever was going to happen was going to affect her, but decided there would be time for that as it all unfolded.

So, like that? she thought to herself.

She stood up, did a 360 degree turn taking in the beauty of her surroundings, dusted off her knees and butt and made her way down the mountain.

5

April 1974

All Kinds of Trouble

"So, what are you going to do?"

"I seem to be getting that question a lot," Davis said to Mary.

"I think it's good to be prepared for whatever is coming next."

"I agree. Until something comes along you thought was resolved and rears its ugly head again."

"It turned out OK last time; maybe that'll happen again."

"What worries me is there are people out there who were not satisfied with the verdict and never will be and this will never go away until they get what they want."

"What do you think that is?"

"An eye for an eye. Four young people died that day. Like in the Neil Young song, 'What if you knew her and found her dead on the ground?' I can't imagine getting that phone call as a parent that said their child was killed today by a National Guardsman."

Davis had his hands in his pockets and fingered the long, sharp-tipped rifle bullet he kept there as a reminder of that day. In the time he had been "away" as he liked to refer to it, he had taken on a whole different life as an artist. In some ways, that time didn't seem real to him anymore, almost like he had dreamt it. He stood there, his head bowed, his body slumped. Mary came up behind him and slipped her left arm around him with her hand on his belly. With her right hand, she rubbed circles on his back.

She whispered, "Davis, I'm so sorry you have to go through this again." She slipped her other arm around him and pressed herself up against him, leaning the side of her face against his back. They had known each other for just a short while and though their first contact had been physical, it had not crossed over into being romantic or sexual.

Not that it hadn't occurred to either of them; Mary had found Davis attractive from the getgo, but had come to know about his relationship, such as it was, with Becca.

Davis didn't know what he was feeling. Or doing.

Especially in this moment. Any time he talked about the "incident," as he referred to it, it put him in a limited state of perception, not only of his surroundings but of matters at hand, both immediate and long term.

Consequently, what he processed in the moment was going from considering facing the parent of someone his age who had lost their child, wanting some justice and even vengeance for that to the very immediate sensation of Mary, pressing up against him.

Mary pressing up against him felt a lot better than the alternative. He allowed himself to just experience that. It had the palliative effect Mary had intended. But as Davis relaxed into her embrace, something shifted. Davis felt it first as he became aware of the heat of her body against his. Mary was no casual hugger, affectionate with all her friends, male and female; there were no sideways hugs or air kisses. If she hugged you, you were going to get full-on Mary.

He took his hands from his pockets and gently loosened her grip from his waist, but only enough so he could spin and face her. Her full breasts followed his body as he repositioned himself. She was almost as tall as him and it put them face-to-face. Suddenly, it didn't feel like a friendly hug, and neither one of them was attempting to give any ground to move it back in that direction.

There's a certain intimacy about being close enough to someone to breathe their air AND for that person to allow you to do that. Davis inhaled slowly though his heartrate had increased considerably. His arms had found their way over hers and his hands settled against the muscles of her back. She was wearing a soft sweater and he let his fingers indulge there.

He also felt himself getting hard and once he realized it, he pulled slightly away from her hips.

"It's okay," she whispered, so softly he almost didn't hear her despite her mouth being just inches from his. She let her right hand slide farther down his back and pulled him back into her. He responded in kind by dropping his hand down her back until it reached the curve of her ass, spreading his fingers and pulling her into him.

"Yeah. Okay," he said.

"Is it?"

"Okay?"

"Yeah, Okay."

"It feels okay."

"Yeah, I'll agree with you there, but IS it okay?"

Davis realized this was a question that was soliciting a wider perspective.

He released his hold on Mary's butt, and brought his hand up between the two of them, placing his fingers gently on Mary's slightly parted lips. He let his touch linger there and said, "Which part of me do you want to have answer that question?"

She backed away from his touch but not more than an inch. "That's what I thought," she said. "Do you smell that?" she asked.

Davis inhaled but wasn't sure which of the subtle aromas he was experiencing she was referring to. He gave her a quizzical look.

"It smells to me like trouble," she said, the spell broken.

They gently pushed each other away.

Yeah, Davis thought. *Could be.*

6

Tempting

Whenever Davis tried to make sense of his relationship with Becca, he invariably came back to their connection, which existed on so many levels. Sure, there was the mind-blowing sex, but that had a tendency to wane. No, it was more the intellectual compatibility, the mind-and-heart-meld and the amount of plain fun they had together; they liked the same food, the same music, the same ideas. But probably most important to him was the innate trust he had in her. But yet, here he was, wrapped up (sorta) in the arms of another woman.

He felt guilty about that and then proud of himself for not indulging further, but what he was struggling with was the attraction to another woman at all. That was not the way it was supposed to be, was it? *Why am I attracted to other women? Isn't it supposed to be just one man/one woman? I mean, I know other people cheat, but I would never do that...* And there was no denying that Mary, had I encouraged her at all, would have been a willing participant in some kind of funny business.

A devil showed up in his ear: "Man, Becca would never know; you should go for it!"

"Oh, no; you don't understand. She would absolutely know."

"Why? Because of your grafting thing? Shit, she might suspect it, but then all you would have to do is deny it. It's perfect; she trusts you!"

"Isn't that the point?"

"Oh, what? Are you gonna go all 'altar boy' on me now? Are you forgetting she left you back in Ohio?"

"I left her."

"We're splitting hairs here; you simultaneously left each other. But you at least had a good reason; the Man was going to charge you with murder."

"You make a good argument. You should be an attorney."

"Huh, I get that a lot."

"Yeah, that would be some kind of justice, wouldn't it?"

"Sure would. But here's the deal; you don't have to actually fuck her; just play around. Y'know, have some fun while you can. What happens if you end up in jail for the rest of your life? There won't be any Marys in the pokey. For all you know, you could end up <u>being</u> somebody's Mary."

"Thanks for the encouraging scenario. That's just what I needed, a worst-case predilection into the state of my love life going forward."

"I'm just sayin'; you gotta look at both sides. And speaking of both sides, have you seen both of Mary's sides? She's fuckin' hot."

Davis's attention went to a visage of Mary he hadn't known he was carrying around: her height translated to long limbs, especially her legs. Her thighs seemed unnaturally long. Terribly long. Wrap-all-the-way-around-me long. Her skin was perfect, unblemished, well, except for that one chocolate chip mole on her neck. Then there was the cornsilk hair almost down to her waist. Davis thought back to that first encounter when she had found him sobbing near the base of the tree where his bullet had finished its flight and how he had gotten lost in her hair. It was perfectly straight and fine, yielding, insulating, warm... and that smell...

Davis brought himself back to "reality," which was the devil-persuader haranguing him in his ear. Davis said, "I know what you're trying to do."

"Hey, hey, hey; let's not get all judgmental here. I've got your best interests at heart. But if you want to go through life being a goody-goody who never ends up having fun and then ends up being Big George's best friend in prison, that's up to you."

"Do you know something I don't?"

"I'm not saying I do, and I'm not saying I don't, but the fact we are still engaged in this conversation means I must be making some sense, right? I mean, right?"

Davis hunched up his left shoulder reflexively in an unconscious attempt to dislodge his now unwelcome whisperer.

But his relationship with Mary had taken on a new sheen.

7

May 1974

At Least I Got a Song Out of It

Not surprisingly, the very next time he was slated to call Becca, Davis procrastinated. They had gotten into a routine where he would settle in on a Sunday night and call, and they would recount their week to each other. He busied himself with one chore or another and the next thing he knew, he was waking up on Monday and hadn't called. He had gone back to working construction, although everything in his life was secondary to waiting for the trial to begin.

He had gotten home after work and collapsed on the easy chair. When the phone rang, he let his roommate and cousin Tommy answer it, but he knew.

He knew it was her.

Sure enough, Tommy handed the phone over to him without saying a word.

"Hi." Davis injected a little more enthusiasm into his greeting than he was feeling.

"Hi, Davis. How's it going?"

"Good, how about you?"

There was a brief hesitation, then Becca said, "I was kind of expecting you to call yesterday."

"Oh. I... I didn't know it was a set thing."

"It's not, but we had gotten into a routine and I looked forward to hearing about your week. What's going on about the trial?"

Davis explained there wasn't anything new; the date had been set and it was still three weeks before it would start. He switched the focus over to her goings-on.

"Not much, singing and playing a lot. I have a gig coming up on Thursday night down at Claude's in Santa Fe."

"Wow, that's great. It sounds like that's becoming a direction for you."

"Yeah, it seems right. I'm writing some songs but still performing mostly covers: some Carly Simon, some Ronstadt, some Cat Stevens. You know..."

"Yeah."

"So, what else is going on?"

The first thought that popped into Davis's mind was Mary. There wasn't anything to tell, really, at least that was what he had convinced himself, but the fact she was his first response spoke volumes.

Silent volumes. Because that's how it came out: silent.

Then, "Nothing. Just the usual. Work, come home, watch bad TV, read, go to bed."

She knew. She didn't know exactly what, but she knew there was something.

And he knew she knew.

The resulting silence hung heavy on the line, like it had a physical weight to it.

Becca spoke first. "Keep me posted on what's happening with the trial, OK?" She knew it was still a few weeks off, but also knew she wasn't going to hear from him before that. If then.

"Yeah, of course." But Davis and Becca both knew there wasn't any "of course" about it; there wasn't any certainty going forward.

Becca sat staring at the phone after they had hung up, like it was a part of Davis sitting there. While she felt certain something had gone unsaid, and suspected it was another woman, she didn't indulge that speculation. Rather, she sat with what was now becoming the familiar pattern of the two of them coming together then drifting apart.

She reached over to the end table and picked up the spiral stenographer's pad she kept handy.

I might as well get a song out of all of this, she thought. She allowed her confusion to take both sides of what she was feeling: their connection, their closeness and how natural that felt, how easy it was to just assume it would just continue. And the frustration that it didn't.

She scribbled "Long Gone Man" across the top of the page and a song poured out, lost in all they had, and all they didn't.

"Long Gone Man"

Long Gone Man
You've been on my mind
Ever since that line
Long Gone Man
I think you look like him
Whoever he might be
(Chorus)
Long Gone Man
(so) Tall and thin
Won't you let me in?

33

Roman Ramsey

Save me from inside this skin

Let me in

Let me in

Long Gone Man

Where you've been

Hiding all this time

Long Gone Man

Has it found you yet?

What you've been running from

Long Gone Man

Shot at the sky

And now it's falling down

(Bridge)

So long then

My long gone man (2x)

Long Gone Man
Write me soon
Or write me off
I wrote you a song

8

Peter Who?

Becca had wrapped up her gig at the legendary Claude's Bar on Canyon Road and was hanging out after her last set when she was approached by a long-haired man with heavy Buddy Holly-style glasses. "I like your hair," he said.

Becca noticed immediately his hair was also red. "Well, it IS different, until you get two of us standing together."

He laughed. "Hi, I'm Peter," he said and extended his hand.

"Becca," she said.

He shook her hand and then said, "I saw your last set, although it was a little hard to concentrate in here; it's pretty rowdy."

"Yeah, by the end of the night, everyone's pretty liquored up and it gets kinda crazy. There hasn't been a fight yet, but if you stick around, there's almost sure to be some people disagreeing about something enough to want to get physical about it, if that's your thing."

Becca didn't imagine this man standing in front of her was the bar brawling type and was offering up potential fisticuffs somewhat sarcastically.

"Actually, no: not my thing. I'm in the music business. I play too, and sing and write but now I'm getting more into management. Is anyone managing you?"

Becca laughed. "Uh, no. It's all I can do to occasionally book a gig in a dive bar like this; I don't think anyone would be interested in managing this career."

"Don't be so sure. You have something. You're raw, but you can sing and there is a presence about how you carry yourself; you're not afraid to be up in front of people."

"Some of that comes from standing up in front of thousands of protestors with a bullhorn; you learn how to project."

"I noticed you did some covers but also a few tunes I hadn't heard before. Who's writing your original material?"

"Those are mine."

"I thought so. Listen, I'm just passing through and heading back out to the coast. The West Coast. Everything is happening out there right now. LA is hot, and the record companies are looking to sign just about anyone with even a modicum of talent. And you've got more than that."

The noise level had risen considerably and Becca found herself practically shouting to be heard. She had been approached once or twice before to be "represented," but it was usually some drunk guy looking to get laid. This felt different. She drew back a little from Peter, in an attempt to "feel" him, but the atmosphere in the bar was so frenetic she was having trouble doing her usual appraisal.

"LA, huh? I did a swing through California but more up north. I was at Altamont and then spent some time being radical at Berkeley."

"Frisco is still happening, but the scene is really in LA right now. You should be playing the Troubador where all the record execs are looking for talent. Nobody's going to discover you here."

"Damn! I thought that's what you were doing!"

They both laughed over that, then Peter said, "Who knows? Maybe I am. Stranger things have happened. I have to get back to my friends, but, do you have a pen?" Becca scrambled to find one from the bar and a matchbook cover to write on. Peter scribbled his name and a phone number down and handed it to her. "If you make it out there, call me. I know a few people."

"Yeah? Like who?"

Peter opened his mouth to possibly name drop and then thought better of it. "I know a few people," he repeated, then smiled and disappeared back through the crowd to his party.

A seed was planted. Becca knew the music scene was so much more vibrant in the big cites, especially on the coasts, but she hadn't thought yet about making it a career path. She had gotten great responses and ovations whenever she played, but this was feedback from someone in the industry. Wasn't it? She wondered if he was for real and was impressed by the fact he didn't name drop when he probably could have.

9

LA Beckons

As fall settled into winter and the temperature hovered in the 20s, Becca thought more and more about leaving for LA. By January, she had her bus ticket, packed up her few belongings and headed off to the coast, guitar case in hand.

Upwards of twenty hours on buses gave her some time to reflect on what had gotten her to this point, including her relationship with Davis. As much as they communicated both verbally and intuitively, there were always gray areas of understanding. Becca had written most of that off, realizing within her OWN self, there were aspects of cognition, feeling and behavior that were not congruent. She wanted desperately to be able to trust Davis, but her gut was telling her there was something going on he wasn't disclosing. When she went "inside," she saw a woman: tall, blonde, with a bony aquiline nose. She struggled to dismiss the images, writing it off as paranoia and a resulting mistrust that another part of her did not want to acknowledge.

Somewhere around Flagstaff, Arizona, she had fallen asleep, lulled by the drone of the bus engine and the tires gobbling up mile after mile of asphalt. She saw that woman again, in dreamstate, with Davis, and woke suddenly, surprised by her surroundings, but knowing her trepidation was founded.

Out came the legal pad, and she penned a letter.

Dear Davis,

I have left Taos, on my way to Los Angeles to seek "fame and fortune" in the music biz (I'm including quotes around "fame and fortune" for obvious reasons. I can see myself using the airquotes you invented if you were here with me and I was explaining this to you.

But you're not. Here with me, that is.

I don't know what it is that keeps separating us, but here we are again. Apart. And I don't just mean physically; I know you are with someone else, the way there are things I just KNOW. And it pains me you haven't told me.

I know you have other issues you are dealing with around the trial and everything attached to that and I know you probably haven't told me out of a desire to not hurt me. I know, I know, I KNOW.

What I wanted for us was to have the kind of love that transcended all of that—all of everything else, that we KNEW the other was there when needed. I wanted that for me, and every bit as much, I wanted that for you, but apparently, you have turned to someone else. For comfort, for companionship, for sex, for ego—it doesn't matter—you turned to someone else.

I'm letting you go. This is too much uncertainty, too much drama, too much of not enough.

Something shifted in me, too. Around music. I'm thinking I DID get some of your music gene in our graft and it is driving me (literally, as I feel this bus propelling me forward) to fulfill whatever is going to look like. It also feels natural. And easy. I'm writing songs and when I sing and play, it feels joyous, and that's good.

I will continue to fret over your future, that is in the hands of others. You must know I want the best for you. I am aware of your demons as I know you are. I hope sometime soon you will be rid of them and you find a purpose in life; you have so much to contribute.

Thank you for the gifts you've given me; you will always be (in more ways than one) a part of me.

And I will always love you.

Becca

10

Goodbye Again

When Davis received the letter, he was both surprised and not. What he struggled with was a sense of frustration over not being able to control his emotions and subsequently, his behavior. More and more, he became aware there was not a one-way-or-another approach to anything in life, that most of it got lived in the middle, there were no absolutes.

He sat down and crafted a response to Becca's letter.

Dear Becca,

(and I DO mean that sincerely-you are dear to me)

You're right, of course. You're (almost) always right. I both love and hate that about you (kidding). Actually, not kidding. While I have loved how much you know about the world around you and inside of you, it sometimes leaves me feeling less than. Not stupid, but ignorant, out of the loop.

While yes, there is someone else, it's not the BIG someone else. I haven't cheated on you. But there's a part of me that wants to. Not to cheat on you, because I don't want to hurt you, but to be with her.

And I don't like that, so I have resisted it. But you must have picked up on all of that. Right now, she is just a friend, and a good one. Here. Where all of this trial shit is going on.

I know you offered to come with me, and I probably should have taken you up on that, but I felt like I needed to deal with this on my own. Why? I'm not sure. But I see that it has pushed you away. I get it. Now, you don't want to be with me, and I get that too. There are times when I don't want to be with me.

But I will stop whining (for now, anyway).

I'm glad you are pursuing music. I wish I could hear you sing the songs you've written. I fully expect to hear them come across the airwaves someday: your familiar voice, raised in song (probably about your wayward ex-boyfriend). I hope you did get that music gene from me; at least it won't go to waste (and there will have been at least some benefit to you for having spent time with me).

I feel like my life is on hold for now, just waiting to see what my fate will be. I want so much more, but I can't even allow myself to consider what that might look like, if I end up in a prison cell.

I know that all sounds very "woe-is-me" but it is also part of my reality right now.

Take care of yourself. Write good songs. Sing with your whole body.

I will miss you, but maybe our paths will cross again. They seem to have a way of doing that.

Davis

He folded the letter, put it in an envelope, sealed it, wrote her name on the front and then realized he didn't know where to send it.

Another "failure to communicate" he thought. Well, she reads my mind anyway; she'll know what I meant to say.

Yeah.

No.

Regardless of whether Becca got the "message" or not, Davis felt a sense of closure. It felt empty.

Without sitting down and mapping out a way to deal with that, there was a part of him that knew the perfect way to fill that void.

Mary.

11

You Don't Know What You've Got' til It's Gone

For Davis, not knowing exactly where Becca was, physically, geographically, further solidified the feeling they were indeed done, that she was gone. In the last time they had been together, when Becca had gotten more into astrology, she had talked about their signs: her being a Scorpio and him a Pisces. While it made for a fiery and passionate union, it was pretty clear who was going to wear the pants, and that was her. Yes, he had left her behind in New Mexico, but in his mind, he had never thought about that being permanent, unlike Becca leaving him, which seemed very permanent indeed.

Davis felt increasingly like his life was out of his control, so, now that he had an opportunity to seize some control—by pursuing a relationship with Mary—he took it. Mary was hesitant again, knowing that Davis was carrying a torch for Becca, although she didn't know much. He explained the letter to her and how they were done, and while she worried about being the "rebound" woman, she saw his advances as sincere, which they were, albeit, on some level, conflicted.

The next time he saw her, he gathered her in an embrace, which she half-heartedly resisted.

"Whoa, what's this about? I thought we decided this would be trouble," she said.

"Yeah, but I've been thinking; it'd be good trouble."

Mary was skeptical. "Uh-huh." She was still somewhat resisting his embrace. "What changed? What are you not telling me?"

Davis loosened his hold just a bit, somewhat frustrated. "Why does everything need to be 'told'? Why can't we just be in the moment and just accept what's being presented to us?"

"Oh, you mean like a snake? Or a fish? Just react, using our primitive reptilian brain?"

"Yeah. That's it. I just want to be like a frog on a lily pad. And a fly goes by and I fling out my long adhesive tongue and snatch it out of the air and I'm happy. Just sittin' there on my lily pad."

Mary extended her arm and place her hand sideways on Davis's shoulder. "So, let me get this straight. You are equating a potential escalation of our human relationship with an amphibian—not reptilian, by the way—desire to satisfy your appetite?" She placed her finger across her lips and gave him a quizzical and slightly amused look.

"When you put it that way, it sounds a little less romantic than I am envisioning."

"Oh. Ya think? And you see me as a fly, do you?" She was teasing him, but Davis knew he had to be careful.

"Yeah, but not just any fly: not like a housefly. More like a beautiful dragonfly, with coppery wings and a long iridescent body."

"I'm not sure you are helping your case here, mister."

Davis moved in closer until their faces were just a couple of inches apart. "Ok, how about YOU be the frog. Aren't there things you want to do with your tongue?"

"You mean this tongue?" Mary placed the tip of her tongue gently against the top of her upper lip.

Davis immediately tried to bite it but she retracted it too quickly and pulled away just a couple of inches.

She said, "It's a frog's tongue; you gotta be quicker than that."

"Point taken. Next time I will be."

Mary pushed off from Davis's shoulder and stuck her tongue out to its full length. "You can't catch me," she said.

Davis decided not to pursue, just stood there and smiled. "Yeah, we'll see…"

Davis had told Mary about Becca and their past, not in much detail, but enough for her to know there was someone else somewhere who was potentially going to usurp his attention away from her. Once Davis realized this was the obstacle, he removed it from the equation. He didn't show her the letter, but alluded to it, and that was all Mary needed.

Her tongue was unleashed.

Unfortunately, not in the ways Davis would have most preferred. You see, Mary was a licker. After a few-too-many wet tongues in his ear and the resulting recoil, he decided he had to let Mary know verbally that those particular advances were not welcome, risking hurting her feelings, which it did.

"Oh. OK. I thought you liked me licking you."

"I do, just not there. Like that."

"Are you saying I'm not a good lover?"

Oh geez, thought Davis. *Here we go. This is why I didn't want to bring it up in the first place.*

Mary wasn't done. "You know, I don't like everything that you do."

Now Davis was hurt. He had figured, with the empathic feedback he had from Becca, that he knew what it took to please a woman, but what he was finding out what he knew was how to please that woman.

While this particular lovemaking session was essentially ruined, they figured it out enough, but what Davis was going to realize over time was because of their graft and the information they shared as a result, no one was ever going to be able to push his buttons like Becca could. He found himself vacillating between the musical messages from Stephen Stills and Joni Mitchell: 'Love the one you're with' and 'Don't it always seem to go, that you don't know what you've got 'til it's gone.'

He decided to forge ahead with the former and try not to focus too much on the latter.

Which wasn't always easy. Like when Mary questioned Davis about the grafting scar on his thigh.

"What's this from?"

Davis hesitated. His relationship with Mary was much different than with Becca. Davis and Becca shared an interest in the esoteric, always considering explanations and "truths" about their existence outside of the norm, more on the fringes, the edges of perception. Mary was much more... "normal" was the word that came to mind when he had previously made the inevitable but unfair comparison.

How to explain grafting to Mary, the uninitiated? He plunged ahead. "That is a skin graft that I performed with Becca."

"Because...?" Here Mary stretched out the word wondering why there would be the need for that particular medical procedure.

"It was part of an ancient ritual. A way to take get a fuller understanding of the other person's inside world."

Mary looked silently at Davis, blinking four times as her mind tried to process "what in the world" would possess two people to undertake a completely unnecessary procedure that involved not only the cutting of human flesh, but exchanging it.

"It was something she had learned when she was in Africa with the Peace Corps," Davis offered as a way to explain it away.

"And she wanted to do this with you?"

"Well, actually, it was my idea, once she had told me about it."

"Really? Did it do what you thought it would?"

"Actually, yes, although it wasn't absolute. But it did give us a fuller understanding of each other." Davis wisely decided right then to omit the part about experiencing each other's orgasms, but felt compelled, against his own better judgement, to provide yet more information. "You can also take on aspects of the other person."

Mary again paused, processing. "Like what? What did she get from you?"

"It looks like she got my music gene, which I didn't have much use for."

"And you? What did you get from her?"

"That's a little less clearly defined. It's hard to explain, but I can 'hear' colors, and that factors into my painting. And I think she may have passed on some of her ESP faculties."

Again, the silence from Mary, this time with her head nodding slowly. Then she said, "Just so we're clear, there won't be..."

Davis interrupted her, "No, no. I'm done with that. I'm perfectly fine with us getting to know each other through our thoughts and deeds. And conversation. Conversation is good."

"Yes, conversation." said Mary, while in the back of her mind, wondering,

Who IS this guy?

12

1974-1977

The Wheels of Justice

The specter of the impending trial loomed large. At the end of March, 1974, the Guardsmen were officially indicted and the idea that Davis could end up in jail became a very real prospect to him. Mary was a supporting influence, knowing his side of the story, which helped his overall state of mind.

They talked about that openly, and it gave each day a kind of sweetness that manifested as a mutual appreciation for each other as well as an urgency he had not experienced before.

But the wheels of the legal system turn slowly. And just when you might think they have stopped, and ended the journey (metaphorically speaking), they have a way of starting up again.

The Guardsmen were acquitted in November of '74.

Then in May of '75, a civil trial began, which ended with an acquittal in August. But there were still rumblings about appeals. The prosecutors were not done. In September of '77, an appeal was granted and the whole trial was to begin over again. All of this hanged over Davis's head, not knowing what his future held. The trial based on that appeal would not start for another fifteen months.

Mary was a rock, despite not knowing what HER future would be in terms of their relationship.

13

October 1978

It's Over, Again

The trial didn't start until October 21. The Guardsmen were charged with "violating the civil rights" of the four slain students. To Davis, the actual charge didn't sound all that ominous. What did was the potential sentence: life in prison. The Justice Department would present 33 witnesses and 130 exhibits. Davis was hoping the rumor about the weapons log, cataloging who had which rifle assigned to them, was indeed true. He was perfectly willing to take his lumps for his part in what happened, accidental, inadvertent or otherwise; he just didn't want those lumps to last the rest of his days.

A jury was chosen. Part of what the prosecution had planned was for the jury to visit the scene and have the sound of the shots simulated for them. He was hoping he and his fellow defendants would not have to be present for that—he could conjure up the cacophony of those thirteen seconds at will—he didn't need to have them simulated.

Federal Court Judge Frank Battisti presided. Though Davis could not read him at first, the judge's influence would loom large in the proceedings. After three weeks of testimony, the judge himself, although there was a sitting jury, acquitted the Guardsmen, ruling the prosecutors failed to prove the charges, that the Guardsmen did not "willfully intend" to deprive the students of their rights. On the flip side, although it didn't carry any consequence, he also declared their use of force "excessive and unjustified" and further admonished authorities his decision did not authorize the use of such force going forward.

Just like that, it was over for the Guardsmen and all the other public officials who had been charged. But for the families that had lost members and those that were injured, the process would drag on for years through ANOTHER civil trial, ANOTHER acquittal, then an appeal to THAT decision and then YET ANOTHER civil trial that finally ended with an out of court settlement for a measly grand total of $675,000, to be distributed amongst the families and victims.

That settlement would be the end of the legal proceedings, although at the time, because of all that had transpired over the nine years since the shooting, in the back of his mind, Davis felt like another appeal or lawsuit or claim somehow tied to the event could somehow materialize and send his life back into uncertainty.

Despite that trepidation, he felt like he had paid his debt. He knew his bullet hadn't found a human target and once a settlement was reached, he felt like he could finally let it go and get on with the rest of his life.

"What do you want that to look like?" Mary asked.

"That's a good question. I haven't allowed myself to entertain what that might be. I didn't want to consider it and then have it taken away. I'm 28 years old and part of me feels like an old man."

"I can understand that, but you have the rest of your life to live. We. We have the rest of our lives to live."

Mary was fishing for some kind of validation for the two of them going forward. They had moved in together years ago and their lives were intertwined but the subject of marriage had only come up once in their six years together, when Davis had dismissed it due to his uncertain future, stating that if he was going to "The Big House" (as he half-jokingly referred to prison), he would not expect Mary to dutifully visit him and live the rest of her life as the chaste wife of a felon.

"Yes," he replied, gathering her up in his arms. "Our lives."

Mary returned his hug, ardently, but couldn't help feeling his tone was not as enthusiastic as she would have liked.

14

A Proposal (sorta)

Davis had written back and forth with his mom over the years, filling her in periodically on the progress of the trials, although she kept abreast of the news, with it being a national story. Watching Cronkite when the story about the settlement came on, she closed her eyes and wept, knowing the turmoil for Davis was over, finally, but she also felt for the families of the victims. Her son having been so closely involved in the event, she had gobbled up every story, every tidbit of information about the case.

She had accepted at face value Davis's claim his bullet had not struck a human target. He had never shared with anyone his surety about the trajectory of his round had come from Becca's encounter with a dark entity. In his most critical moments, he had trouble himself believing it himself, but as much as anything, it fit what he wanted to believe, and that's all he needed.

Brenda Filkins got a rare phone call from her son on the eve of the announcement.

"Hi, Ma. I suppose you heard the news."

"Oh, Davis, it is so good to hear your voice. Yes. It sounds like this ordeal is finally over."

"Yeah. That's what they say, now that there was a settlement. It seems like history now, and I guess that's true; it will become part of the fabric of who we are going forward. I can't help but believe maybe some things have changed significantly because of it, too."

"I agree. It was a high cost to pay."

"Yes. For some more than others. I think back about not wanting to serve in 'Nam and where it landed me. I guess sometimes we make decisions without knowing what the outcome will be."

"Oh, Davis, we never really know. We do our best to imagine what outcomes will be, but we never really know."

Davis noticed a sense of resignation in his mom's voice. She sounded tired.

"How are you, Mom?"

"I'm OK. It's been hard making ends meet since your dad passed away and I get lonely, but y'know, he wasn't around much at the end anyway. I've been alone for a while."

"Maybe Mary and I will come and visit. We should have some more free time now."

"That'd be great, dear. How is Mary?"

"She's doing fine."

"When are you going to marry that girl?"

"Things are different now, Ma; you don't have to get married to be together."

"That's what YOU say. How does she feel about that?"

"She..."

Davis hadn't thought about that for some time. While the civil trial didn't hold the penalty of life in prison, there had still been that air of uncertainty about everything going forward.

That was gone now.

Davis realized he still hadn't finished his sentence after about a ten second pause. "We haven't talked about the future for a while. Everything's been on hold."

"Well, it's over now. And when you start talking about plans, throw a grandchild for me into the pot while you're at it."

Davis laughed. It wasn't the first time that had been brought up. "OK, Ma. That'll be the first thing I mention to her after we talk about coming to visit. I'll let you know."

He hung up the phone and sat looking off into space. "Marriage." "Children." It all sounded so...

Adult.

The trials, appeals, missteps and dismissals had been a convenient distraction for Davis. He didn't have to grow up: make decisions, take responsibility, because the threat of jail time or some other unforeseen control of his life could wipe all that out in one fell swoop.

That was now removed. His life was "tabula rasa," a blank slate. But it wasn't as if he was starting from scratch; he'd been treading water in his relationship with Mary for years.

"My mom thinks we should get married and give her grandchildren."

Mary had been tending to some houseplants, but stopped, considering this could be a conversation that demanded her full attention. She put down her watering can, wiped her hands on her jeans and came over to Davis, took a deep breath, shook the blond tresses away from her face and planted herself in front of him.

"Why, Davis," she said, affecting a southern accent. "I do believe that sounded like a proposal of marriage." She batted her faint eyelashes in exaggeration.

"Uhh... not exactly, but..."

Mary gave him a quick out; she dropped the façade and said, "Davis, honey, relax. It's me, Mary." She gently slapped the sides of his face. "Snap out of it, brother." She was smiling, trying to ease his obvious discomfort. It was part of what Mary did.

Some of the blood returned to Davis's face. He realized also, though, the possible effect of his stammering and hesitation and wanted to atone. "Well, shit, Mary; I'd marry you."

Mary raised an eyebrow. "You sure do know how to charm a girl, don't you?"

Davis was slowly coming back to full consciousness. He placed his hands underneath her hair. Oh, how he loved that hair, feeling it interlacing between his fingers, the warmth of her neck against his fingertips. "Would you?"

"Would I what?"

"Marry me. Would you marry me?"

"Are you asking me if I would, or are you asking me if I will?"

Davis was on a downbound train now and there was no stopping him. "Will you. Will you marry me?"

Now it was Mary's turn to be on the spot. But for her, it wasn't as if she hadn't thought about the possibility. Yes, feminism had pushed women's rights and roles forward, and they weren't just relegated to being wives and mothers anymore, but that didn't mean she didn't want the security of a commitment. It wasn't as if she hadn't considered, if they did get beyond Davis's albatross, the idea of spending the rest of their lives together.

The look in his face was serious and she was done teasing.

"Yes, Davis. Yes, I will."

Davis pulled her closer and kissed her gently on her mouth. He had always loved her full lips and in the moment was experiencing them anew. Mary returned his fervor. They held that kiss for a long time, neither one wanting to break the spell.

Mary did though.

"Let's back up a minute, though. I love you. You. That's the "me and you" part. Have you given any thought to the rest of your mom's request? And not that this is about what your mom wants, but what we want. Have you thought about children? We've never talked about that. What do you think about a houseful of little Davises and Marys running around?"

It was true; they had never talked about it. The conversation was getting more "adult' by the moment.

Images of children flooded through Davis's mind: babies, children who some of their friends had, kids he had grown up with, images of his own, only-child-hood. Dozens of children, running, smiling, crying, raising a din in his head, and at the front of the hoard was the image that Mary had suggested: a tiny little Davis holding hands with an even smaller Mary.

It was not an unpleasant picture for him.

"You're right. We haven't talked about that and we probably should." He smiled broadly. "And, I have to say, first impression: I like the idea of little Davises and Marys." His mind expanding to the concept, Davis then said, "What about you? What do you want?"

Mary had thought about it, and she knew her answer. She had come from a big family—four siblings—and her childhood had been fairly functional. She was the youngest and she already had two nieces and three nephews. Her answer was immediate, premeditated and rose from a place deep inside her: "I'm in."

In a span of six minutes, after being on hold for so long, their future was cast.

15

April 1979

No More Dead Bunnies

The engagement was short. They got married in the small Wisconsin town where Mary grew up. It was largely attended by Mary's family, sparsely by Davis's, if for no other reason, Davis didn't have that much family. They flew his mom in; it was the first time she had ever been on a plane.

Davis was shocked at the state of his mom's health. She walked slowly, bent over and extremely frail. After the initial bloom of the wedding was over, a decision was made for them to move to New Jersey to take care of her. It was a difficult decision for Mary to be farther away from her extended family and her job, but being the caregiver she was, it overshadowed her loss.

Davis's mom insisted they take the master bedroom and she moved into Davis's old room. It felt like adulthood was being thrust upon him, but it also felt like it was time.

There were reunions with some of Davis's old friends, although not as many as he had expected. Some had moved away. Gene had been drafted to go to Vietnam and had come back completely messed up.

Davis found employment at the local Nestle plant and came home smelling of coffee every night. Luckily Mary loved the smell and always inhaled deeply upon hugging him when he got home. Mary found a job at the local community college in the admissions department and they settled in, but that didn't last long. Davis's mom's condition worsened and in a matter of 8 months, she had passed away from cancer that was later attributable to a nearby Superfund site from chemicals that had been dumped on nearby property for years.

Davis's dad, Tom, had long since left their home. Having started out as a classically trained symphony musician, once he was exposed to jazz, got lost in the bop and the lifestyle, including the drug use that permeated its seedier environs. A heroin addiction eventually took his life.

The house and all of Brenda and Tom's belongings were left to Davis, including Tom's extensive jazz record collection from the 50's and 60's. The collection included more than 5000 titles and took up the entire living room wall. Tom had been extremely fastidious with his records, only taking one out at a time, carefully replacing each on in its sleeve before removing another. Not only were the big names represented, Miles Davis (Davis's namesake), Coltrane, Parker, Chet Baker and Ella Fitzgerald, but plenty of obscure names Davis had never heard of: Lenny Tristano, George Russell, Bud Powell, Tal Farlow and Ahmad Jamal.

Tom disdained rock 'n' roll although there were some early examples in his collection of musicians crossing genres and experimenting with what was referred to as race music: rhythm and blues, straight blues and even some acapella doo-wop. The collection had lain dormant for the years since Tom's death. Brenda had never touched it and actually changed the house very little after Tom moved out, taking only his horn and a few clothes with him. She didn't even know he had died until months later when a family friend mentioned his passing, assuming she knew. She had packed up his clothing and sent it off to the Salvation Army but otherwise left the house as it was.

Now, Davis and Mary were left with a home that was almost completely somebody else's. There were some memories there for Davis but absolutely none for Mary. They set about cleaning everything out except for the record collection which both of them took to exploring at every opportunity.

That music became part of a soundtrack to their new East Coast lifestyle. Mary, in particular, had adjusted quickly and enthusiastically to an East Coast sensibility. Once she got over the population density and the pace, she felt like she was in her element, quickly outgrowing her rural roots. She fell in love with New York City, the two of them taking the bus up almost every weekend. Clubs, museums, concerts, restaurants, Little Italy, Chinatown and especially Greenwich Village, which everyone referred to simply as 'the Village.'

And movies. They especially loved going to small theaters to see independent films. One of their favorites was "Harold and Maude," a black comedy about a rich, morose eighteen-year-old boy and a full-of-life 79-year-old woman who have an unlikely love affair until she deliberately takes her life at the end on her birthday, feeling like 80 years was a good, appropriate run. As sad as the ending was, they would both often recall her last words after Harold professes his love for her on the way to the hospital: "Oh, Harold, how wonderful. Go and love some more."

They talked about moving up to the city and decided to sell the house for a tidy profit and find a loft downtown in Soho. Mary applied for a job at Barnard, a division of Columbia University tucked into the middle of Manhattan, and with the profits from the house, they bought out a small used record store on Bleeker Street in the Village and stocked it with much of Tom's collection.

They were blissfully happy. Once Davis had the cloak of the Kent State incident lifted from his shoulders, he felt himself open up to the possibilities that life had to offer. He contacted Gloria Westin, the gallery owner who had represented his paintings in Santa Fe and she introduced him to some of the major players in the international art scene based in NY. Davis hadn't painted since he had left the Southwest to return to Ohio, nor did he have an inclination to do so, but he found that he liked hobnobbing with creative and quirky individuals.

The record store, called Whirled Records, had an established following, but really took off under Davis's management. It became the "go-to" place for musicians coming through the city. Davis had an ear for what was collectible and cool, but also for what was new and upcoming.

Three months after they had moved into the loft, which was classic New York chic—a fourth floor walk-up with worn marble steps, an antiquated cage-like elevator, brick walls, a fire escape, exposed ductwork with lath and plaster walls—Mary missed her period. She did not report it to Davis right away, not wanting to jump the gun on any biological conclusions. Deep inside herself though, she knew she was pregnant and it did her heart good. It just felt like the natural order of things. She waited a couple of weeks to let Davis in on her secret until it felt like it was really *their* secret and her period was not going to show up anytime soon.

She purchased a home pregnancy test, which had hit the market just a couple of years earlier, but decided to wait until she and Davis were together to perform it.

She unpackaged it and waited for him to get home from work. She had it hidden in her pocket and waited for him to flop down on the couch and open up a beer. She brandished it like a magic wand before him, with a mischievous grin and said, "Do you know what this is?"

"No, I don't."

"I'm going to pee on it."

Davis chuckled, but not having been exposed previously to the machinations of an E.P.T., wondered why his wife would want to pee on anything.

"O...kay," he said, drawing it out. "And why would you want to do that?"

"Because when I pee on it, it will turn colors."

"Besides yellow, you mean?"

"Yes, it will turn pink or blue."

"Ah, the wonders of modern chemistry. And you would want to do this because...?" again, drawing out the last word.

"Because if it turns blue, that means we are going to have a baby."

Davis had no idea where the conversation was headed, and certainly wasn't expecting that direction. A smile spread across his face. "No shit? You mean, they don't have to kill a rabbit anymore?"

"Nope, no more dead bunnies."

The ramifications of what they were about to learn was catching up to Davis. "Well, do you feel like you need to pee?"

"I've been holding it for hours," Mary exclaimed, heading for the bathroom. She closed the bathroom door behind her and held the stick under her urine stream. She knew from the instructions that it took a minute or so for the results to show, and she wanted for them to discover together what she already knew. She kept the stick hidden in her hand and opened the bathroom door. Davis had been waiting there in anticipation, still grinning, which, to Mary, was a positive sign about what was going to be a positive result.

She held her hand out, palm down and then turned it upright. Her eyes were closed as she slowly unfurled her fingers from around the stick. "Well? What's the verdict?"

"What color is it again for a positive result?" Davis teased.

"Blue. Blue. Is it blue?"

Davis dropped to his knees and pressed his face against her belly. Though somewhat muffled, she could hear him say,

"Yeah, baby, it's blue."

16

1980

For Those About to Rock

Becca was no stranger to new places. That nomadic part of her sought out the novel and unfamiliar, so when she arrived at the bus station in downtown LA, it was with no small amount of excitement tempered with just a hint of trepidation. While the music in her felt sure, it also felt partly "borrowed," from Davis, as part of their graft, and her acceptance of everything around it was based on pure faith.

Nevertheless, as much of a dreamer as she was, she was also a pragmatist and part of her time on the bus was spent in preparation for when her feet hit the ground. First was going to contact Peter, who she had met back in Santa Fe. That and find a place to live. She wanted a place that felt like home, a sanctuary she could come to that felt safe and certain with all that was going to be new coming her way.

She rented a motel room so she could park her stuff: her guitar, of course, and one large suitcase filed with what she hoped would be weather-appropriate clothing. She had gotten rid of the coats and sweaters that were necessary in the high desert of New Mexico winters, except for the ones she wore on the trip. She imagined she would be retiring them shortly.

She felt a need to go as far west as she could, which meant finding a beach. She would soon discover the waves would have a hypnotic effect on her and would find many places along California's coast that would lend themselves to her meditative lifestyle. She was not alone in having the beach be a mecca for just about everyone in California; they flocked to the beaches because they could.

When she got to the shore, she removed her shoes to be able to feel the sand on her feet, walking to the edge of the water and looking out at the great expanse of the Pacific, stretching far beyond what she could see. She rolled up her pant legs and ventured out just enough so some of the waves would lap around her ankles. Planting her feet in one spot, as the waves receded, she could feel herself sinking into the beach, grounding, but at the same time, getting just a little dizzy as the water rushed back to its source. The rhythm of the surf shut out all other sounds save a few seagulls in the distance. She could feel the pulse of the city at her back and the force of nature in front of her and felt the balance.

She had arrived.

It didn't take her long to make some acquaintances. There was an openness to the culture among the young people there. She was reminded of her time in northern California, in Berkeley, although the vibe there was different: more serious, intense. Here it felt looser. She put feelers out for where the music was, and everything pointed to The Troubador, a club in Hollywood that had been the epicenter a decade earlier for the folk-rock movement, where the Jackson Brownes and the James Taylors and the Linda Ronstadts had moved through on their way to the top of the charts. Speaking of Ronstadt, Becca came to realize the Peter she had met would end up managing her and had HUGE influence in the business starting with the Beatles.

To Becca, Los Angeles and Hollywood in particular was synonymous with the movie industry, but being physically there, it became less of a mythical, ethereal idea and more of a physical place complete with concrete sidewalks, palm trees and lots and lots of Californians, both native and imported. She immersed herself firmly in it.

The music industry was going through another incarnation. The 70s had seen the end of the big rock era. Morrison, Joplin and Hendrix had died, and pop music seemed to perish along with them. Disco topped the charts which led to a counter-movement: punk. Starting in London, then New York, it was a return to a hard-edged rock sound, but even simpler, with harsh rhythms, three chords and a violent undertone that spit in the face of disco.

One of the proponents of this sound was Chrissy Hynde, an American from Ohio who had gone to England and cycled through a number of collaborations until she put together a band called Pretenders. Their debut album had been released right around the time Becca hit the West Coast and hearing it was transformative to her. Her own music had been folk-based, soft, gentle, played on an acoustic guitar. When she heard (most people ended putting a "The" in front of their name) Pretender's "Mystery Achievement," it would change her own music going forward. A lyric in that song would resonate with her:

"...where's my sandy beach?"

Becca went into one of the pawn shops on Vine St. and picked herself up a beat–up Fender Mustang and amp. Her first attempts going electric were tentative and largely an extension of how she played her acoustic Yamaha. She was surprised at first at how much heavier the Fender was, being a solid body with pickups instead of a hollow box, especially when she stood to play, which she realized would be the case. No one, that is, not ONE self-respecting rock guitarist sat down to play their guitar when performing. There was no shortage of examples of how to play rock guitar, except they were almost exclusively by men and so much of what they were doing was posing.

She became a student of rock guitar styles, attending as many performances as she could. She recalled too, how enthralled she was at seeing Johnny Steele for the first time. With him, there were no extra histrionics. There didn't need to be—he was a virtuoso. But that didn't stop his performances from being visually compelling. The guitar was an extension of his fingers and his fingers a part of the rest of his body and the body an extension of the soul that went into his music.

She found too her fingering on the neck of the electric had to be different since it wasn't sitting on her lap anymore. Luckily, she had long arms and fingers and she could wear the guitar low. She experimented with new chord fingerings including using her thumb along the top of the neck. What irked her though, once she would strap on the Mustang, was the derision she would get from some of the men about a "girl" playing an electric guitar. Once she had been exposed to that a few times, it was all the impetus she needed to not only keep doing it, but to flaunt it, and flaunt it not like so many of them did, as an outward masculine extension of their sexuality, but more of a yin approach, taking IN the energy of the audience and then throwing it back out.

The other aspect that was an adjustment was the idea of playing in a band. It was no longer just her. There were plenty of musicians around to collaborate with, the challenge was finding those with a common perspective. That synergy was the key. She looked for it in the music she watched and heard, both recorded and live. She watched for musicians having fun, experiencing joy in their collaboration, as well as the personality types that went into creating the whole: those that had to assert, those that were willing to be part of the background and those that wanted the collective to be the end result.

And then there was the question of talent. Who could really play? Becca took to music like she did everything else: full on. She saw it as a discipline, as a concept, as a language, a form of expression. In likening it to a form of communication, she realized t there were those who were more articulate than others, but that took on many forms: sheer virtuosity, passion, verbosity. Ha! Verbosity. She recognized those players that would try to cram asmanynotesasfastastheycould into any given space versus those who understood the value of spacing, silence and feeling, where less could be more.

She got a job tending bar at one of the clubs, which gave her constant access, not only to the music but the musicians and the river of information and creativity–so incredibly rich and full of content. She absorbed every bit of it like a sponge so it would in turn be expressed in HER music. She had a small memo book in the back pocket of her jeans that she would scribble in whenever an idea struck her that could work its way into a song.

She became part of a tribe that played and sang constantly. She was invited to stay at what became just a flophouse right on the beach in Malibu. The cast came and went. Instruments were shared, food was shared, bodies were shared. Not that everything was blissful. In any group setting, personalities were going to clash, egos inflated, agendas pushed, hearts broken, but Becca came into it all with a wider perspective and kept herself apart from most of the petty bullshit that went on. She was able to use her intuitive skills to steer clear of the toxic aspects of communal living. After all, she had been through it numerous times before.

The big difference in the lifestyle for Becca was the pace and the energy. At times she felt like Dorothy in the Wizard of Oz; "Toto, we are NOT back in New Mexico anymore." No, she was in Los Angeles, one of the most dynamic cities in the world, arguably the center of the entertainment industry. Just about every waiter, store clerk and hairdresser had a screenplay, story or song they wanted to pitch. The competition was fierce. What Becca found, however, was so much of what was being proposed was derivative. For her, the challenge was to take what had been done before, internalize it, then push the envelope and synthesize a new product no one had ever seen or heard before.

Back in Taos, so much of her time was spent alone up in the mountains and that introspection was important for that time in her life, but now, the socialization, the combining of the thoughts and ideas of others, the alliance, fed her. Now she was embracing the idea of being pushed and inspired by others.

The jams and the parties at the Beach House were virtually non-stop. Most of the action occurred at night or, more accurately, in the early morning hours. Daytime is when most of the inhabitants slept, which, for Becca, would often be literally on the beach, letting the waves lull her into not just a somnambulistic state, but a meditative one as well. She found the sound of the waves hypnotic. Their continuum, the idea that they kept coming, regardless of what else was going on, was reassuring to her, reminding her if an aspect of her life was stalled or not getting the outcome she wanted, the rest of the world kept going.

While Becca enjoyed the idea of musicianship in playing the guitar and piano, her real joy came from singing, from being able to take a deep breath, formulate the idea of what words she was about to sing and then have them be expressed through her voice. Since that moment in the shower when she realized she could sing—really sing—it gave her intense pleasure to explore the range of where her voice could go, especially when she got the chance to sing with others.

At the beach house, musical coalitions were being formed all the time. Sometimes those unions were forced, usually when two egos competed for who was going to dominate, who was going to be better, as opposed to how the different parts would come together to create the whole sound. Not being classically trained, Becca was behind the curve of those who did have an idea of music theory and concept.

Bobby Sawyer was one of those music savants; he could play just about any instrument: keyboards, strings, horns, it didn't matter. Growing up with piano lessons, he was one of those kids who mastered scales and beginning techniques until he eclipsed most teachers. Not only did he understand the structure, the language of notes and keys and their sounds, he was able to translate them to different instruments, including the human voice so that when those instruments came together, they made a harmonious, joyful noise.

He became the de facto teacher to some of the other, less educated musicians, and for those who were open to his coaching, the whole of their joint effort always became more than their individual contributions. He taught Becca how to sing harmony, then, once he realized the scope of her voice, sang harmony parts to her lead. Then he would get others to join in, like leading a choir, the results echoing off the walls of the house until the whole structure hummed in one melodious vibration.

Word of these jam sessions got out and people would pack into the house on weekend nights, wanting to be part of what was happening. They would play covers, but also started incorporating some of Becca's new songs, finishing one of those to an enthusiastic response when one of the attendees remarked, "Wow, you guys are too much."

Immediately, someone responded, "Ha. That would be a great name for their band."

Becca glanced over at Bobby. A core group of them had been playing together for a few months and while there had been no discussion about actually forming a band, now that the idea was out in the open, it made perfect sense.

"Too Much" was formed that night and it wasn't long before they were playing some of the smaller clubs in LA. Word got out and a local promoter offered them a gig opening for Pat Benatar at the Troubador.

Sort of.

On the strength of their local following, a promoter, Chad Adams, had approached Becca after of their gigs and offered to represent them. Becca knew at some point they were going to need some representation if they were going to get anywhere. Part of her was still holding out for Peter Asher to take them under his wing, but he had committed to managing Linda Ronstadt and that seemed to be going quite well for both of them.

Chad was fairly new to LA, but he seemed to know the business and he dropped all the right names. "Yeah, I know Peter," he said when asked about Asher, but Becca suspected the reality was more like "I know OF Peter." Having been in LA for long enough now, she was getting an education about industry "types:" charming, smooth-talking persuaders who would lie as easy as opening their mouths. He had the look, he had the feel, he had the moves and the laid-back lines of just another West Coast shyster, but he had a sense of self-deprecation that allowed Becca to put her guard down. When she tried to go inside and size him up, though, she was not able to get a read on him; it was like her intuition, her radar, around being able to assess his intent was blocked.

Pat Benatar's first album was a hit behind John Mellencamp's song, "I Need a Lover (That Won't Drive Me Crazy)" and so it would be a coup for Too Much to get billed as the opening act. Becca wasn't about to commit to anything without talking to Bobby and the rest of the band first, but when Chad dangled the possibility of a Troubadour gig, they all got more interested, and when he came through with the Benatar booking, he became more than just talk. Chad, (who the band privately would refer to as "Chadams") had proposed the Troubadour gig as a "what if?" to the band as a requisite for becoming their manager and now, here it was; they were getting set to play in front of serious music critics, record executives and other bigwigs in the business.

Audiences at the Troubadour, especially during an opening act for a major headliner, could be dismissive, but they also knew their music, and if whoever was on stage had the goods, they would rise to the occasion and be incredibly enthusiastic.

With no preamble, no "Hello, LA'S," no gradually building of their set, Bobby launched into the anthemic intro to AC-DC's "Highway to Hell." After Bon Scott's death in February of that year, playing this song was either going to come across as sacrilege or tribute, so it was a risk, especially in front of this audience, not to mention having a woman out front, but once Becca launched into the vocal, the entire room was transfixed in a deafening, gut-punch/body-shakin' exorcism with all the rock demons invited in, not out. Their set was eight songs, without a ballad to be heard and barely a break in between songs. When they were done, the crowd erupted in one solid roar of approval.

They had a song selected for an encore, but Chad had greeted them backstage and said, "Go back out there, line up in front of the stage and just take a bow. Leave 'em wanting more."

It was a legendary debut. They were written up in all the trade rags, and the record execs came clamoring. Chad had come through and now it was time to not only shake hands, but sign papers. Bobby was the musical leader of the band, but Becca was the head, the face and the voice. The rest of the band was unanimous in wanting to move ahead. Becca was on board too, despite her slight misgivings on not be able to "read' Chad. The Troubadour gig was just a few days behind them, but offers were coming in and Chad wanted to make sure HE struck while the iron was hot.

He arranged for them to meet at a swanky Hollywood lunch spot, wanting to make sure they were seen.

They sat and ordered, then Chad began. "So... pretty cool, huh? You guys did it. You fucking kicked ass."

"Yeah, it still doesn't all seem real yet."

"Well, it's Hollywood; don't get too invested in the hype, but this IS wanting to happen. The question is, do YOU want it to happen and maybe a bigger question for today is, are WE gonna make this happen?"

Becca knew she had the band's blessing, and she was all set with her yesses. A remote part of her checked in again to see if there was any resistance and came up empty.

"Yeah. Let's do it. You're our guy. You did what you said you were going to do."

Chad smiled his LA best and extended his hand across the table. Becca took his hand in a firm grip. His hand was warm and soft, but strong. Their eyes locked while Chad held the handshake a little longer than necessary, and for a flashing, split-second moment, Becca felt a chill and a tiny but significant gnaw in her gut. It was so short as to almost not register and passed as quickly as it came, leaving her making a deal that would catapult her onto the national stage.

17

The Usual Song and Dance

Chad ended up being a mover and a shaker. What he lacked in the way of big-time contacts he made up for in his ability to get his foot in the door, and once it was in, he knew what to do with it. He also had some leverage because he had what everyone else wanted: Too Much.

He signed them to a mid-sized label that would provide enough distribution and support for a tour. Becca and Bobby collaborated on all of the writing; he had an understanding of where a song could go and combined with her sense of where it should go, they had more than album's worth by the time they hit the studio.

The rest of the band, Brian on drums, Caleb on bass, Jim on lead guitar and Alex on keyboards had all played around in other bands. Brian was a black-dyed-hair guy who had a reputation as a madman, but was really just a shy kid from Decatur until he got behind his kit, and then his sense of rhythm pushed their music forward. He never missed a beat. Next to Bobby, Jim was the most accomplished musician. He spent time with Becca on her guitar playing and ended up being as good a teacher as he was a player. There was no excess with him; his playing was precise and if there was a note that sounded discordant, it was because he wanted it that way. Caleb was the pretty boy in the band and played to an audience of admirers every night from which he chose partner after partner. Alex was an adequate keyboard player but what he really brought was a background vocal that made their sound distinctive.

Studio time was expensive and Chad wanted everything ready by the time they got in there, so every hour that wasn't spent at a local gig was spent at the house, polishing up the songs. The label had their engineers and producer in place and the self-titled album was cut in two weeks, but not without a considerable amount of conflict over the content.

None of the band had dealt with the music industry on the recording side before and while they all had preconceptions about what it might sound like, when they got to the studio, they were treated like the neophytes they were. They had been playing their songs a certain way and expected them to be recorded that way. The producer, Larry Westridge, an industry type that the label had chosen, asserted himself immediately in a heavy-handed way.

His very first order, after going through the songs the first time was, "The drummer's got to go."

That obviously didn't sit well with Brian, but the other band members bristled as well. They held firm but valuable studio time was being wasted over who was in charge. Then it became about the arrangements. They had laid down some tracks and when it came time to listen back in the sound booth, they had been layered over with strings and special effects.

"What the hell is that?" Becca demanded, "That's not what we sound like. And what the fuck is up with all the cowbell? We don't need any cowbell in there. What are we, Blue Oyster Cult?"

Chad answered, "Some people think you can never have enough cowbell." "Then he added, "but maybe that's a subject for another venue."

Becca looked at him like he had two heads. "What are you talking about?"

"Never mind; I just thought that was funny."

"Well, it's not. These are OUR songs," Becca contended.

"Not any more they're not, honey," Larry gestured towards the door of the sound booth with his head, meaning, get her out of here.

Chad spent some time with the band, explaining that, especially for a first-time artist, the record company had artistic control over what was going to on the final recording. "It's in the contract," he said.

"No, it isn't," Becca replied.

"Uh, yeah, it is." Chad knew exactly what was in the contract, including how he got paid (royally) and exactly the amount of control the record company had including rights and royalties to all the songs.

Truthfully, Becca didn't know what was in the contract. There had been a whirlwind nature leading up to the signing and she had trusted Chad despite her intuition telling her to get someone else to look at it.

Chad was able to convince the band how valuable studio time was, so they put the arguments somewhat aside and were able to lay down enough tracks for an album. What ended up being released was a watered-down version of what the band brought to the stage.

"They know what sells," Chad argued.

"This isn't about selling, it's about music, creativity. Art."

"I agree," said Chad, "but if no one gets to hear it, what then?"

"It was still created. And whether or not something sells it no barometer of quality."

"Do you think what you have created is good?"

"At the risk of sounding less than humble, yes, I do. But now it's been bastardized. It's one step away from Muzak, for crying out loud."

"What they are trying to do is expand your audience. When you get as big as the Beatles, you will have total creative control. Once you're popular, you can do whatever you want."

"I'm not so sure I WANT to be popular."

"Then why are you doing this?"

"I'm an artist. I am creating."

Chad looked at her askance and chuckled. "OK, let's stop the bullshit." And for a brief second, Becca saw that flash—no, not a flash, the opposite of a flash—the void, in Chad's countenance she had ignored before. "I've seen you onstage. I've seen you soak up the adulation. I've seen you get all puffed up by the recognition, the validation, the JUICE you get when those fans are yelling and screaming for you. In that moment, you are someone; you are significant. There's power in that, big power. Fans, Becca... you have fans, and you really like that. And don't try to tell me otherwise."

Up until that moment, Chad had been the placater, the glad-hander. He hadn't confronted Becca before and she wasn't prepared for it. Worse yet, she knew he was at least partly right. What she felt up on stage was no different than the feeling she used to get being in front of a bunch of protesters—she was being heard.

It took her a long couple of seconds to gather herself. "We're talking about two different things. There is the creation of the product, then the product itself and then there is the dissemination of the product. I won't sell out!"

Then, with his very practiced, controlled inner censor, Chad thought to himself, You already have; you just don't know it yet.

It was a classic case of a naïve performer getting fleeced by the recording industry. The record was panned by critics, but it sold. Unfortunately, Becca and the band saw very little of the profits from that. They hit the road to promote it and their live shows got rave reviews, which helped to promote the album. Becca and the band had no idea for quite some time how much of the revenue they were generating was going to the label until Bobby talked to some of his contacts who saw their numbers on the charts and had the nerve to question him about exactly how much of that was ending up in their pockets.

Even worse, they had signed a three-record deal. Too Much was a hit, but by the third release, their hearts were not in it: Becca and Bobby were just churning out remakes of the original material. Their inclusion in the world of rock and pop music in the 80's was not exempt from the usual trappings of drugs and groupies, music business egos, mistrust and broken promises. Before they had gone into the studio for the third record, the band talked about just not doing it, but lawsuits were threatened and Becca had taken responsibility for signing the contract without getting other representation.

Needless to say, their relationship with Chad had soured considerably, but he always managed to toe the line between giving the "suits" what they wanted and making the band feel like they should stay in the game.

Oh, and yeah, during the tour for the second album, Becca got pregnant. I forgot to tell you that.

18

August 1979

A Dangerous Place

Mary skated through the morning sickness. She wasn't going to allow it to diminish her bliss. Friends said her optimism reminded them of Mary from the Mary Tyler Moore Show. She had always seen herself as a mom. Their routine didn't change much, although even though she had pooh-poohed the concept of pregnancy cravings previously, she found herself absolutely having to have the cheesecake from Katz's. Davis was happy to indulge her. He was just happy in general.

"They're telling me now they can tell through an ultrasound if the baby is going to be a boy or a girl," Mary announced after coming back from a doctor's appointment.

"Really? So? Did you find out?"

"I thought about it, but decided we should talk about it first and be on the same page about knowing."

Davis took Mary in his arms and kissed her gently. "That's sweet; to consider what I might want."

"Of course, silly. This is OUR baby. Our child. I want all of our decisions about him or her to be made together. I think you are going to be a great dad and I want us to raise our child together."

"What makes you think I'll be such a good dad?"

87

Mary didn't hesitate, as if she had considered the question ahead of time, which, frankly, she had. "You have a sense of honor, of doing the right thing. You're gentle and kind and you think about others. Those are all traits that translate into good parenting, I think."

Davis actually blushed a little. "Wow. This Davis character sounds like an alright guy. Maybe he would make a good dad." Then, feeling a little self-conscious, he brought the conversation back around to the baby-gender. "It'd be kinda cool to know ahead of time."

"Yeah, it would, but at the same time, I kind of like not knowing: having it be a mystery. A surprise."

"I've been wondering about that—what it would be—a boy or girl," Davis said.

"Do you have a preference?"

"I don't know. On the one hand, I would love to have a son. Ever since you mentioned 'a little Davis' running around, I've had that in my head. But when I think about 'a little Mary,' I love the idea of that, too. How about you? In a perfect world, boy or girl?"

Mary put her hands on her belly. "It doesn't matter to me. And as much as I would love a daughter to dress us and brush her hair and do girly things, I would love for this child to be a boy."

"Really? Why?"

"I just think we need more good boys."

In that simple declaration, Davis saw Mary for the first time in her wholeness, the depth of her love not just for him and their family but for the collective, their place in society.

It warmed him.

"You're the one that's going to be the awesome parent. Mama! Mama Mary."

He took her in a full hug and for the first time consciously embracing the idea of what family could be.

He whispered in her ear, "Did you hear that?"

"What?"

He exaggeratingly cupped his hand over his ear and said, "I do believe I heard the sound of the little bell over the door in Katz's." He sniffed the air. "It must be; I can smell a fresh cheesecake just out of the oven."

Mary inhaled. "I do believe you're correct, sir." Her eyes twinkled. "Let's go!"

As he was closing the door behind them, Davis said, "I think we should wait."

"You tease!"

"I don't mean about the cheesecake; I mean about knowing the gender. If you want it to be a surprise, so do I."

Mary smiled her biggest Marysmile. "Good," she said and grabbed his hand pulling him. "But for now, there's a big fat slice of sweet cheesy goodness that's calling me."

They walked the familiar route hand in hand down the sidewalk. The streets were crowded as they came up to the corner of Houston Street and Avenue A, waiting for the light to change.

Traffic charged mere inches in front of them at the usual breakneck speed everyone just took as a given.

It was New York.

Without warning, there was a crumple of metal as one of the city's ubiquitous bicycle messengers cut off a taxi gambling wrongly he had enough time and space. The cab struck the bike sending it careening skyward and forward into the crowd packed together at the street corner. Davis heard the sound and reacted immediately, placing himself in between the impending bike and Mary. Her hand slipped from his and she lurched forward.

Right into the path of the oncoming taxi.

New York is a place of constant motion and sound, but for a few brief seconds, at least in a radius of about twenty feet, everything stopped and went deadly quiet. The taxi driver has already been braking after making contact with the cyclist otherwise he would have completely run over Mary. As it was, she was wedged under the front bumper. Davis was disoriented from the impact of the bike but quickly picked himself up and ran over to Mary, crushed and bleeding under the yellow cab.

Not sure what else to do, he tried to lift the car off her, to no avail. The driver had started to get out of the cab and Davis screamed at him, "Back up! Back UP!" The driver reversed the vehicle slowly but it pulled Mary with it.

"Stop! STOP!" Davis yelled and was able to release her from the mangled front of the car. Mary's eyes were closed, but she was breathing. "Somebody call 911! Somebody. Please. Help me. HELP ME!"

19

November 1979

Beep... Beep... Beep...

Davis had injuries of his own, ending up with his arm in a sling and a bandage around his head. The side of Mary's face had taken first impact with the front of the car and she had been knocked unconscious immediately. After she was wheeled out from surgery, part of her head had been shaved and she was still unconscious. Davis kept a bedside vigil for two days.

 It was about 2:00 in the morning. Davis had dozed off in a chair next to the bed, holding her hand. He woke, thinking he had heard Mary calling him. When he looked at her in the dim light of the still beeping heart monitors, he thought he heard her voice again, although her lips were not moving.

Davis. Davis... our baby.

Their little one had been miscarried shortly after Mary had made it to the hospital. Mary's poor, collapsed body had all it could do to try and support her own life, never mind another.

Davis placed his hand on her belly, but she still did not move.

He closed his eyes, knowing her voice wasn't coming from her lips, knowing it wasn't something he could see, but also sensing it was indeed Mary communicating with him.

He's gone, Davis heard.

He opened his eyes and looked at Mary's face. The side that had been smashed and then operated on was away from him and in the dim light it was hard to see anything different than just his normal beautiful Mary.

"I know," Davis whispered. "I mean, I know our baby is gone. I didn't know he was a 'he', though."

Yeah. He was a "he"' And he was going to be something, I'll tell you what.

"Zat so?"

Yeah. Just a sense of him, a goodness, is what I saw. Someone fair and just and strong. Like you.

"Well, once you're up and out of here, we'll just have to go back to work and make us another one."

Davis didn't hear any reply. He stroked her hair. "Right?"

Mary responded, *No, honey.*

"Don't be silly..."

She interrupted him. *I can't.*

"You can't what, Mare? Have any more babies?"

No, honey, I can't... I can't come back.

"Yes, you can." Davis was speaking in a regular voice now. "Oh, yes you can. We've got shit to do, you and I. We've got a family to make and the rest of our lives. We've got..." and Davis started sobbing. Sobbing like the first time they met. "You saved me. You can't go anywhere. Let me save you. What do I have to do? Tell me."

I'm sorry, Bud. I can't. But we did good in our time. 'Well.' We did 'well.' We loved. You can't ask for any more than that.

"Yes, we can. We can ask for more of it. I want more. I want more with you. I love you."

She was silent for a moment and then said, *Go out and love some more, Davis.*

"Ah, see?" Davis could see her smiling, although her face has not moved a muscle. "Life imitating art."

The beeping of the monitor stopped for a second then became a solid tone—the cliched prompt in every hospital show to send all of the medical personnel scrambling with their life-saving machinery.

He stayed holding her now lifeless hand, somehow knowing no amount of screaming for the crash cart was going to bring her back.

20

December 1980

Oh, THAT Chapman

The bottomless glass of Jameson's that welcomed him somberly back at the loft every night led to Davis dragging himself into work at various hours, more out of habit than with any purpose. Since Mary's death, he had mostly gone through the motions running the store. Luckily, he had competent staff that recognized it and allowed for it, tiptoeing around him, none of them having the sort of connection to Davis to be able to intervene.

Davis had dragged himself in to open at noon. Store hours were generally from 12 to 9 PM. He had stationed himself behind the counter on the stool and immediately placed Miles Davis's "Kind of Blue" on the turntable. The staff had secretly taken to trying to hide the store's copy of the album to keep Davis from playing it all the time, but he kept finding it.

And playing it.

Over and over.

Traffic early in the day was generally slow but picked up after lunch. Davis looked up as the front door announced the first customer. It was a young man, slightly heavy, wearing yellow tinted wrap-around sunglasses. He walked around the store and then came up to the counter asking for a copy of John Lennon's newly released Double Fantasy album. The bulk of Whirled Records' business was in the collectible inventory but they also carried some new releases, both Billboard top sellers and obscure material that Davis and the staff felt like promoting. In the same way that FM radio had been making musical careers for the last twenty years, Davis ran his store like an art gallery, with him being the arbiter of what was cool.

The man seemed strangely familiar to him, but Davis just assumed he had been in the store previously. He directed him to the new releases section.

As the customer was paying, Davis again got a feeling he had not only seen this person before, but met him.

"You look familiar. Have we met?"

"I don't know. You look familiar, too. I'm just visiting the city from Hawaii. I'm hoping to get John Lennon to autograph this album today up at the Dakota."

"John and Yoko come in here from time to time. They're pretty low key."

"I'm a big fan. That is, I used to be, before he started spouting off about how the Beatles were bigger than Jesus."

Davis had no rejoinder for that. He bagged up the album and handed it to the customer. "I hope you get your autograph. Seems like a long way to come just for that."

"I've been planning it for a long time."

The customer took the album and cradled it in his arms, standing awkwardly, seeming to want the conversation to continue but not offering up anything further to that end.

"Thanks," Davis finally said after a long pause and the customer turned and left the store.

Odd duck, Davis thought and turned his attention back to nothing.

Later that night at home, watching Johnny Carson before passing out, a news bulletin came on about Lennon being shot four times in the back at the entrance to his home at the Dakota. They showed the perpetrator, who had remained at the scene after the shooting.

Jesus, Davis thought, *That's the same guy who had been in the store.*

The man was identified as Mark David Chapman.

The guns. Nutbags with their fucking guns, thought Davis and took another slug of whiskey from his tumbler, but in the back of his mind, he was nagged by the thought he had met him before.

The next day, as Chapman's photo was splashed across every newspaper available, Davis went back to the short conversation he had had with the assassin and remembered his comment about coming from Hawaii. *Hawaii...*

Then he recalled a vision he had had—no, it was not just a vision—an out-of-body experience. Where he had intervened in a young man's suicide attempt, how the young man had "seen" him and how at the time he remembered their paths had crossed one time earlier—at the shooting range in Georgia when Davis had been on his road trip running away from the National Guard.

Holy shit. I saved the life of the man who would go on to shoot John Lennon? What is it with me and people with guns? It was a rhetorical question, but one that would come up again in the not-too-distant future.

The news story revealed the shooter had actually met Lennon earlier that day and John autographed the very album Davis had sold. *I wonder where that album is now?* Davis thought, disliking himself for considering the macabre collectible value of what might have been not only the last autograph Lennon may have signed, but also the most notorious.

The city, the world, mourned the death of one of its most famous and beloved songwriters. Davis, being a purveyor of those songs, couldn't get away from the immediacy of it, especially considering his indirect role in it. It got him thinking about cause and effect, fate—the interconnectedness of the smallest action and the outcomes of what sometimes seemed like tiny inconsequential deeds. He was still struggling with the death of Mary and his unborn son, and while Lennon's murder did not come close to matching the emotional impact, it certainly did nothing to lift him out of what was becoming a depression. Not only did he feel a lack of control over external events in his life, but even the events in his life that were seemingly IN his control were going haywire.

Chapman's copy of the album that had been placed in some bushes near the Dakota was found by a mourning Beatles fan the next day and turned into the police as evidence. They traced its purchase to his store and an officer came by and asked questions, but Davis had nothing to contribute he thought germane to the case, not to mention certainly not wanting to get involved in another trial around someone getting shot.

Christmas in New York is usually a magical time: the stores festooned in the most imaginative decoration, the excitement of gift-giving and its connection to the mighty god of retail. The always bustling city gets buzzing even more, but Lennon's death cast a pall over the holiday season and the music business in general. Ordinarily, the busiest time of the year for record sales, Davis made sure to be stocked up with the current best-selling titles: Pat Benatar, The Cars, The B-52s, Dire Straits and the like but also knew enough to be offering some of the new music that was coming out: Pretenders, The Police, Tears for Fears, The Dead Kennedys. Store hours were expanded to accommodate the crush and it kept Davis from wallowing in his loss, but he mostly went through the motions then crawled back into his bottle at night.

Once the new year rang in, the reality of winter in the city took over: dirty snow piled high on street corners, frigid, damp air blustering in off of one or the other of the rivers depending on which way the wind was blowing, channeled down the valleys of skyscrapers, the cold stored in millions of tons of concrete and asphalt waiting for spring to bring a renewal.

Which wasn't coming for another couple of months.

Central Park in New York is a huge, sprawling oasis smack in the middle of the island. Davis and Mary loved visiting there throughout all the seasons of the year. It always amazed Davis it was allowed to remain a park, considering it sat on what was arguably the most valuable real estate on the planet: six percent of Manhattan's land area (843 acres), 2.5

miles long and a half-mile wide. Mary had particularly enjoyed all of the statues but especially Alice in Wonderland that had been worn through in parts of its bronze patina by millions of children (not to mention Davis and Mary) climbing on it.

Davis left the store early one day and trudged over seventy blocks to the statue just off of 74th Street. Snow had gently begun to fall, creating a hush that dampened the harsh edges of the typical urban cacophony. He had underestimated the distance; they usually took the subway to get uptown, and the now slippery sidewalks made the trip that much more difficult. When he got there, the snow had created pristine white hats for Alice and her cohorts: the Mad Hatter, the March Hare, the Cheshire Cat. Davis did not know what had compelled him to make the trip, but now he was faced with this reminder of what had been taken from him. He proceeded to make a pile of twenty, maybe thirty snowballs. It was the fluffy but wet kind of snow that packed really well. Then, his arsenal ready, at a distance of about twenty feet, he unloaded at the statue, his icy missiles finding their mark more often than not, flinging with all his might. After the last one, he walked over to the statue, sat dejectedly on one of the large mushrooms that made up the sculpture and allowed his sorrow to pour out, which he had not been able to do since Mary's passing. His arm and shoulder hurt and his legs ached from the trek, his feet were freezing and wet, his hands practically frostbitten. He tried climbing up on the statue, not being able to get much purchase at all, slipping and falling, determined to remove the residue of his barrage. One by one, he wiped down the faces of the characters, then slid back down the biggest mushroom, then walked over to Fifth Avenue, hailed one of the ubiquitous Yellow cabs, went back to his loft, turned up the heat on the ancient radiators and splashed his way down into the bottom of the latest bottle of whiskey.

The winter wore on through February into March. Friends tried to call Davis but he seldom answered the phone anymore. They would stop by the store, but as often as not, he wasn't there. Towards the middle of March, the weather had been letting up and the first signs of spring began to show. In a man-made world of concrete and steel, nature still asserted herself wherever she could. Daffodils and crocuses pushed up, trees budded, the weather warmed in the cycle of renewal.

Davis received an invitation in the mail from his artist friend Tschuck; he was to have a major opening in Washington DC at the end of the month. It brought him back to his time in New Mexico: what a different existence it was on so many levels. He remembered how he would escape into the high desert with his easel and his paints. He decided he would attend the opening; it would be great to see Tschuck and get out of New York for a few days. It was around the time the cherry trees blossomed in DC, which he had never experienced. His staff at the store enthusiastically supported his decision; they had been worried about his morose slide and he had become more difficult to be around. The opening was on a Saturday night. Davis decided to surprise Tschuck and not announce his attendance. He booked a room near the gallery.

Tschuck was an imposing figure: Native American, with long black hair and his signature lone dangling earring. Davis approached him well after the event had started, watching the well-wishers pay tribute, which meant the Davis was already half in the bag. He came up behind Tschuck and slapped him roughly on the back, saying, "Gee, they let..."

That was as far as he got. Davis, knowing some of Tschuck's history, didn't know about his military and martial arts training. Reacting to what appeared to him to be a strike, Tschuck swung his elbow widely, clearing out his attacker to the rear. Davis stumbled backward, lost his footing and his drink and plowed into Tschuck's latest work, "Wounded," ripping a giant tear down the middle of the canvas.

The buzz of the room stopped abruptly, appropriately. Davis slumped to the floor and Tschuck stood looking at him, finally realizing who it was.

"What the fuck? Miles?"

21

March 1981

An Opening

"Jesus, Miles, I didn't know it was you. Are you OK?"

"You sure know how to greet a friend you haven't seen in years," Davis (or Miles, as Tschuck knew him) said, rising to his feet. A bit unsteady, he looked behind him at the large canvas on the wall, torn and askew, realizing the gravity of his position. Every single eye in the room bored into him.

Davis turned to the painting and straightened it on the wall, but that was not going to have any effect on the two-foot gash he had created in a $38,000 work of art. He fingered the edges of the tear when security stepped in to escort him away. (Ironically, Tschuck had a weaver friend sew up the canvas, leaving the stitches deliberately visible, and because of the story behind it, the work eventually sold for many thousands more).

Tschuck stopped the security people. "It's Ok. He's a friend of mine." Tschuck took Davis in a bear hug, "What are you doing here?"

"I couldn't have you showing on the East Coast and me not show up."

"Right. You sure know how to make an entrance, pal."

Davis hung around until the closing was over and went to the after-party at Tschuck's suite, where he passed out and spent the night. They tried to connect the next morning, over breakfast, but Tschuck was burdened with numerous hangers-on and orders-of-business. He sensed his friend was going through a tough time and persuaded Davis to hang out through Monday so they could catch up.

Over lunch on Monday, Davis told him all about the intervening years: the trials, meeting Mary, the store, the accident, their unborn son.

Tschuck just listened, like a good friend should, without passing any judgement on how Davis (again, Miles to him—since Davis had been on the lam in his time in New Mexico) was coping.

It felt good to Davis to have someone removed, but close to him, to unload on. When he was done, Tschuck sat across their lunch table and remarked, "Those are some hard times, my friend."

"Yeah, well, into every life some rain must fall, huh? How about you? How are you doing?"

"Everything's good. My paintings are selling like crazy overseas. It's been good." He paused. "You inspired me, man. You took my work in another direction. Thank you. What about you? Have you been painting?"

Davis chuckled. "No, I haven't dipped my fingers in any paint since that last one, 'The Cross.' Shit, I don't even know where that painting is now."

"Are you kidding? Gloria still has that hanging in the gallery in Santa Fe. She could have sold that dozens of times, but it's still hanging in that same place. It's become kind of an icon."

"Huh." Davis allowed himself to revisit his time back in New Mexico. There was silence at the table.

Tschuck said, "Let me call you when I get back home. You can come and visit. We'll go out in the desert, do a sweat, clear your head. Take a break, bro."

"That's not a bad idea. It'd be good to get out of the city for a while."

They exchanged contact information and Davis left their meeting feeling connected, lightened, not knowing what was ahead, but feeling optimistic about it. He decided to walk the streets of Washington before heading back to New York. It was a pleasant spring day and he set off just walking, nowhere in particular. He noticed a gathering of people near a hotel complex and curious, moved ahead to see what was going on.

"President Reagan just gave a speech and should be coming out any minute now" a bystander replied when Davis asked. Not being especially political, especially after his Kent State experience, Davis got caught up in the anticipation of the crowd, which wasn't very large. There was a ripple of excitement as the president's entourage exited the side door of the building. The crowd surged forward to get a better view and Davis got swept along with it.

Davis could see the commander-in-chief's signature pompadour just above the crowd when his attention diverted to the man standing directly in front of him.

The man had reached into his jacket and Davis could clearly see what looked like a .22 pistol being raised to shoot. Reacting instinctively, he brought his arm forward to divert the man's wrist downward. He made contact and as he did, he heard six shots ring out. Bedlam followed. Some of the Secret Service agents immediately wrestled the shooter to the ground while others dove in front of the president and pushed him into the waiting limousine. Davis immediately retreated. The very last thing he wanted was to be involved in yet another shooting. He backed away and melded into the crowd of people now gathering to see what the commotion was.

Are you fucking kidding me? Went through his head. *What is it with me and these guns?!*

He continued to back away from the scene and once he had retreated a half block, turned and continued walking away, slowly, making sure he was doing nothing to draw attention to himself. His mind was racing: *Why? Why the guns? Did I have any connection to this one?* Nothing was coming to him as far as any connection. He wasn't political, he had no opinion of Reagan or his politics and as far as he knew, there was no connection to the shooter.

Davis would find out the next day Hinckley's first shot, the one he altered, had hit White House Press Secretary James Brady in the head, leaving him partially paralyzed. A local police officer and one of the Secret Service agents were also wounded. Reagan was not directly hit but Hinckley's last shot ricocheted off the limousine, hitting Reagan in the side, puncturing a lung.

Davis took the next train back home to New York. This latest episode just contributed to his sense of helplessness.

And he never even got to see the cherry trees blossom.

22

September 1982

Gravid

Being the frontperson of the band, Becca got a lot of attention: a LOT of attention. It was seductive, both in the traditional sense—men came on to her all the time—but also on a deeper, more psychological sense. At first, Becca let her gut be her guide and that had governed her decisions up to this point, dictating how she would respond to the attention she got both on and off the stage, but after a while, the sheer volume of affirmation was too intoxicating to ignore and she let herself succumb to it.

She had never had trouble attracting the opposite sex, but what was coming at her now (pardon the pun) was different: rock stars, TV personalities, celebrities of all ilks. By virtue of HER celebrity, she now qualified for a higher tier of interest. Where she shrugged off advances at first, when she got approached by people she admired, her guard went down, and once it was down, it stayed down.

The band had been swinging through the South as part of the tour. Sometimes the gigs were just on the way to someplace else—but they had wound through Memphis and played to an enthusiastic sold-out audience. It was Memphis, after all; they knew their music.

There was a gathering at a venue downtown after the show. It was early morning, but the scene was just getting started. Becca was approached by the largest man she had ever seen. He was not just tall, but wide, easily 6' 6" and at least 250 pounds, with not an ounce of fat on him. He stood right in front of her and stared down at her, a smile on his face.

While not afraid of him, he was an intimidating presence, although his smile softened any actual fears she might have had.

"Uh, you're blocking my view," she said, half-jokingly.

"Yeah, I get that a lot."

"I'll bet. I'm not going to make any tall jokes, though."

"It might be a little late for that, but I'll chalk that one up to my girth, not my height."

He stood there, expecting to be recognized, then realized that wasn't forthcoming. Becca extended her hand. "I'm Becca. With the band. Too Much." His hand engulfed hers.

"Too Much, huh?"

"Yeah, we played at The New Daisy tonight. Did you catch the show?"

"No, I didn't." His hand was still holding hers, and as white as Becca's skin was, his was just as dark. "You don't know who I am, do you?"

Becca was put off by the audacity of the question and pulled her hand back. "No, but I am guessing I should."

"Maybe, but I guess we're even. Here you are a big rock star and I didn't know who you were, either. So, I apologize for that."

"Are you going to tell me?"

"Actually, I kind of like that I can be just another guy. Give me a name. What do you want to call me?"

"I'd like to call you my bodyguard, quite frankly. 'How about Beauregard?'"

"Beauregard the Bodyguard? I like the alliteration, but it does smack a little of southern plantation. How about 'Bojangles?' Sho' nuff, Missy; I could do a li'l shuffle fo ya." With that, the imposing big man affected a deep southern accent and actually did a short dance.

Becca looked up at the man's face in front of her and was able to read his anger. "I apologize," she said. "Often my attempts at snappy repartee end up going in the wrong direction, and this one has gone WAY off the rails. I assure you, there is not a racist bone in my body."

"That's easy for any white person to say once they're called on it."

Now Becca bristled.

She immediately thought back to her time in the Peace Corps and the friends she had made in Africa, especially Embartu, the shaman she had grafted with in their ceremony. Maintaining eye contact with the person who had now become somewhat of an adversary, she rolled up the sleeve on her blouse, until she knew the fabric had passed the point where she knew her skin graft was visible.

"You see that?"

The man's eyes tracked up the freckled line of Becca's arm and stopped at the small rectangle of dark skin looking like a tattoo on her upper arm.

"What's that?"

"That is an implant of my friend Embartu's skin. She was a shaman with the Shimbaru tribe in Somalia. We exchanged grafts in an ancient ceremony when I was there a few years ago."

The man's gaze came back to Becca's. "I would imagine there's a story behind that."

"Yes, there is," said Becca softly. "So, can we start over?" Becca extended her right hand. "I'm Rebecca. Most people call me Becca."

The man took her hand. "Jackson. And that's what people call me."

Becca could sense other people watching them. Now she was curious about who he was, but decided to give him what he wanted—a bit of anonymity. She relaxed into the person he was and the next thing she knew a couple of hours had flown by. The party was winding down somewhat and Jackson proposed they go someplace else.

They did.

She was thoroughly charmed, bordering on seduced, and it wouldn't be long before that was accomplished too. She had never been around any man who so epitomized masculinity. She found herself at times wanting to match it, but that didn't feel right, natural. When he suggested his place, she didn't hesitate, although there was a part of her that was actually a little afraid of him.

And she found that exciting.

With a couple hours of social foreplay under their belts, they had both sent out appropriate signals; they were going to get naked and see what it looked like from there.

He bent over to kiss her. His lips were full and large, like the rest of him. She locked onto his kiss, all of her attention on his mouth and promptly got lost there. The next sensation she felt was of being lifted, effortlessly. She wrapped her legs around his waist and her arms around his muscular neck, allowing herself to be carried over to the bed.

Clothing was quickly dispatched, some self-shucked, some assisted with. Becca had a distant voice in her head, telling her to be careful. It was little more than a whisper; she had a dozen thoughts swirling around her; his body—he had to be a professional athlete, who IS he? Who cares? His skin was perfect and the body underneath it was... Jesus, so... fucking hard. She found herself exploring places on the male body she hadn't realized before. And then there was his erection. Holy shit! What am I supposed to do with THAT?

Meanwhile, Jackson was engaging himself with Becca's parts. He was obviously practiced.

"We OK?"

Becca's overmind interjected: Fuck! Birth Control... She did not want to interrupt what they were doing, but...

"Yeah," she said. She made a move to slink out from underneath him to retrieve her diaphragm and he stopped her. "Where you goin'?"

"I... I... nowhere." Her mind did a quick calculation around rhythm, somehow... Yeah, we're OK... I think...

He kissed her again and she slipped back into their abyss.

When he entered her, she felt that sense of fear come up again. She had never been with a man so large. It took one stroke for her to realize those fears were unfounded. His weight was not fully ON her, but his size engulfed her. She had some thoughts about flipping him and getting on top. He was having none of that. He was fully absorbed with his own agenda now and it was getting intense. Again: a little scared, totally turned on.

This was different from any other sexual encounter she had ever had. From early on, Becca had taken full part in everything that transpired, and had often initiated. This was different; she was being taken. She thought to resist, then realized she didn't want to.

She allowed herself to succumb to it, to receive it, what she would later reflect upon as the absolute "yin" of it. His orgasm was intense. She felt him come in her, his whole body wracking, releasing.

He pulled out and collapsed next to her. It became apparent there would be no tending to whatever needs she might have. But for now, that didn't matter. It had been extremely pleasurable, in a different way from what she was used to.

The next day the band was on to another city. She wouldn't see him again.

Becca decided she didn't want to know his true identity, just to keep that air of mystery about it. She was able to nip every inquiry in the bud about who she had left the club with, but she overheard a certain name come up numerous times in other whispered conversations.

So much for mystery...

She had gone off the Pill about a year earlier, not liking the effects it had on her body. The Pill was so easy, taken as part of a morning routine. She took to using a diaphragm. It made sex a bit less spontaneous, she was able to make it work and remain ungravid.

Until she wasn't.

She had told herself if she would ever become pregnant, she would have the baby, regardless of the circumstances. Now, over two months in, and sure of her state, it could not have come at a more inconvenient time. The tour to support the second album was set to start and being pregnant did not fit the rock n roll image she, the band and Chad had forged.

She spoke to her friend Margie about it.

"Just get an abortion," was Margie's initial reaction.

"I don't want an abortion. I don't believe in it."

"What part don't you believe in? You weren't consciously trying to make a baby, were you? You don't have a religious argument, right? Do you know who the father is?"

Becca reddened a bit, dodging the question. "I have my suspicions," Becca answered.

"You little slut," Margie responded, laughing.

"Hey, hey, hey. The men can sleep around, and there is no judgement around that."

"I'm only teasing. Besides, I'm not one to throw any stones."

Becca was aware of Margie's proclivities; they talked about their partners on a regular basis.

"Have you ever had an abortion?"

Margie immediately got serious. "Yes." She hesitated. "A couple, actually."

"Margie..."

"I know, I know..."

"What was it like?"

"It sucked. Ha. No pun intended. It was awful. Invasive. And sad. One of them was the hardest decision I have ever had to make because I knew who the dad was and I thought we were going to get married. Until he learned I was pregnant, and then he started singing a different tune."

"Margie, I am so sorry."

"Hey, it's part of our lot in life, y'know? We bear the children. The men have it easy. If they get someone pregnant and don't want the baby, they can just leave. And that's what he did. But you know what? I don't regret it. Either one. Could you imagine me lugging a child around?"

Becca didn't answer Margie's somewhat rhetorical question, but it planted the seed in her mind about the reality of motherhood at this point in her life.

"I just don't want to make the wrong decision."

"It's not about 'right' or 'wrong.' You don't know what the consequences of your decision will be, either way. We never know. We try to kid ourselves into thinking we know, but it's all an illusion. Who knows? I may never get pregnant again and end up a shriveled old maid with eleven cats. But you, Becca, if you have a child now, what happens to Too Much? Can you keep your career? Do you even want to be a mom?"

That night, Becca walked down to the beach and sat for hours, poring over Margie's questions and more. She tried going "inside" and communicating with what she felt was already perhaps another entity inside her but her efforts were one-sided. Are you a person yet? she asked.

She got no response.

In the band, she was closest to Bobby, even though a while back, she had had a short fling with Brian the drummer. She told Bobby she was pregnant.

"Hey! That's great!" was his response, until he saw Becca didn't share his enthusiasm. "Or... not so great."

Ultimately, Bobby was clueless. All he knew was music. When Becca finally went to Chad with the news, his immediate response was she had to have that "taken care of" as soon as possible.

Being fairly certain of the dad, she struggled with the prospect of having him be part of the decision-making process, especially when she had convinced him they were covered as far as birth control. She thought back to the conversation she had had with her mom, years ago, about somewhat similar circumstances and how bitter she had been about keeping that child.

Her.

She made an appointment to have an abortion. She had to go to a counseling session first, which just made the decision all that much harder, but she still showed up for the procedure. When she got there and disrobed, then got on the table, she was still conflicted. The doctor came in snapping on some rubber gloves. "Ready?"

That's when it became clear. "No. No, I'm not. I can't." Becca sobbed.

The doctor took off her gloves, came and stood by her side and put a warm hand on her shoulder. "I watch women go through this every day. For some, the decision is easy, for others, like you, it's much harder. Your heart is telling you what to do and you have to listen to that."

Becca left the clinic. She had told the band and Chad what she was going to do, now she had to tell them something different.

The band's feelings were mixed; they wanted to be supportive, but knew this was going to affect them in some way. Chad was incensed. He went on a tirade, telling her she had to make another appointment and "do the right thing," that she was in "breach of contract."

Ultimately, Becca stuck by her guns. They toured for a couple of months until the situation became untenable. For her, it wasn't just about how it would look, being up onstage with her big belly. She didn't want to be up there, front and center. She wanted to nest somewhere, now that she had made her decision, to nurture the life inside of her and just take the time to engage in one of the most natural acts possible.

Becca gave birth to a baby girl.

Mayah.

23

October 1983

What Do You Mean "She's Gone?"

"You signed a contract."

"So sue me. You can't get blood out of a stone. The big contract you got for us has barely given us enough to live on, so if you want to sue me, go ahead and see what that gets you."

It was just a month after Mayah's birth and Chad was already after Becca to take the band out on the road to support the album, which was getting close to no airplay. He didn't have a lot of leverage, though, outside of the fact Becca had no money coming in either, nor did the other band members, outside of some side gigs they were playing.

Meanwhile, Becca was firmly ensconced in motherhood. She had not expected her maternal instincts to kick in the way they had, nursing and nurturing; it was all-encompassing. It wasn't until Bobby came to her after the second month that she realized the reality of her financial situation.

"Bec, you know we love you and we love little Mayah, too. But we need to figure out what this is all going to look like. We've got rent due on the house and all of the other bills. And we signed that contract, too. Are you done with the band or is there some kind of timeline going forward for when you will be back up on stage?"

Standing up to Chad was one thing, but having to disappoint Bobby was another. For the first time in months, Becca began to have a sense of her responsibility to the collective. And she realized she had been using Mayah as an excuse to not have to go on the road and rehash the songs on the second album, which had been produced very much like the first and unlike the vision Becca had for her music. Chad had pushed them to write the songs and then had rushed them through another contentious recording period.

"Look, we can go out on the road, and rearrange the songs like we did for the first album. Play 'em our way. There's nothing Chad can make us do once we are on stage. Besides, there's nothing that says you can't be a Rockmama out there. We'll bring a nanny along with us. We can make this happen."

Becca took Bobby's words to heart. There was a financial reality to deal with and so it was decided; Mayah would come with them on tour.

Having a small child along on a rock tour changes a lot of perspectives, but it wasn't along the lines of "sshh-the-baby's-sleeping." Quite the contrary. Mayah loved the noise, in particular, the rhythm section, notably Caleb's bass playing. There were numerous times when he was called upon to put Mayah to sleep. It was comical to see a smile come across her face when he would play and then her eyes struggle to stay open until they couldn't anymore.

When she was really tiny, they would fashion a crib out of a guitar case, and countless photos of that got circulated. When she got bigger, (and it didn't take long) one of the gear crates the band equipment came in became the substitute crib. And of course, many photos of her sound asleep in a Too Much-emblazoned equipment box also made the rounds.

The biggest change was in the typical sex and drugs atmosphere. Not that Mayah was going to be aware of any of that tomfoolery, but it was as if a certain amount of respect was being paid to her existence. One of the roadies, Billy Ashcroft, a bearded, long-haired biker-bear of a man really took to her and he could be seen carrying her around cradled in his forearm like the footballs he used to carry. Even though there was a full-time nanny, Jenny Tutonia, taking care of Mayah was a collective effort, the 'village' before 'it takes a village to raise a child' was a thing.

The band would do encores and then, as often as not, come out for a final bow with Becca holding Mayah on her hip. She became a part of the band; crowds would chant her name at the end of the show to get a glimpse. The noise, the lights, the bedlam became part of the environment she was growing up in. As a result, when it was time for her to sleep, she could sleep through anything. The rule with the designated gear case that was to be used as the surrogate crib was the top, which was latched, not hinged, was never to be closed during a gig, whether Mayah was in it or not.

She was one happy child; the kind everyone wanted to hold. She smiled easily, as if she was just comfortable being alive. As soon as her baby fat burned off, her face was dominated with an almost unnaturally deep dimple on the left side. She went to strangers without a fuss. As long as they were going to provide attention, she was all in.

So, when Jenny came back to the "crib" after having been called away for a few minutes, she didn't worry when she saw it empty; she just assumed Billy or one of the other roadies had taken her. It didn't take long for panic to set in, though, when a quick search came up empty. Billy rushed to the stage to see if she was out there with the band, but it was obvious she was not. Word spread quickly backstage to look for the child. Though she was just beginning to move about on her own, it would have been almost impossible to get out of her crib without help.

The band had been headlining a medium sized renovated movie theater in Minneapolis. There were a half dozen dressing rooms that had been set up backstage, and they were quickly searched while the band played on, oblivious to the scramble that was going on behind them. Billy rushed outside one of the exits, opening onto an alleyway and saw nothing, then sprinted to the street to see if he could get a clue to Mayah's whereabouts. There were a few people walking around, but no one furtively slinking away with what may have looked like a baby wrapped in a blanket.

He ran around the entire block that surrounded the theater and went in through the front lobby, his eyes searching frantically everywhere for a sign of the missing girl. He entered the theater, the band still playing as if nothing were amiss. He ran up the aisle to the front of the theater, casting his gaze from side to side, finding no sign of a child. Making his way all the way up to the stage, he stood stock still, frozen and breathless, looking up at Becca, not able to say anything. The band finished their song, and Becca, not expecting to see Billy standing on front of her, locked eyes with him. It was obvious from the look on his face something was wrong. He beckoned for her to bend down so she could hear him from up on the stage, which was elevated about four feet.

Becca's eyes got large. "What do you mean 'you can't find her?'" she screamed. In a single motion, she unleashed herself from the Mustang around her neck and was already two steps towards the back of the stage by the time it clattered to the floor, sending feedback through the system that echoed the gravity of the situation.

A hush grew over the crowd. Billy jumped up onto the stage and followed after Becca, praying in the time he had made his circuit around the building that Mayah had shown up.

That was most assuredly NOT the case.

Jenny was hysterically crying. She, after all, was responsible for watching Mayah at all times. It was her one job. Billy found the person in charge of security at the venue and filled him in. "Every exit gets monitored and no one leaves until we find her."

The promoter came on stage and said there would be a short intermission and the band left the stage. He came back a short time later and made the announcement that Mayah was missing, in the hopes there was some benign explanation for the disappearance and someone in the building would find her.

That did not happen.

Becca was a mess. The tour was cancelled. The police were brought in, hell, the FBI got involved. The story made all the trade journals and local papers, even some national news. There were very few clues. Jenny said someone had told her there was a phone call for her and she had checked Mayah who had been sound asleep. She couldn't have been gone for more than a minute and a half, since, when she got to the phone, there was no one on the other end.

There was no ransom call forthcoming, there were no cryptic clues about who might have done this. Mayah had simply, calculatingly, been abducted.

24

January 1984

Shades of Robert Johnson

Chad had unsuccessfully tried to make a case for the tour to go on. He knew he had to tread lightly.

"You're fucking kidding me, right?" Becca had screamed at him.

"Look, it's not as if you are going to be out there physically beating the bushes looking for her. It'll take your mind off of it to have something else to do," Chad had argued, however feebly.

Becca looked at him like he had two heads. "Really?! Somebody out there has my BABY" she literally screamed the last word, "and you want me to go up on stage and what? Sing?"

Chad opened his mouth to speak and a few words tumbled out: "You know... you..." and then he stopped, having the sense to know when he had reached an immovable object. His gaze had been downward, towards the floor, and he shook his head. Without moving his head, he glanced up at her, his expression unchanged. "It didn't have to be this way," he said.

"What are you talking about?"

His visage went stony and cold. "Nothing. Nothing at all. Just... this all could've been easier."

He got up and quickly left the room, leaving Becca to ponder how to possibly move forward.

The authorities were getting nowhere. The woman who had summoned Jenny to the phone was not anyone associated with the theatre or the security team, although she had what had appeared to be backstage credentials. Beyond that, she could have been a ghost.

Becca decided she wanted to seek the services of a medium. She found a woman who had worked in similar cases that had some success in finding lost individuals.

Her name was Leslie Kellerman, a middle-aged woman who looked like she could have stepped out of any suburban household in America. Becca was a little disappointed and it must have shown.

"Not what you expected huh? I get that a lot. I thought about sporting a turban or a crystal ball but they clashed with my housedress."

Becca colored a bit. "No, no. Actually, I'm aware that psychic powers come in all shapes and sizes."

"Yes, Becca. You of all people would know that."

Becca thought back to a previous encounter she had had with the psychic Madame Marie years ago, when she had immediately recognized Becca's own powers.

Leslie asked her, "What are you seeing? When you go inside?"

"I can't tell. It's like I am too close to it. I see her, I see my Mayah, but I can't tell if it's just a memory, or wishful thinking. I believe she is alive, but I don't know where or who she's with." Becca's emotions swelled and tears poured freely down her face, with no other visible signs of crying.

"Let's see what I can pick up. You just stay with where you are; I want that connection."

Becca allowed herself to stay in that moment, accessing a state she used to meditate and sometimes "travel." Leslie guided her back to the night of the concert, but there was nothing there for Becca to recall. She was regressing her further when Becca lost all sense of her physical body and felt herself slipping into a layer of darkness.

When her eyes adjusted to what little light there was, she saw a field stretching off in all directions at the intersection of two country roads. A fence ran along one of the roads, disappearing into the darkness. Sitting atop one of the fenceposts was a huge owl.

Not surprisingly (to Becca, anyway) it spoke to her. "Well?"

Becca's first thought was *Really?* But she also knew enough to trust the process if she asked the right questions. Owl's voice was extremely deep and rumbling, and... familiar. Familiar in a way she did not want to acknowledge from episodes with the dark entity she had in the past.

Becca figured she might as well take the bull by the horns. "This is kind of clichéd, don't you think? I mean, c'mon... crossroads? The owl's a new twist but, really? Are you gonna ask for my soul next? Maybe it's time for a new shtick."

Owl rumblelaughed. "Ah, the same old smartass Becca. Yeah, maybe it's a little hackneyed, but hey—you recognize it when you see it, don't you? Maybe it's time YOU came up with a new shtick. From where I am sitting, you're the one whose power seems to be getting her nowhere."

Becca watched as the image of Owl spread its massive wings and morphed into an all-encompassing blackness, only to revert to birdform but with human faces: the first of which was Chad. There were no voices, only expressions, none of them benevolent.

Owlface came back and spoke again in the rumblevoice: "Don't think you can turn to your 'angels,'" spitting that last word out. "That may have saved you the last time we met, but those two chumps are in no shape to be helping you now." Becca flashed back to the time she had encountered this entity before, when Davis and her dad were somehow present to extract her. Not believing the dark entity, she attempted to bring up an image of either of them, to no avail.

Owl chuckled, raspy and phlegmy. "What? Didn't believe me? Look, Missy; I tried to make this easy for you. You could have had it all. I just would have needed a few," and here it hesitated, then, "concessions on your part. But you wanted to do it your way. Well, guess what? You don't get to have it all—not without my help. That's not the way it works."

Becca's mind was racing. Is this really happening? Is this my version of Robert Johnson making a deal with the devil at the crossroads? This is just me making up some cheesy metaphor, right? At the same time, she recalled other experiences she had she knew were not dreams, not figments of her imagination, scary and malevolent, and this was certainly fitting into that category.

Owl seemed to read her mind. "Uh-uh, dear. Not a dream, not a figment. You must know if you fuck around in other dimensions, there will be times when you cross over into my turf. Welcome to my little corner of hell."

Becca gathered her wits. She was lucid and remembered she had entered into a session with that women. Leslie.

She was aware of Leslie, standing impassively down the road, about fifty yards away, realizing she wasn't going to be any help at all.

Owl snapped her out of her reverie. "Let's get down to business. I believe you lost your baby."

Now it had her attention. "No accident, that. You would think you would have learned your mama's lesson, but no; you had to screw around, and then think you could just go on living your life and everything was going to be hunky-dory."

Owl's face cycled through the faces of her lovers, some more familiar than others. She had gone through her own version of this, once she had become pregnant, but had decided there wasn't anyone on the list she had wanted to co-parent with. She wasn't even completely sure back then she wanted to be a mother.

Until she was. Sure, that is.

And then everything changed, and it was all taken away. It had been about three months since that gig at the theater, that horrible, horrible night.

And now here was this darkness, bringing it all back, not that she hadn't spent every single minute of every day since, wondering where Mayah was, and if she was even alive. All this passed through her mind in an instant, and somehow the entity was privy to it all.

"Yeah, that was some nasty business," Owl said, deliberately understated.

Becca lunged at him, but he was ready for it; one flap of his wings set him up just high enough to be out of Becca's grasp, not that she knew what she would do if she had been able to reach it. It's talons were bigger than her hands. She launched into a tirade of expletives, laden with "fucks" and plenty of "goddamns" just in case this really WAS the devil.

Owl floated just above her without having to flap its wings. In the back of her mind, Becca wondered HOW it could do that, giving some credibility to its otherworldliness.

She grabbed at one of Owl's feet and it retracted briefly then lashed back with one razor-sharp talon, raking across the back of her hand, which only exacerbated her rage.

She could feel it churning inside her, but also knew she was up against a power and strength far beyond her physical prowess. She closed her eyes and gathered herself. "Alright. Alright." She paused. "Alright. What exactly is it you want from me?"

Owl settled back on to the fence, with as smug a look as an owl's face can have. "That's a good start: a little fealty, a little humility. I'm always looking for minions, and there are many who will sell their souls for little more than a metaphorical piece of candy. But they are chattel, mere placeholders and they have very little power. But you, dear lady, you were blessed with charms beyond those of most. Simply put, I want you on my team. I want you to wear the dark cloak."

"Will you give me my baby back?" Becca's voice cracked as she made her request, as much as she wanted to portray a sense of strength.

"Getting right down to the details of the negotiation, are we?" Owl let a silence settle in for a few beats. "That can be arranged, yes."

A sob wracked Becca's whole body and then she gathered herself again. "In exchange for what?"

"Nothing. Right now, that is. At some time in the future, I may call on you to do my bidding, and I need to know that I can depend on you to do that."

Becca snorted (she couldn't help herself). "What are you, some fucking Don Corleone?"

It was Owl's turn to laugh. "No, little girl. Don Corleone was me."

There was another pause and Owl continued, "Or, more specifically, he was one of mine, or a depiction of one of mine, but we are splitting hairs here. The question is, are you in, or out?"

"In. When do I get Mayah back? I want her back NOW!"

"You'll get her back when I am good and ready to give her back, and not a second before. It may be tomorrow, or it may be years from now, but you are hardly in a position to demand anything. Meanwhile, go about your business. Give Chad what he wants; he often speaks directly for me."

Owl could see Becca was a little behind on some of the information he had been throwing out. It said, "What? Chad? Yes, that's right; he's one of us. But deep down, you already knew that, didn't you?"

Becca allowed herself a brief moment to go inside, to that place where she KNEW, and realized Owl was right.

Owl brought her back. "G'wan now. Run along. I have more important matters to deal with." It gestured with its massive wing. "Your 'helper' is waiting for you. You may want to tend to her. She is a little out of her league on this one and she may be a little shaken up."

Owl raised up both its wings. "Just remember; you're mine now, Red. I'll hold up my end of the bargain. If you want to see your little girl again, you'll hold up yours."

It brought its wings forward together and dissipated into a mist of black particles.

Becca turned and saw Leslie still in the distance, useless observer but somehow a facilitator. One step at a time, feeling defeated, yet somehow optimistic, she made her way back.

Owl was right; this was beyond any session Leslie had ever been a part of.

Right down to the gash across Becca's hand.

25

April 1981

Back "Home"

The Reagan shooting put Davis over the edge. While he had some closure around his part in the Kent State shooting, it was troubling to have been connected, however remotely, to John Lennon's murder and now this. He felt there was a force connecting him to gun violence without his intent. He personally had no qualms about guns, having joined the National Guard and excelled in the training they had given him, but he wasn't a gun fanatic. He didn't even own one, and now he was feeling a definite push to be as far away from them as possible.

He went back to New York on the first train out, not wanting any witness to the assassination attempt to identify him. He absentmindedly fingered the bullet he kept in his pocket and thought, *That would have great: for them to hold me at the scene and then find this cartridge to an M-1 in my pocket...*

He wasn't even sure why he kept it. It was like a good luck charm in reverse, a talisman, a reminder of everything that had happened at Kent state and how figuratively, he had dodged a bullet, but now he wondered if keeping it was just attracting more of the same. He promised himself he would get rid of it at the proper time.

When he got back to New York, he went to the record store to check in. The employees were used to him not being around much but he had given a core group of them part ownership in the business, so he knew it was in good hands. After chit-chatting about the recent store traffic and what was new in the business, Davis browsed the racks to see what had come in. The bulk of their inventory was used records brought in by people cleaning out their attics and garages. Though somewhat jaded at being exposed to the entire spectrum of recorded music, there was still a 'collector's thrill' when a piece popped up that was truly rare: the Beatles "butcher cover," early rockabilly stuff, 50's doo-wop and the like. They had a rack with a few new releases, usually not the big mega-hits, but more obscure, small labels and sometimes some promo items that record companies were eager to push.

And sure enough, you guessed it; there was a copy of Too Much's first album displaying a picture of the band with Becca front and center. Davis held it in his hand, knowing exactly who he was looking at, but having a bit of trouble connecting the idea of 'his' Becca to 'this' Becca.

He turned to Jack, who was working the register and said, "Have you heard this?"

"Yeah, they're pretty good. The lead singer kicks ass. She's got a great voice."

Davis split the shrink wrap as he walked over to the front counter. There was always something on the turntable, often cranked up to concert level. He removed the record that was on, a release by a new band from Dublin called U2. He dropped the needle down onto the vinyl and found the two antique easy chairs that had been set up to afford customers the maximum listening experience, settled in and closed his eyes.

The first song had an acoustic guitar intro, and then, clear as a bell, there she was: his Becca, singing something about going home. Her voice lifted him out of the chair and into the speakers, through the wires and the electronics of the stereo system, out to the turntable, spinning a perfect 33 1/3 revolutions per minute into that stylus with its diamond needle, the hardest substance on earth, holding its ground while a platter of polyvinyl chloride rotated, etched with a continuously descending spiral of grooves that reproduced through vibration, amazingly, the tones, the notes, the sounds that human musicians and singers had created.

Not just any musician, either. Here, after all these years, was his Becca, singing. To him. It was unmistakably her voice from the first note, but now it had taken on a different timber. Melodic, yes, because she was singing after all, but there was a different quality to it, and the message had a truth and a soulfulness that belied the amount of time she had been at it.

The songs were good, the band adequate. The production sucks, he thought, but that was just an afterthought. All of his attention was on her, as if she were right there in the room with him. The record played through the first five tracks on side one and the resulting silence snapped him out of his otherworldly experience. He got up and went to the turntable, flipping the record with the practiced dexterity of having done it hundreds, if not thousands, of times before, dropping the needle lightly, expertly, in the leading groove, then racing back to the chair to resume his aural journey to a place both in the past and very VERY much in the present.

The record played through and Davis sat in the chair, reliving his connection with the woman he had literally shared his flesh with. He fingered the spot on his thigh where they had grafted, creating another spot of connection. At various spots during the playing, he felt a welling of emotion, not out of sadness but sheer joy over the sound of her voice, her progressions, chord changes and the soulfulness of her delivery.

Becca, Becca, Becca... he mused. *You've got it.*

He asked Jack, one of the store employees, to keep the record playing, flipping when necessary, until he asked him to stop. He wanted the songs to become familiar to him, so he could recall them at will. He situated himself back in the easy chair, his feet propped up on the worn coffee table in front of him, closed his eyes and retreated back into his other world, a world away from music idols and presidents being shot at, a world where taxis didn't career past stripping away your family, a world that was safe. Part of him knew it was a fantasy; he was after all, living in one of the largest cities in the world, with literally millions of people stacked on top of one another, all vying for the same resources. It was a wonder there was as much order as there was.

Time apart had made Becca that safe place for him. Oh, sure, they had had their differences and seemingly couldn't stay together for very long, but in those times when they were, there was a connection, a completeness that was unmatched anywhere else.

He let her voice transport him back to the times when they were in harmony. The voices on the record helped him with that as they wove together. All the way back to Woodstock—talk about a fantasy time. And then meeting back up again after Kent State and how, despite her political leanings, she had allowed herself to open back up to him. He put a filter in place—a good-times filter—and just allowed that to balance out the confusion and heartbreak he had experienced over the last couple of years. Part of him knew it was false, that he was creating an illusion, but he didn't care. It was an escape, pure and simple, an indulgence, a palliative.

When he had cycled through the infatuation, the passion, the safety and sanctuary he wanted to remember, he opened his eyes and just held up his hand to Jack signaling it was enough. He didn't know how long he had been in the chair, how many record flips Jack had performed for him, but it didn't matter. He got out of the chair, walked out into the street, teeming with people and cars, the cacophony of the city. He walked. And walked. Through neighborhoods and parks, along the East River for a while, all the way uptown, into the night. He cut through Central Park—not the safest place at night—but it didn't matter, past museums, galleries, restaurants. It was his version of an urban walkabout, with no destination in mind, just one foot in front of the other. He was in a benevolent mood, and saw the city in that way, soaking in all the parts of it he loved.

Ravenous, he stopped for a slice of pizza from one of the corner shops that populated the city—their ubiquity belying their status as world's best pizza—dripping grease, parmesan and oregano suffusing his nostrils.

He walked all night, stopping to appreciate the architecture of the public library and its commanding lions out front and center, then made his way through Grand Central Station, staring up in awe at the constellations on the ceiling twelve stories up, listening to the echoes of the billions of people that had made their way through that cavernous room on their way to somewhere else.

Just like him.

Mesmerized by the old-fashioned destination board that had arrivals and departures constantly flipping new alternatives into place (*how do they DO that?*), he chose one and got on a train. Six days later, he was knocking on Tschuck's door in Tesuque, New Mexico. A train here, a bus there, hitchhiking, walking, just basically locomoting any way he could, he arrived at his friend's doorstep, unwashed, unshaven, in the same clothes he'd had on for the past week.

Tschuck opened the door as if Davis were expected and beckoned him inside, neither of them saying a word. Davis himself had barely uttered a hundred words over the whole last week, communicating only when absolutely necessary for food and travel considerations.

Tschuck had a large adobe house he had built with the profits from his paintings. He steered Davis to the guest room. Davis stripped and got in the shower, sloughing off days of road and rail, then found the bed, collapsed in it and slept for 12 hours.

When he woke, he barely remembered where he was. It was midday. With no immediate alternatives, he reluctantly put on his dirty clothes and made his way through the winding halls to the kitchen. There was a note from Tschuck:

Make yourself at home.

Eat. Relax.

There's a robe hanging on the chair.

Use it, Wash your clothes· Please·

I'll be back around 6 PM with chili rellenos·

We'll drink beer·

Welcome back·

Davis found the laundry room, stripped and put the washer to its unenviable task. He padded around the house and found Tschuck's studio. The large northern window had an unobstructed view of the Sangre de Cristos, the Blood of Christ mountains—the tail end of the Rocky Mountain chain. He remembered his forays into those mountains and the surrounding desert and the peace that came from being in the wide-open spaces.

I wanna paint, he thought.

And he would.

He let the southwest re-adopt him—the landscape, the clean air, and in Santa Fe, the openness of the culture. Unique in its acceptance of the fringe elements of "normal" American culture, the city had become a mecca for the effete, the downtrodden, the creative, the outsiders, the... odd.

Davis realized he had become that. Odd, that is. Knowing that in Santa Fe, he was not going to stand out but rather blend right in, he let his peculiarities flourish. They were not outlandish, like some. No, his uniqueness was subtle to the observer, mostly because it was internal. He did let his hair and beard grow wild and taking a cue from the relative silence on his recent sojourn, he rarely spoke. Even his internal dialogue was largely silent; he was content to exist in the moment. He allowed himself to become engrossed in various esoteric spiritual practices that flourished in the city's freedom.

When he would paint, he bordered on a fugue state, whether he was expressing his vision of the landscape or sitting on the plaza rendering the likeness of some usually clueless tourist taken aback by his interpretation of their outward appearance. Instead, he was displaying another side of his subjects that many of them were not even aware of. While not necessarily Picasso-esque, they were hardly realistic images. Davis would work silently, often manically, brushless, his hands daubing, slashing, not just the tips of his fingers but knuckles and wrinkled backs, even palms.

He would charge modestly for these efforts and they came across largely as entertainment for the visiting masses, the paintings often finding a trashbin nearby, which ultimately would only add to the value years later of those paintings that survived.

Occasionally, a subject would sit for him he found intriguing, and he would take more time, even engage in light conversation, sometimes just to hear their vocal inflections. Other times he would probe and push a bit in his conversation to get a bit of emotional reaction he could sense and then interpret.

Most of his landscapes would end up in Gloria's gallery (she had also re-adopted him). She was a good promoter and a good friend, giving him a position as a caretaker on her ranch, with lodging and an income so his day-to-day concerns were minimal.

Most of his time was spent alone, and he liked it that way. He felt now, even more so than before, like he had told Becca: "people disappoint me." That assessment extended beyond just relationships for him, to life in general. As his spiritual boundaries expanded, he allowed that perhaps his expectations were too high, so he found himself lowering the bar, and taking delight in the mundane: nature's kaleidoscope of color, a perfect musical composition, even, upon reflection at bedtime, a day without torment or tragedy.

He became a fixture around Santa Fe, sometimes seen on the trails up above town in the Sangres and on Canyon Road, capturing the local flora and rising-out-of-the-earth adobe architecture. More often than not, though, he wasn't seen, as he would go off on remote hikes into the high desert where no one could disturb his solitude to record his perspective on canvas.

He never planned his days ahead, except for chores at the ranch, caretaking. Other than that, his time was freeform, based on mood and sometimes the weather, although the constant sunshine afforded by the southwest rarely restricted him.

His appearance became somewhat feral; he let his hair extrude into whitemandreads, although he would take scissors to it to keep it out of his face on those rare occasions when his reflection in the bathroom mirror would catch his attention. He still bathed and showered, brushed his teeth, practiced normal hygiene, but he had no concern whatsoever for what others might think about his appearance. His beard, though not a full-on ZZ Top, grew long and scraggly. One local referred to him as Cragnon Man, a bastardization of Cro-Magnon man.

He took his place among the Santa Fe misfits, content to just be. Many of the non-conformists who had come before him were trust-fund babies who had been sequestered there by well-to-do families from the coasts, embarrassed by their offspring who just didn't fit in—gay, creative, bohemian, offbeat, oddball, sometimes a little crazy—that made for a patchwork quilt of disenfranchised individuals who accepted, applauded and often celebrated each other's individualism.

Ironically, in his detachment, Davis fit right in.

26

May 1982

Reunion

Davis's non-routine routine became his way of life. Every day was a new canvas, figuratively and sometimes literally. His paintings were sometimes finished in a single day, while others were works in progress, depending on his source of inspiration. He'd been back in New Mexico for about a year, keeping largely to himself. The idea of romance or relationship seemed alien to him. He had extended his "never-again" mode into a mantra that wasn't going to let a woman affect him in a way that was going to create the kind of heartbreak he had experienced with Mary.

Days turned into weeks turned into months. His life took on a Walden Pond quality: simple, uncluttered, taking pleasure in the most ordinary experiences.

It was spring in New Mexico. At the southernmost end of the Rocky Mountain chain, Santa Fe sits at over 7000 feet, which delivers very unpredictable weather; it can (and often does) snow all the way up until the middle of May. But this spring had been unpredictably spring-like. The fruit trees had blossomed and there had been no killing freeze, so fruit had set. Up in the mountains above the city, the aspens leafed out and each day warmed slightly, inching towards summer.

Davis had procured an old Toyota Landcruiser for his forays into the wilderness. He didn't have to go far; the mountains above Santa Fe afforded numerous trails and ways he could get far enough away to paint in peace.

He had found a spot and set up his easel along one of his favorite spots: seldom used, isolated, in the middle of an aspen grove he and Becca used to frequent. He had set out right before dawn, wanting to experience the early light coming through the newly emerged leaves, hoping to find a combination of colors in his tubes of paint that would capture that quality. He brought a canvas with him he had started the previous day he wasn't entirely pleased with. The temperature was perfect, the air almost perfectly still. The stream bubbling nearby exuded an earthy humidity. He walked to the edge of it and squatted, sinking his fingers into the cold mud, wanting to take a small quantity of the silt to incorporate into the actual painting. He closed his eyes and said a short blessing for his humble existence—his health, his solitude, the resources he had that allowed him to live the lifestyle he had, the beauty of his surroundings.

Coming back to his easel, he let his intuition guide the paints that made their way onto his palette. His fingers went to work, layering, combining, embellishing. His eyes took in the whole of his surroundings. He was always disappointed he could not capture all of what his senses did in the moment, but he had come to terms with that about his art and was content to hope to capture some element, some aspect of it for the next viewer.

His perspective switched back to the canvas and he felt it was done. He put his palette down and cleaned his hands on the rag he had brought for that purpose.

He was just slightly startled by a voice from behind him. "It's beautiful."

He did not turn around to see who it was; he didn't have to; the voice was practically as familiar to him as his own. The question now became *Am I imagining her or is she really standing behind me?*

The voice continued, "Aren't you going to turn around? It IS you isn't it?"

Davis had gotten used to his solitude and the voices from his past that would often present themselves. He wondered sometimes if he was going a little batshit, as he liked to refer to it. This voice has a different quality to it though. It was unmistakably <u>her</u> voice, but what would she be doing here?

He also didn't want to start entertaining imaginary friends. If he turned around, was he was giving credence to that diagnosis? Or was it the other way around?

He didn't imagine the touch on his right shoulder, though, but still didn't turn around. He was not afraid at all, but in a moment of considering all the ramifications of what her return back into his life would mean, he was flooded with emotion. He turned his shaggy head slowly in the direction of her touch and sure enough, the first hue on the edge of his vision was the unmistakable red nothing else came close to.

It <u>was</u> her.

Here. Not a ghost, not an apparition. His Becca, in the flesh.

He turned fully, their eyes met, the years and miles that had elapsed between them melting away. His arms opened and she entered them. For her, the beard and hair were a bit alien, but the rest of him was Davis.

Their hug went on for a long time, neither of them wanting to break it. Not a word was spoken. Those would come, but this was healing, this was reconciliation, this was rejoining and exclusive of everything else but the embrace of a loved one. Eyes closed, wanting no other sense to enter but touch, they held their bubble, experiencing the meld that what once so familiar, back again, every angle and curve of each of their bodies conforming to the other until they were one.

Again.

Davis let his sense of smell be included and it confirmed the reality. Gradually, his other senses came around and finally he opened his eyes. The light green glow from the aspens filtered through the red of Becca's hair. They broke their hold simultaneously, instantly back in sync after all their time apart and both spoke at the same time:

"What the fuck?" which sent them both into a fit of laughter, much the way it had always been between them. Except for when it wasn't, but that wasn't the predominant feeling either one of them was experiencing.

No, this felt like home.

27

Of All the Aspen Meadows...

"I knew it was you... But, how...?"

"I've been working on my teleporting skills. Pretty good, huh?"

Davis paused for a second, knowing Becca had some serious metaphysical abilities, and considered she might be telling him some new truth, but then he saw the twinkle in her eye and knew she was putting him on.

She continued, "Nah... astral projection, maybe, but I haven't figured out how to physically WILL myself from location to location just yet. Actually, I was in town for a show at the Lensic and stopped by the gallery. I was able to walk by your painting of The Cross without passing out this time and talked to Gloria about your whereabouts. She mentioned an aspen grove and I wondered if it was this one we used to come to so often." She tugged on his beard and dreaded hair. "So, what's all this? Going for the rasta-mountainman look?"

Davis felt a blush underneath all of his head hair and hoped it wasn't too obvious. "Personal appearance has not been high on my list of priorities lately. I've turned into a bit of a hermit."

Becca did a quick 'read' on him and felt his loneliness. "Yeah, well, all that human interaction crap seems great at the time, but I'm starting to think it's grossly overrated."

"If you remember some of my feelings about human interaction in general... It's gone downhill from there." He stopped to take her in. "Except for right now, in this moment, it feels pretty good."

"Yeah, it does."

"How long are you in town? We have some catching up to do."

"We're heading out tomorrow. We have the tour to finish up. Another couple of weeks of dates and that's the end of it."

"That's right. Too Much." He took a step back and feigned a surprised look. "Wait a minute. You're that singer. You're Rebecca Lakaris!"

"Oh, you're familiar with my work?"

"Am I? You betcha," he said faux-exuberantly.

"Did you come to the show?"

"I guess I am not that big of a fan. I actually didn't even know you were playing." Then, by way of excuse, "I don't get out much. You know, "out" out."

"We DO have some catching up to do."

They found a comfortable spot to sit in a small meadow nearby and spent the day listening to the travails of each other's journeys. Becca with her music and the band and then Mayah's abduction, Davis about Mary and the baby, the record store, the Lennon and Reagan shootings and ending up back in New Mexico. The sun worked its way across the sky in a flawless arc. They sat in constant physical contact, taking short breaks to pee and stretch their legs. Davis had brought water and snacks. Eventually, the sun ducked behind the mountain as late afternoon crept in and the temperature dropped.

"We'd better head back into town. I'm sure the band's wondering where I slipped off to."

On his drive back into town, Davis's head was filled with thoughts of what this fortuitous reunion meant and where it would lead. There had been numerous times over the years when he had lamented letting Becca go, going as far as to consider her the "love of his life." On the other hand, he recalled how many occasions their paths had gone in opposite directions, sometimes by his choice, other times hers. Now that their paths had crossed again, would they find a way to stay together?

Maybe.

As was often the case, their thoughts were now traveling on parallel trajectories. Their individual losses had created emotional voids for them and their once-familiar-now-familiar-again connection was not only intoxicating but fulfilling on a deeper level.

Becca did not go a single day without thinking about Mayah and when she would be returned to her. After all, she was fulfilling her contract with the "Shadow" as she had come to refer to the entity that had intruded on her life.

She had hunted Jackson down, the baby's biological father, as a possible suspect. While not the only man she had been with, he had been the only one she had not practiced birth control with and even more obvious, the only man of color. While Mayah's striking light blue eyes could have been from Becca's genetic pool, her beautiful brown skin certainly was not.

Becca had to do some minor sleuthing to find her one-time sexual partner, but it didn't take a Columbo; even though he wasn't in the upper echelon of notoriety in the athletic world, he was recognizable enough. She didn't approach him directly, not wanting him to know he had fathered a child if he indeed was NOT the abductor, but had him watched. There did not seem to be any signs of parenthood in his daily routine.

The trail was ice-cold beyond that. The authorities had been called in, but they had come up empty as well. It truly seemed like her little girl had simply disappeared. Her conversation with Davis brought it all back up—front and center—and made it seem raw all over again. Davis was the one person she could talk to, though, about the Shadow, after one of her previous encounters with it had led to epiphanies around Davis reconciling the firing of his rifle at the Kent State shootings. For the two of them, the Shadow was not just a subconscious figment of Becca's fertile imagination.

28

Milk Carton Blues

Many saw Davis living the life of a hermit, therefor had no idea what his daily existence was like. His scraggly appearance led most of those who considered him to assume he lived in a ramshackle hovel somewhere, devoid of amenities, with trash strewn about and cockroaches having free rein. The opposite was true; his casita at Gloria's ranch was maybe not neat as a pin, but orderly. Upon rising every day, he made his bed. He never left dirty dishes lying about and he had decorated the space tastefully, though sparingly without much clutter. There were stacks of canvases, but even those were neatly arranged.

He had given Becca directions on how to get there. She had wanted to meet up with the band members to let them know where she was before she rejoined him. Davis parked his car in his usual spot and entered the unlocked front door. He looked around to make sure the place was presentable, then made his way to the bathroom. He stood in front of the mirror and for the first time in a long time, assessed the image he saw there. On most days, if there was even a glance at the looking glass, it was cursory. Now he stood there, taking in the image of an unkempt, disheveled hippie-gone-awry. His matted hair hadn't experienced a comb or brush in quite some time, although he washed it once a week, whether it needed it or not. His beard was almost as bad, although he had taken scissors to it at random intervals, not so much for appearance as convenience around eating.

For the first time in a long time, he saw himself through the eyes of another, and not just any other; this was Becca. What he saw embarrassed him.

"Where are those scissors?" he actually said aloud, and found the orange-handled Fiskars in the junk drawer in the kitchen area. He went back into the bathroom, confronting the task at hand. He pulled the small wastebasket close by and fingered the most prominent rope of gnarlytwistedhair, pulling it away from his head. Scissors poised, he considered where to make the cut. *It's ALL gotta go, right?* he thought.

That seemed extreme, so he positioned the blades to leave about four inches—I can always cut more—and squeezed the handles to make the first cut. The resistance surprised him, feeling the blades trying to labor through what was not really hair anymore but some strange combination of randomly interwoven fur, oil and dirt. He found he had to make repeated cuts to work through the hank. After three passes, the dread came away in his hand and he stood there looking at it like some Medusan appendage that had grown out of his head. He inspected the elongated fuzzy hairball then tossed it into the metal wastebasket where it landed with a muffled thud. *That's one*, he thought.

Turning his attention back to the mirror, he was now confronted with a four-inch stub sticking out at a right angle from his head. *Now I'm gonna look like Alfalfa.* He set the scissors down and tried pulling the shorter dread apart with his fingers. He had some success, but his hair was not used to ANY kind of attention or manipulation. He realized he didn't even own a comb or brush. He picked the scissors back up and attacked the corresponding snake on the other side of his head. Can't stop now.

After that one landed in the trash, he made eye contact with the image in the mirror and he started to laugh. Really laugh. And he realized he hadn't done THAT in a long time. He went after the remaining skeins and was about halfway through when he heard a knock at the door. *Fuccckkk!* He looked at his reflection in the mirror. *What was I thinking?* Laughing again, he realized he might as well go for full humorous impact, so he made whatever was left into a mane of disaster and went to the front door. He pulled it open with a flourish, expecting Becca. Instead, there stood Gloria, the only other person who might be knocking, but he hadn't considered. At first, there was a shocked look on her face, then she burst out laughing. Davis had the presence of mind to give her a deadpan look and said, "What? What's so damn funny?"

He joined in her mirth and then she explained Becca had come by the gallery looking for him.

"Yes, she found me up on the mountain. She's on her way over here, so I thought I would just neaten up my 'do' a little bit."

"OK," laughed Gloria. "I'll leave you to that, then. Do you want any help?"

"No, I'm good. It looks great so far, don't you think?"

Gloria laughed again. "Yeah. Great. You missed a spot or two, but it's going in the right direction."

Just then, they heard the sound of car wheels on the gravel road and could see Becca behind the wheel of her rented car, pulling up. Davis ducked away from the open door and Gloria motioned for Becca to come over to the casita. Just as Becca had made her way up the two steps onto the porch, Davis popped out looking like Bozo meets Bob Marley in a hedge clipper fight. Becca, ever the one to be amused, spluttered and howled appropriately.

"Oh my god," she said. "I can see we've got some work to do here..."

She came forward and grabbed his protruding locks, pulled him into her and kissed him full on the mouth. She pulled away and said, "You goofball. God, I've missed you."

Davis stood there with a grin on his face—the first one of those in a while, too—and said, "Yeah, me too."

Gloria said, "OK, I will leave you two to your barberous, uh, challenges, if you will excuse the pun. Let me know if you need anything." She turned and walked away.

Davis pulled Becca into the casita, kicked the door closed and returned the kiss she had given him. When they came up for air, he said, "Will you help me with this?"

"Yes, of course, but we may have to get you to a proper barber at some point."

For the first time in a long time concerned with his appearance, he said, 'Yeah, but I can't go out in public like this."

"If worse comes to worse, we can always resort to a hat. You live in New Mexico. You must have a cowboy hat."

"Nah. Got the boots, but that was as far as this Jersey boy could go."

"Well, let's have at it and see what we come up with."

Davis perched himself on one of the stools from the kitchen counter and let Becca hack away at the rest of his dreads, cutting them to within an inch of his head. His eyes devoured her when she was in front of him but when she moved behind him and pressed up against him, he let his other senses take over: her smell, her touch. She was giving him a running report of her progress and her voice sounded like music to him.

"Will you sing for me?" he asked.

"Not now; I want to concentrate on what I am doing. But later, sure..."

When she had chopped off most of the snarls, she stood before him, inspecting the carnage. Her eyes dropped to his beard. "What are your thoughts about this?" she said, grabbing a handful.

"What are YOUR thoughts about it?"

It was long: a good five or six inches in length, and full. "It could be a little less 'Smith Brothers,'" she said, referring to the brand of cough drops that were popular when they were kids.

"Have at it," he said.

She did, cutting it to within a half inch of his face. Her attention was fully on her task. His attention was fully on the woman yielding a sharp object so close to him.

So close to him. The one person on the planet who was closest to him was SO close to him.

148

"There you are," she said when she was done with the scissors.

"I can't believe you are here," he said.

"I know, right?" This is all a little surreal."

There was hair everywhere. Becca had aimed for the wastebasket with the big hunks, but there were clippings all over the floor and both of them. Davis ran his hand over his head. Some of the hair was still matted. "I think those will relax once you wash it," Becca said.

Davis got the broom and dustpan and completed the cleanup. "I think I need to get in the shower," he said. He went over to the cupboard and pulled out a bottle of wine and a couple of mismatched glasses. "I haven't ever had anyone else ever here," he said. "Can you stay for a while? Let me get cleaned up and we'll figure out dinner."

"Yeah, sure."

He poured wine for the two of them.

"To reunions," he toasted.

"Yes, and reconnecting."

Davis headed off to the shower. A few minutes later, soaping up his head, he heard a knock on the door. "I was thinking you might need a professional shampoo to go with that haircut,' Becca said.

"Oh? Did you find someone lurking about who might be willing to perform that function?"

"Still a smartass, I see. I'm coming in."

Davis cleared the soap away from his eyes but not before he felt Becca's arms reach on either side of his waist, followed by the once and now again familiar feel of her breasts on his back and her pubic mound against his ass.

He said, "If this is how they do a professional shampoo, I clearly have been missing out."

Becca laughed, her voice echoing off the Mexican tile. Liking the acoustics, she launched into one of her songs, using the shampoo bottle for a microphone. It was the most fun Davis had had in a long, long time. They soaped, they rinsed, they soaped again until the water eventually got cold. Davis found as many mismatched towels as he could to accommodate them, but they got hastily dropped in a heap by the side of the bed as they continued their reacquaintance.

They made love, talked, slept, woke, made love, talked, slept some more. Morning came. It was all Davis could do to find something suitable to use as a coffee cup for himself, having given Becca's his one and only. They talked about Becca's obligations with the rest of the tour. Hanging over them were the times before when they had separated, and they both had a sense, however unspoken, they wanted a different outcome. Luckily, Davis's time was his own, and he agreed to follow them to their next gig: a theater in Tucson.

The eight-hour drive gave them a chance to catch up on each other's stories, cementing their individual desires to keep their reunion euphoria going.

Despite Becca's best efforts, Davis's hair was a mess. When they got to Tucson, he used their rehearsal time to find a barber and get a buzz cut and decided to do away with the beard too.

Having memorized all of their songs from their records, Davis was familiar with Too Much's material. What he was not prepared for was the energy of their live performance. He was blown away, not that he probably wouldn't have been anyway, in the state he was in. The band, protective of their lead singer and ever wary of outsiders looking to steal their "girl" away, warmed up to Davis anyway and he to them, rediscovering social skills that had gone dormant in him for a while. He became part of the tribe, being careful though not to impose his perspective on music into what they were creating.

The tour wound down back in California, having buoyed sales of the album enough it didn't lose money for the label, but there was a general feeling of relief to have it be over. A couple of the band members had slipped into drug use and general debauchery after Mayah's abduction, Chad wanted the band disbanded anyway and Becca's heart just wasn't in the music anymore; every day that went by without her daughter contributed to her accumulated pain. Davis's reemergence into her life was serving as a temporary band-aid, but Mayah's absence and all of the uncertainty around it created an empty place in her heart nothing else could fill.

Becca placed a lot of credence in her vision, her meeting, with The Dark. She felt like she had fulfilled her part of the bargain and now it was time to get her daughter back, although she carried around an additional sense of dread around what that might look like.

She and Davis were sitting around the breakfast table one morning back at the beach house in California. Conversations about what was coming next were met with general "I-don't-know's" from both sides, neither wanting to upset what felt like a delicate balance around not repeating their past history with each other.

The living situation at the beach house was still largely a communal affair. Alex, the keyboard player, had come downstairs and was fixing himself a bowl of Cap'n Crunch, his favorite hangover cure, which made little sense to anyone, but it seemed to work. He plopped down at the large kitchen table with a box, a bowl and a half gallon of milk and silently started voraciously wolfing down his bowlful of cure. Becca was used to his routine: his long hair getting splashed with milk, his head bent over the bowl as he heaped spoonful after spoonful into his mouth, one after the other, shoveling more in before he had completed the last. Davis watched him, somewhat appalled by the lack of manners. Alex lifted his eyes to meet Davis's stare, suddenly aware he was being observed.

"What? I am getting a sense you are not aware there is a methodology to breakfast cereal consumption. What may look like gluttony is actually science. You have to prepare just the right amount of cereal to milk, and then it has to be consumed in a certain amount of time, otherwise the milk gets too warm, tainted, if you will, and more importantly, the cereal gets too soggy. It IS, after all, Cap'n Crunch, not Cap'n Munch."

Davis said, "No, no; I get it. I didn't realize there was a precise ritual to it all, but, by all means, carry on..."

Which Alex did. Davis glanced over at Becca and gave her a raised eyebrow over the top of his coffee cup after which his attention strayed across the breakfast table and was caught by a single word emblazoned across the side of the milk container:

"Missing."

Beneath the heading was the picture of a young boy and a short description of him and his last whereabouts. Davis reached over, grabbed the container and presented it to Becca so she could see the message. "Hey! What if..."

Becca practically leapt out of her chair. "I can't believe I haven't thought of that. It's brilliant! Somebody out there HAS to have seen her."

Their next steps were figuring out how to get Mayah's case considered for inclusion. The missing-kid-on-a-milk-carton program had been instituted by the National Child Safety Council in an effort to help law enforcement find missing children in cases just like Becca's.

Borden's loved the idea once it was pitched: there was a notoriety to it that could certainly sell more milk. It took almost a month to implement, but it got done and then there was the matter of wading through the crackpot calls from false leads.

There were plenty of those.

At first Becca had been encouraged by the positive response, but her enthusiasm waned when there were dozens of hits from all over the country about her one tiny girl.

Some people say all babies look alike, which is certainly not true to the parents of those children. Becca was further dismayed by photos that came in that looked nothing like Mayah. Still, like Davis constantly reminded her, all it would take would be the ONE real lead, and she could have her daughter back.

Woven through this time for Davis and Becca was deciding about their futures: Davis had a very loose obligation to caretake Gloria's property and she had been willing to give him some free rein to temporarily 'join the circus' with Too Much, but her generosity would wane at some point. For Becca, the tour was over, her contract with the label was satisfied and now her attention had been diverted, and rightly so, to finding Mayah.

The bond between the two of them continued to grow. It went beyond the sex, which they quickly remembered how to engage in. They had glommed back onto each other coming from very different perspectives.

"I don't want for us to be apart again, not even for a short while," Davis had admitted to her, adding, "It seems like once we part, something happens and we stay apart for too long a time."

Becca smiled at him. "It's not like those times apart have just 'happened.' We made decisions that led to them, both of us."

"Agreed, but some of them were more conscious of consequence than others. When we parted at Woodstock, I fully expected to see you again, and soon."

"Woodstock. That seems like a few lifetimes ago already, doesn't it?"

Davis let his mind drift back to those first infatuous days when they had met. "Yes, and here we are now. Again. Together. Looking back, I feel like I like the times better when we were together than when we were apart," Davis said, going for the deliberate understatement.

"Really? What about your time with Mary?" Becca knew she was trodding in delicate territory, but it was a sticking point for her; essentially, Davis had decided to stay in Ohio with Mary instead of returning to New Mexico to be with her, or inviting her to come there.

Davis immediately felt a rise of emotions; not just one, sorrow, but also anger, not just at how Mary and their unborn child had been taken from him, but also towards Becca for ripping the scab off that wound.

He was silent for a moment, allowing himself to refeel those emotions and was able to compose himself. "I made the decision I did back then, as who I was at the time. I've thought about that decision many times, and about the ramifications of it and how it affected not just Mary and I but also you. Had I known—had I been—more aware, I would have chosen differently."

"What does that mean?"

"I would have asked you to come back to Ohio. I should have asked you to come back. Mary was a wonderful person and I loved her, but..."

"But, what?"

"You and I have something I think is beyond what most people get to experience. I don't know if I believe in soulmates or 'finding the ONE,' but when you located me back on the mountain, which, in itself was no small feat, I didn't even have to turn around; I knew it was you. And it was instantly as if we had never been apart. I don't know if it's because of our graft. Maybe. But I think it goes beyond that. We hadn't grafted when we met at Woodstock and look at how we connected."

"Back then I think you were just enamored with my cut-offs," Becca quipped.

"That's true; I WAS enamored with your cut-offs, or more correctly, the legs sticking out of them. But look at us. Time and time again we are apart, and when we come back together, it's right. We fit. We're a team."

Somehow, in that confession, whatever seed of doubt Becca may have had about Davis had dissolved. "Yeah. You're right. We are."

29

December 1983

Will You Mmma...?

The next days, weeks were blissful. Not only had they rekindled their infatuation and passion for each other, there was something more... mature about it this time, not the least of which was dealing with adult issues. Not that they weren't dealing with serious issues before; Davis possibly being tried for murder is right up there, but who they both were in terms of how they were going to address them was different.

Decisions were made around Becca's music; the band would go their separate ways and she would take a sabbatical of sorts, at least until she got her daughter back. And in Becca's mind, there was no doubt Mayah was alive and she would indeed get her back.

Davis had some passive income from the record store and from his paintings. They also decided to move back to the casita in New Mexico and have that as a base for their operations. For all of the time they had spent apart, now they were inseparable. Despite how good their union felt NOW, there was a fear in the back of both of their minds one or both of them would revert back to "flee" mode.

Davis was the first to address that, and he had plans to take it to extreme measures.

Ring and all.

"I don't want for us to be apart again. Ever."

"Nor I. I feel like our being thrust together so many times is a sign we are supposed to be a couple." As soon as she said that, Becca felt a

155

nervousness on Davis's part. She tilted her head and gave him a wry smile. She said in a sing-song voice, "Are you getting ready to propose to me?"

Sensing his thunder completely stolen, he said, "Well, not anymore."

"Not anymore? You were! You were going to!"

"Yeah, but you stole my thunder. Now it's kind of after-the-fact. There's no surprise. No romance. The moment has come and gone."

"No, no, it's not. Were you going to get down on one knee? What were you going to say?"

"Forget it. The window has passed. I can't just re-conjure up the moment after you..."

"Re-conjure? Is that a word?"

They both knew where this was headed and they were both having a little fun with it.

"Sure. 'Re-conjure: to conjure again.' Totally a word. I've got lots of words."

"Yeah? How many?"

Davis had to think for a second and also count on his fingers. "Nine. I've got nine words for you."

"Go on..."

"Please spend the rest of your life with me."

Becca had been grinning through this whole exchange.

"Yeah. OK. I can do that."

"I mean legally. Spiritually. Soulfully. Committed. You know, the whole 'til death do us part' thing."

"You mean "marry?" That word?" Becca placed her hand around his mouth and playfully tried to get his lips to utter the word. "C'mon," she said, "you can do it... 'Mmmm' 'mmaa...'"

Davis decided to play along and mouthed a series of "m's". Then, with her hands still on his mouth, he pulled her into him so their faces were not even an inch apart. "Flesh with my flesh. Breath with my breath. Heart with my heart. Marry me."

"Well, ok, if you put it that way, sure."

The weeks that followed were filled with discussions about what "'til death do us part" meant and also practical considerations like their vocations, lifestyle, money and children. They agreed the search for Mayah would be renewed with a vigor and when—not if—they found her, Davis would take on the role of her father.

"What about more children?" Davis asked.

"I've thrown that around in my head and heart for a while now. Having Mayah gone feels like there is a hole inside of me. And I don't want to consider having another child just to fill that void. But when I think about a child coming forth as a result of our union, having parts of us and taking that forward, I like the way that feels. Besides, I've seen you around kids; you're a natural. You would be a great dad."

"You think so? I guess... I like kids. Well, most kids, anyway. There are some demon seeds out there but for the most part they are these open, innocent souls with no guile."

"I don't know about that. I've seen some kids who were pretty-damn-guileful."

"Just part of the human condition; trying to get their needs met. But how about if we were to meet those basic needs? Just love 'em to start."

"You mean get the stuff we didn't get?"

"Yeah, like that."

They agreed to each come up with questions, concerns and ideas for what their married life would look like and not surprisingly, their blueprints were not very far off.

"What about fidelity, monogamy?" Davis asked.

"Do you trust me?"

"You know I do."

"Then you shouldn't even have to ask."

"Lives change. People change. Circumstances change. We've gotten "used to" (and Davis made the airquotes gesture he had come up with years ago had now become part of the general culture) each other in the past and was enough to send one or both of us scrambling in the opposite direction."

"I like to think we've gotten that out of our systems. We're not a couple of teenagers at Woodstock anymore."

"I agree. We are a little more set in our ways. At this point, we have "ways." But you and I are a little different. I'm a bit of a hermit, while you are a lot more social, more group-oriented. You get off on being up on stage."

"Are you OK with that? Because I think you're right and I don't see that changing."

"It all comes down to trust. That is at the core of who we are together. If we have that, I think anything else is negotiable."

"I promise you, Davis. I swear to you on all that is holy to you, and you know how I mean that... I will never do anything that would compromise our relationship, that would violate that trust."

They locked eyes and shared the serious moment until Davis, in an exaggerated show of frivolity, said, "OK, then, I'm in!"

Becca gave him a knowing smile, knowing his heart and how important that vow was to him.

They decided to have Tschuck perform a ceremony for them with just a few friends. They wrote out long elaborate vows until they decided those were superfluous.

"What was it you said to me when you proposed? That was pretty damn poetic."

"Oh, that 'Flesh with my flesh. Breath with my breath. Heart with my heart' thing? That?"

"Yeah, that," not surprised he had memorized it verbatim. "Why don't we just say that? And maybe add something like, 'within you, never without you. For the rest of our lives.' Something like that."

"Good. Perfect. Succinct. To the point."

Tschuck performed the short ceremony for them at the place in the mountains where Becca had refound Davis.

They were done being apart.

30

February 1984

Greetings From Chimayo

Once the idea of Mayah-on-a-milk-carton got into Becca's brain, she was not going to stop until she walked into the supermarket and saw her baby's face staring back at her in the dairy section. She had just enough notoriety to pull it off, too, although there was resistance from some quarters. The program was more regional than national and there was a lot of lobbying around exactly who was going to get their missing child's face in front of America's breakfasters. But when Becca put on her relentless hat, there was no stopping her and the day came when she went into the Piggly-Wiggly, pulled the half gallon off the shelf and saw her little one staring back at her. Through the campaign to get "accepted," she had kept a cautiously optimistic attitude. Now that it had come to fruition, the stark reality of having lost her child overwhelmed her. Clutching the container to her breast, she sank to her knees next to the shopping cart and sobbed.

Customers came over to comfort her and eventually management had to come and "clean up" in the dairy aisle. Now it was a waiting game. The milk carton campaign had given them leads which the FBI had followed up on, to no avail. Most of those calls came from well-meaning fans wanting to help or wanting to <u>want</u> to help.

Every time Becca, and Davis, for that matter, went to the store, they checked the dairy case and were somewhat comforted to see Mayah looking back at them. Davis went as far as to rearrange the cartons so the missing child side was facing out and even surreptitiously move the particular cartons with Mayah's photo up to eye level for maximum exposure. He would step back to examine his display, multiple images of this child he had never met boring into his brain. *Where ARE you?* he would wonder, only to be met with Mayah's silent stare.

Two months went by. No viable leads came as a result and the day when Becca went to the store and inspected the milk only to see the face of a strange boy smiling back at her, she threw the container down to the floor. While the cardboard carton did not produce the satisfying shatter a bottle would have, the force of hitting the floor was too much for the peel-back-then-pull enclosure and Becca got drenched. Now there really WAS a clean-up in the dairy section.

Despondent, Becca considered "contacting" the Dark, but was afraid of what that might incur. She spoke to Davis about that. He had only dealt with that evil force peripherally, but his forays with Becca into various esoteric and metaphysical realms gave him enough healthy respect for the shadow world he encouraged her to concentrate her efforts in the physical world.

When Becca talked to her contacts from the milk carton campaign and why Mayah was no longer represented, she was simply told hers was only one of many missing children and other families had to be given equal time. She would learn later other reasons went into that decision, some nefarious, not the least of which was the color of her daughter's skin.

"Now what?" she asked Davis, "We can't just do nothing."

He had nothing to turn to but blind optimism, his response being "Something will turn up. She's out there, and she will come back to us."

Becca, though hardly religious, had taken to visiting the local Catholic churches, finding solace in their earthen structures. The Santuario de Guadalupe, the San Miguel Mission, the San Francisco de Asis Mission Church made famous by Georgia O'Keefe and Ansel Adams, the Loretto Chapel and the St. Francis Cathedral all made her list as well as many of the lesser-known chapels, to her, the smaller the better. She would pray. Not in the normal sense of reciting rote passages of religious doctrine, but appealing to a higher power to return her child.

The ringing phone always carried a bit of foreboding, ever since Mayah had gone missing, but Becca was not fully prepared for the heavily disguised voice on the other end. "Mayah is safe and I know where she is. Do not disclose this message to any authorities. Some of them are not working in your best interests. Your prayers will be answered."

She heard a click on the other end. Her hands were shaking as she replaced the handset, then her hand went up to her mouth and her eyes welled with tears.

Davis went into rational mode. "What exactly did they say?"

Becca recounted the message as well as she could. Davis wrote it down. Neither of them was satisfied with the work the authorities had done, so they didn't have any problem with keeping it quiet, but the "prayer" part had them both a little rattled. "Do you think someone is following me?" she asked, thinking back to her church pilgrimages. "What do we do now?"

"There's not much we can do. Unless someone is playing a nasty trick, it sounds like someone is trying to help—we just don't know who." For the next couple of days, whenever they were away from home, both Becca and Davis kept an awareness around strangers, but their vigilance was not rewarded.

Becca made a trip up to the Santuario in Chimayo. She loved the chapel there but also loved the grounds with its small river running nearby. She would always stop at the small room over on the side and get some of the sacred dirt that was rumored to have healing qualities. She wasn't sure she believed that and even knew workers there had to keep replenishing the dirt to satisfy the demand of all those who went away with their handfuls, but she was always buoyed by the faith of those who came to the tiny town to have their prayers answered. The 'dirt room' was cramped with a low ceiling and small doorways that one had to stoop to exit. Pilgrims had left crutches behind as evidence of having been healed as well as other mementos and blessings. As she was making her way out, a boy about eleven years old came running up to her and handed her an envelope. She grabbed his arm as he went to turn away.

"Wait. Who gave this to you?"

The boy was Hispanic, with jet black hair and eyes to match. His face scrunched up into an expression of "I don't know" and as he shrugged his shoulders, he broke Becca's grip and ran off. Becca looked around to see if there were any likely candidates, but whoever had employed the young boy to deliver the letter was obviously long gone. The plain white envelope had no markings on it at all. Typewritten on a single sheet of paper was the following:

I AM MAKING ARRANGEMENTS TO HAVE MAYAH RETURNED TO YOU, BUT YOU MUST FOLLOW MY INSTRUCTIONS.

SHE IS WITH A FAMILY IN NEW ORLEANS THAT DID NOT KNOW SHE WAS ABDUCTED, BUT ARE WILLING TO RETURN HER. HOWEVER, HER RETURN HAS TO BE HANDLED VERY DELICATELY.

THOSE RESPONSIBLE FOR HER BEING TAKEN WILL NOT BE HAPPY WITH HER BEING RETURNED, BUT I AM TAKING STEPS TO INSURE THEY WILL NO LONGER INTERFERE.

YOU CANNOT GO TO NEW ORLEANS. YOU ARE TOO VISIBLE AND THE INITIAL RETURN HAS TO BE LOW PROFILE. SEND DAVIS. WHEN HE GETS THERE, HE WILL BE CONTACTED ABOUT WHAT TO DO NEXT.

Becca's heart was beating a staccato rhythm in her chest. She drove back to the casita, where she and Davis immediately made plans for him to go to New Orleans and hope whoever their avenging angel was would follow through on their promise. Their only alternative would have been to do nothing.

Neither of them was willing to consider that.

31

April 1985

Meeting by the River

Having never been to The Crescent City before, Davis was unsure of where to stay, to go, to do. It was a strange feeling to know someone was watching him, knowing who he was, but he didn't know who they were. He watched for suspicious activity, but wasn't even quite sure what that might look like: basically, someone watching him who had no reason to, which would be anybody. Tall and fairly attractive—his hair having grown back some—Davis might attract some attention, but in a busy city like New Orleans, everybody had their own agenda. Davis was used to the pace of New York City, where little, if any, eye contact was ever made with strangers. This wasn't much different.

His purpose for being there made everyone a potential contact and he wanted to make himself available. He booked himself a room in a motel just on the outskirts of the French Quarter, and decided he would spend as much time in public as possible to allow whoever was going to contact him the easiest access. Every child he saw became a potential target, and being in Louisiana, there were a lot more black children to choose from.

Coming from the arid southwest, the air felt different to him: heavier, sweeter, certainly more humid. It seemed to damp everything down: movement, speech, everything was just a bit slower. His move to New Mexico had slowed many of his east Coast sensibilities, but this was a different level. He found the slower pace gave all of his senses a chance to linger and savor. He knew New Orleans was famous for its food and the smells emanating from the restaurants he passed as well as the street food carts certainly supported that.

Then there was the music. Davis had no idea how long he was going to be there before he was contacted, but he had a purpose and a focus, with no plans for entertainment. He also didn't want to be distracted from his mission, to bring Mayah back to Becca.

But there was no escaping the music. He didn't have to go to any of the clubs or concert halls to hear the richness of sound the city had to offer. Practically every street corner had someone playing all manners of music, although, of course, being in New Orleans, there was a lot of jazz. It brought him back to his childhood and the sounds of his father's trumpet.

In his aimless meandering, he stopped in Jackson Square to listen to a young woman sing, completely unaccompanied, her naked voice just feet away, unabashed, unfettered and strong. She had a broad-brimmed hat on a bench in front of her, sprinkled with bills and change. When she finished her song, someone requested "God Bless the Child."

Davis was standing not five feet from her. He watched her eyes light up at the suggestion and saw her change in posture. In a voice like melting butter on a beignet, she began to sing:

"Them that's got shall get

Them that's not shall lose

So the Bible said

and it still is news

Mama may have, Papa may have

But God bless the child that's got his own

That's got his own..."

Ever wanting to support musicians, Davis dropped a fiver in her hat

The message of the song did not apply to Mayah, but it got him thinking about her, and what she might be experiencing. *Was she safe? Being cared for? Loved?* He was optimistic this exchange was going to take place, but what effect would it have on her? Would she remember it? Probably not, he thought, but he wondered what it was all going to look like.

Most of his attention was focused on the major aspects of getting Mayah back—the actual physical exchange: *Will she even want to come with me? A complete stranger?* but some of the smaller details lurked in the back of his mind: *How big will she be? Do I carry her? What does she eat? Is she potty trained?*

Davis spent the first whole day meandering about the French quarter, playing tourist but staying alert for some sort of contact. There was none. Bored and frustrated at not being contacted yet, he saw a flyer for a jazz band playing at a dive bar he thought might be promising. He went and nursed a couple of beers without any sign his presence was going to be rewarded.

Not wanting to be impaired, he left without finishing his last beer and walked back to his motel. Having spent so much time in New York, he was used to moving about in a city late at night without any fear, but he also knew having that attitude was part of being safe; predators could smell weakness, and while Davis would probably not be characterized as a typical alpha male, his size and his military training gave him a certain carriage that exuded a best-not-fuck-with-me vibe.

Still, he was in unfamiliar territory, and realized in making certain turns it was very easy to cross over from a relatively safe tourist areas to a pretty sketchy one just a block removed. He could feel that heavy air closing in around him, trees blocking out intermittent streetlights creating shadows filled with uncertainty and malice. His whole reason for being there certainly added to the sinister atmosphere: *Who steals a child?* All the accompanying questions cycled through his mind as well: *who is wanting to give her back? At what cost? Why now? Why all the secrecy?*

Lost now, he found himself getting deeper into what seemed like a place he shouldn't be. Recognizing his fear for what it was, he straightened up his spine and focused on his surroundings rather than his inner thoughts.

He felt certain that someone was following him but did not want to turn around to validate the thought. He stopped at the next intersection of streets and gathered himself, then closed his eyes and imagined himself out in the middle of the rolling hills of New Mexico—at times truly lost—but able to navigate himself back by getting a sense of where he had been.

If he reversed his direction and someone truly was following him, their paths were almost certain to cross. That felt like the right move, but retracing his steps, he did not come across anyone that seemed to have any interest in him, other than he stuck out like a tourist who had gone off in the wrong direction. He found his way back to the Quarter and then to his hotel.

Frustrated there had not been contact, Davis flopped on the bed and contemplated calling Becca to report in when the phone jangled loudly, startling him. Thinking it was Becca, picking up on him wanting to call her, he answered, "I was just going to call you."

Instead of Becca, a male voice answered, "I doubt that, but listen to these instructions. Write them down if you have to. Do not deviate from them in any way or you may not get Mayah back."

Davis scrambled to get the pen and paper hopefully supplied by the motel. "OK, go ahead."

He was given instructions about where to meet a woman in a park down by the river. She would have Mayah and would simply let him take her. He was to leave immediately for the rendezvous, and then leave the city right after.

It was about a ten–minute walk. Davis moved briskly, sometimes even breaking into a trot, then wondered if that might bring attention to himself, so slowed his pace a bit. When he got to the waterfront, from a distance he saw a black woman about his age with a young girl sitting on a bench. The woman had cornrows in her hair and so did the child.

Mayah.

The girl was seated on the very far end of the bench with the woman next to her. He approached them and sat on the opposite end of the bench, making eye contact with the woman.

"Davis?"

"Yes. I'm sorry, I don't know your name."

The woman hesitated, seemingly not sure if she should give out that information. She seemed to be sizing Davis up. "Leticia. My name is Leticia."

"And this is Mayah?"

The woman gathered Mayah up in her arms and placed her on her lap, smothering her in a hug that was certain be one of their last. 'Yes, this is our Mayah."

Mayah returned the familiar embrace. Leticia held the hug for a long time, then pulled Mayah away at arm's length. "Baby, this nice man is named Davis. He is going to take you to your other mama."

Mayah looked confused. "You're my mama."

"I am, Sugah, and will always be. But some lucky children have two mamas, and you are one of those lucky ones."

Mayah looked at Davis suspiciously. Obviously, this had not been discussed prior to this moment. Davis was not sure about how to proceed: extend arms? Say something? What?

Mayah broke the silence. "That's OK. I don't need two mamas. I just want you." She proceeded to hug Leticia while keeping a steady gaze at Davis.

Leticia broke the hug and proceeded to whisper into Mayah's ear, Mayah the whole time staring at Davis. Davis could not hear what she was saying, but Mayah nodded her head numerous times and put a thumb in her mouth.

"OK. Mama," Mayah finally said.

"Give me one more hug, for now, Sugah."

169

Mayah did, breaking her gaze with Davis, which gave him a chance to look at Leticia. Her eyes were closed, with tears streaming down her face. She stood and handed Mayah over to Davis where she latched onto his neck. Leticia also had a large canvas bag with a long strap and a folded-up stroller she placed over Davis's free shoulder. "She loves the Goldfish and she will sleep every night with Poohbear."

"Poohbear!" Mayah said and reached out for her favorite stuffed animal. Leticia fished it out of the bag and then rezippered it. Mayah took the bear and pulled it into her face, then resumed her position on Davis's hip.

Davis locked eyes with Leticia. "Thank you."

Leticia put her hand on Davis's upper arm and closed her eyes in a silent blessing. She squeezed his arm, then turned and walked away, not once looking back.

Davis turned his attention to the girl clinging on to him. "OK, young lady, we have a long trip ahead of us. Are you ready?"

Mayah nodded into Davis's neck.

He took off quickly in the direction he had come.

32

The Bullet as a Weapon

He hadn't gotten more than a block when he heard a voice come out of the darkness: "And just where the fuck do you think YOU are going?"

Davis spun, clutching Mayah close to him with his right arm in a paternal hug he didn't know he had in him. His left hand rested on the stroller and the bag that contained Mayah's stuff. Turning towards the voice, Davis immediately interpreted the question as rhetorical and malicious. He decided not to answer.

"That baby is not leaving this city. She didn't belong with that nigger-lover to begin with and she aint goin' back."

The rational part of Davis's brain was temporarily satisfied to know this wasn't a random mugging and they were finally getting at least some sort of motivation for why Mayah had been abducted to begin with, but that satisfaction echoed WAY in the back of thoughts that were far more "fight or flight," like *Who is this guy and how do I get away from him, especially holding Mayah?* He looked around for avenues of escape. There was very little light and no one else around he could see. "Flight," especially carrying a child, seemed unlikely to be successful, and "fight" seemed to present an even dimmer prospect, especially considering the size of his opponent—the guy was easily a few inches taller than Davis and a good forty to fifty pounds heavier. Plus, much of Davis's focus over the last five years or so had been steered towards a decidedly non-violent bent.

"What do you want?" Davis asked, more to try to buy some time than to elicit an actual answer.

"Just hand her back to me and walk away and no one gets hurt."

171

"Yeah, I had a feeling you were going to say something along those lines. What are my other options?" Davis's flippancy surprised even him.

"Other options? Oh... other options... There are no other options, asshole. You never should have come here and if I find out how you got this far, there is going to hell for somebody else to pay as well."

Davis backed away slowly, but the man was keeping pace with his retreat. Davis could also see the man had a baseball bat gripped in his right hand and was now clearly brandishing it as a weapon.

"Look, what is your problem? Are you related?"

"Related? Do I look like a jungle bunny to you? No, I'm not related. The problem is that white women should stay with white men and there shouldn't be any racial mixing. That little niggerbaby should be with its own kind. You should have just let it be."

"But who ARE you? Why is this any business of yours?"

"It's my business because if we keep letting this kind of nonsense go on, it'll be the end of the white race."

"Do you know her mother?"

"I know WHO she is. One of the whitest white women there are. And it's a sin for her to be carrying a black baby around, parading it like it's normal."

"Maybe it's the new normal—the way things are supposed to be. And maybe you should just mind your own business." As soon as that last sentence slipped out, Davis regretted it, but there was no taking it back now.

"This IS my business, jerkoff. I'm FBI." And with that, the man flashed his shield, or something that looked like it could be a shield; it was still fairly dark.

Now Davis was confused. "Wait a minute. You're law enforcement? Shouldn't you be working to get this baby back to her rightful parent?"

"Yeah, sure. I'll get right on that. So, hand her over."

The man took a step forward, covering the ground between them. Davis pivoted away, still holding Mayah and with his left arm swung the stroller at his assailant. The man blocked the carriage easily with the bat, distorting it almost beyond recognition. Continuing the sweeping motion, Davis laid Mayah on the grassy ground then sprung back up, figuring he might have the element of surprise on his side. He charged the man in a football tackle. Clearly, "fight" mode had taken over. Davis got him to the ground and knew he had to stay out of the way of that bat. He swung out to punch him but missed and the man used that force to reverse their positions, now with Davis on the bottom. He could hear Mayah squalling in the background, behind the blood pounding in his ears.

Luckily, in the reversal, the bat had ended up underneath Davis, and while it was uncomfortable, it could not be used as a weapon. Unfortunately for Davis, his attacker actually <u>was</u> FBI and had the martial arts training to go along with it. He had his left forearm across Davis's throat, his right arm pinning Davis' left arm to the ground. His left knee prevented Davis's right arm from having much movement. Davis struggled, twisting, trying to buck the heavier man off him, recognizing that the biggest threat was the pressure on his neck.

Davis tried to free his right hand and momentarily was able to grip the bat but realized the weight of his body was rendering it useless. Along with all of the other pains he was experiencing, he could feel a piercing in the area of his right pocket. Squirming, he was able to dig his hand in there and felt his fingers wrap around the pointed, three-and-a-half-inch long bullet he still kept as his talisman, the reminder of his role in the Kent State shooting. Rolling his body to the right, then quickly to his left, he was able to free his hand from his pocket and lashed out sideways, the quite sharp, elongated point of the bullet protruding slightly beyond his fist.

His first strike hit bone, skull, something hard, and he kept lashing out, how many times he could not recall, but after four or five blows felt a lessening of the pressure on him as he continued to strike out. He felt a sticky warm fluid envelope his hand, making it harder to grip his weapon, but the damage was already done. In a burst of blind fury, he pushed the man off him and continued to strike.

In the diminished light, his attacker, now victim, lay in an increasing pool of blood. Heaving breaths, Davis scrambled to his feet, aware of Mayah's cries not very far away. He crammed the bullet back in his pocket. Scooping Mayah up, he walked quickly away, then stopped and surveyed the scene, seeing the bat, the crumpled stroller and the bag strewn about. He picked up the bat and walked over to the man, who was choking on his own blood. Making sure Mayah's face was buried in his neck, he brought the bat down on the man's face in one sickening, obliterating blow.

The spluttering stopped.

33

Now What?

The rest of the night was a blur but for a couple of lucid moments: one, as Davis made his way along the riverfront, realizing he was carrying VERY implicating evidence on him. Carrying Mayah in his left arm, he reached into his pocket and extracted the bloody bullet that out of habit had returned there. It had been with him for too many years now, and he knew it was time for them to part ways. He wound up and threw the round as hard as he could over the Big Muddy.

The bullet hit the surface of the water with a plop and promptly sank, wavering slightly on its path downward, the weight of the brass casing dictating a path to the bottom. The blood quickly dispersed sending increasingly diluted swirls into the muddy current and as it neared the bottom, salt water, creeping in from the Gulf hugging the bottom with its higher density, washed the last of any human remains off as Davis's bullet nestled into the silt. Tides and currents would wash over it for the rest of time. It would never see the surface again.

The bat and the stroller could not be disposed of so easily. The bat would obviously float and while the stroller would sink, it seemed like a critical piece of evidence to be leaving behind. Right now, though, the most damning incrimination was his own appearance. His hands were sticky with blood, especially the right one that had held the bullet. He held Mayah close to him with his left arm. She had clung Velcroed to him when he picked her back up, and promptly nodded off, feeling safe in Davis's embrace, oblivious to the danger around her.

He went down to the water's edge and carefully laid Mayah down. She did not stir. He couldn't see his reflection in the water, but assumed it bloody; he could FEEL it. He washed off as much as he could, thankful for the late hour and the lack of any obvious witnesses. The water sobered him somewhat from his fight or flight high. *Now what? Do I go to the police? Was that guy really FBI? If he was, I am fucking doomed. Is he dead?* Davis quickly recollected the crunching feeling of the bat-blow he had delivered to the man's skull. *Oh, he's dead, alright.*

Davis pulled open the folding stroller and bent it as best he could back into a functioning shape. His hands were shaking from the adrenaline but it also gave him a strength he might not have had under ordinary circumstances. He even had the presence of mind when he placed Mayah into it to strap her with the tether supplied for just that purpose. He took a couple of seconds to situate her and to actually see her for the first time. "Let's get you back to your mama, and then we'll figure all the rest of this out."

The stroller had tiny wheels that dug into the soft earth near the water's edge. He decided to pick it up with Mayah in it, deliberately stamping out any wheel marks he had left. When he found a sidewalk, he placed it back down and started wheeling her, one of the wheels wobbling like a bad grocery cart. *Where am I?* he thought, trying to get his bearings. His plan was to get back to his hotel. The challenge was going to be getting back there undetected. He imagined himself being able to get a birds-eye view of his location and set about making his way back. He had gotten most of the blood off his face and hands, but his shirt was a mess. He came across one person on the way back, but stooped over Mayah in the stroller, pretending to attend to her until the person passed.

He was thankful about his decision to stay at a motel rather than a hotel, where he would almost certainly have had to pass by a desk clerk. He reached into his left-hand pocket for the key and found nothing there, then remembered he had put it in the back pocket of his jeans and was relieved to find it still there, even after all of his physical activity.

He opened the door, pushed Mayah inside in the stroller and quickly closed the door behind him. He realized he had to piss, having held it in for quite some time. He rushed to the bathroom and turned on the light, catching sight of his reflection rushing past the mirror that stopped him in his tracks. His shirt had gotten soaked in blood, which had now mostly dried and stiffening. He had gotten a lot of the blood off his face, but there were still streaks resembling warpaint and his hair was sticking up with in stiff dark spikes that would make a punk rocker proud. "Jesus," he said. Then, remembering why he had gone in there, attended to that. He came back to the sink, removed his shirt and worked on cleansing himself, realizing a shower was going to be his best bet.

He retrieved Mayah, still asleep in the stroller, and rolled her into the tiny bathroom. Careful to face her away from him, he disrobed and turned on the shower and watched as the remaining blood flushed off him reminiscent of the shower scene from "Psycho."

Modestly wrapping a towel around himself, he found his one change of clothes and got dressed, feeling renewed and calmer. He took Mayah out of the stroller and placed her on the center of the bed surrounded by pillows on each side of her so she couldn't roll off. He peeked out of the curtains and saw the first light of dawn starting to beckon. Now what? was the mantra that kept cycling through his brain. He knew he would call Becca at some point, but not yet. His brain was jumbled with the events of the past few hours and trying to cram in what should happen in the next few seemed daunting and impossible. He decided to lay down on the bed next to Mayah, just to clear his head.

He drifted off.

He was startled by a loud knock on the door. He had been asleep, no idea how long. Quickly trying to orient himself into wakedness and away from the darkness that had permeated his sleep, his first reaction was to just ignore whoever was at the door. No one he knew was supposed to know where he was; whoever was knocking could only bring bad news.

The knock came again.

Davis got out of the bed, seeing Mayah was still asleep and tiptoed over the carpeted floor to the door. The third round of knocking startled him, coming from so close. "Open the door. Davis. I'm the person who contacted Becca. Let me in."

177

Fuck. What do I do?

Davis undid the chain he didn't remember having engaged a few hours before and unlocked the door. Bright sunlight flooded in and a single silhouette of a man stood outside. He immediately pushed his way inside and closed the door behind him. Davis put his arms up to defend himself but the man held his left arm straight out in front of him in a halting motion and then put his finger up to his lips. "Don't say a word. I am agent Timmons." He looked over at the bed and the sleeping Mayah. "Is she OK?"

Davis nodded.

"And you? Are you hurt?"

Davis shook his head, not sure if he was still under the 'don't-say-a-word' command.

Timmons motioned for Davis to sit down on the bed and pulled the single chair over from the desk. He leaned over with his elbows on his knees and said, "I am the person who contacted Becca and got you to come and retrieve Mayah. The man you engaged with a few hours ago is dead and this is going to be a major clusterfuck. He was an FBI agent, but a bad one. Away from his job, he is part of the KKK and was instrumental in Mayah's kidnapping. I don't know what happened back there, but somehow he found out you were here and taking Mayah back. Obviously, things got out of hand." He paused, "Jesus, what did you stab him with?"

Davis was trying to process what was happening. Law-abiding (OK, except for the going AWOL and hiding out for years as a potential fugitive part), he was wanting to defer to this authority confronting him but another part of him decided his best path was just to keep his mouth shut.

Mayah stirred on the bed behind him and started to fuss. Reflexively he gathered her and put her on his hip, a move now becoming second nature. Timmons's question hung in the air.

Davis just stared him in the eye, mute.

"Right. Probably better if I don't know," said Timmons.

He glanced around the room, seeing the stroller, the bat and Davis's pile of clothes, all of which were coated in blood to some degree.

"Shit." He turned to Davis and said, "Ok, listen. You are going to have to trust me."

That's all Davis had to hear for him to think *Whatever you do, do NOT trust this guy.* But he didn't have a lot of alternatives.

Timmons continued, "I can't stay here any longer. Here is what you need to do."

Roman Ramsey

34

On the Road Again

Timmons exited the room and Davis rechained the door behind him, realizing how much of a benign, symbolic gesture it was.

Mayah was wide awake now and needing attention.

He had listened intently to Timmons's instructions, not committing at the time to any of it, but also realizing he could have (and should have) been arrested for taking the life of another human being. That is, if Timmons (or whatever his name was) was really an FBI agent at all. His skepticism radar was now fully extended and he was in full survival mode, his mind racing with a dozen contradictory thoughts: *I have to call Becca. But not from here. Mayah's crying; she must be hungry, I have to get her something to eat.* He found the bag Leticia had given him and after rummaging through it, found an almost empty box of Goldfish. That would have to do for now.

Timmons said the guy I stabbed is dead. Fuck. Murder? Manslaughter? No. Self-defense. He told me to trust him. Why should I? He could have arrested me, but he didn't. There's that.

Meanwhile, Mayah's fussing had taken on a more urgent pitch, to the point of him realizing it could draw attention to them. OK, Mayah first. Food. Bathroom. Maybe bathroom first.

He gathered her and they set out in the wobbly stroller. He had wiped it down and what few blood stains remained just looked like dirt now. It took him five blocks to find a Food and Geaux, the local convenience store where he purchased bottles of formula, another box of Goldfish, a cup of coffee, Slim Jims, a package of bologna, a loaf of bread and three dollars worth of quarters. He found a phone booth outside, nestled himself and

Mayah into it and dialed Becca. It took her a few rings to answer but hearing her voice calmed him.

"It's me, Davis."

"Oh, sweetheart; it's so good to hear your voice. Are you OK? What's happening?"

"I have her. I have Mayah."

Becca collapsed, sobbing. When she gathered herself, she said, "Is she Ok?"

"Yes, she's right here, sucking away at some formula. There's more. A lot more, but I am in a bit of a time crunch to get out of town. Let me call you later."

"Are you OK? What happened?"

"Yes, I am fine and so is Mayah. There were some... complications, but we need to get on the road. I will call you later. I love you."

"I love you, too. Oh, and Davis, do you have a car seat for her?"

Davis's first thought was *I just killed a man; how did I not think of a car seat?* Not wanting to open up that can of worms yet with Becca, he merely replied, "Not yet, but I will."

"'Cause it's the law now, and besides, that's how she will be safest."

Davis's ideas about how to keep Mayah safe had not included how to restrain her in a car, but he mentally added it to a list that seemed ever increasing.

Becca sensed Davis's unease. "What's wrong, baby? You sound upset."

"Not everything went as planned, that's all. I will tell you all about it when we get home."

"How long do you think it will take?"

"It was about 16 hours getting down here, and since Mayah doesn't have her license yet, it looks like I'll be doing most of the driving." Davis's small attempt at humor calmed Becca a bit, but she knew there was more to the story.

Part of Timmons's advice had been to leave the city as soon as possible and avoid major thoroughfares. Davis had picked up a map at the Food and Geaux and used it to chart a roundabout way west out of town. He had made a makeshift bed on the front seat for Mayah, who seemed very curious, but comfortable, with him. "Ok, girl; time for us to 'geaux,'" thinking the odd spelling. He was especially cognizant of speed limits and any sign of law enforcement. He passed a sign that said, "Leaving The Big Easy. Come Back Soon." *That's not likely,* he thought. It wasn't until he was an hour away that he started to relax a bit.

He found a K-Mart on the outskirts of Lafayette and purchased a car seat, setting it up in the back seat, again, trying to be a compliant as possible should anyone take notice. Mayah settled right in. Davis, not having spent a lot of time around children was still aware of how uncooperative they could be and was amazed with Mayah's easy nature. He positioned the rearview mirror so he had a constant view of her in the back, not that she was going anywhere, but it just comforted him to have her in his sights. They had a bit of a running conversation about cows and barns, but they both seemed to get bored of that. Most of Davis's thoughts were consumed with what was next: who knew what? Was there going to be a manhunt for him? Was he actually a suspect? *I know I am, but did anyone else besides Timmons know? How much can I trust him? We wouldn't even have Mayah back if not for him, but how long could or would he keep his secret? And what was his part in all of this?*

He thought back to the time when he had gone AWOL after the Kent State shootings and how he was always looking over his shoulder. He remembered how good it had felt to finally turn himself in and take whatever was coming to him in terms of punishment, but also how fortunate he had been to get off so easily. That might not be the case here. That first time, he had no idea where his bullet had landed coming out of the muzzle of his M-1. This time, he knew exactly where it had landed, time and time again, not to mention that last blow with the bat.

Shit! The bat! He had taken the bat, his bloody clothes and the stroller with him, not wanting to leave any evidence behind. He remembered they were still in the trunk of the car, waiting to be disposed of. Mayah let him know it was time for a potty break. He found a Burger King and figured their dumpster was a good enough place for the bat. He would get rid of the stroller at another location, trying to spread evidence as far and wide as possible.

He called Becca again and she got to speak to Mayah. Davis wondered what was going through Mayah's head, hearing a voice that might sound familiar, but certainly not from conscious memory, identifying herself as "your mama." He thought about what Leticia had said about "two moms" and wondered if any of them would ever see Leticia again. Mayah seemed eager to want to share the information about how many Goldfish she had been allowed to eat.

Davis seemed intent on driving the 16 hours straight through, stopping to rest and eat but not check into a motel. He wanted to deliver his cargo and to also be back in the safe haven of his home to figure out with Becca how best to proceed. He considered for a brief second not telling her about the dead man, if for no other reason, to protect her. But of course, that wasn't going to happen. Even if he tried to keep it from her, she would suspect. She would KNOW. It was Becca, after all. The thought of their connection became a beacon for him, a sanctuary. He wanted her counsel, her support. Her love.

Once Davis had crossed into Texas, he figured it was safe to get back on the interstate. He skirted the city of Houston heading north to Dallas and passed to the west onto 287. The farther he got from New Orleans, the more he relaxed, although the amount of caffeine he was pumping into his veins through cup after cup of coffee contributed to jitters of another sort.

Once he hit Amarillo, he realized he had been on that route before: the first time he had come out West, driving his beloved Fairlane 'Lucy' literally into the ground: an arroyo on the side of the road, narrowly missing getting creamed by a semi. To pass the drive time he devised a game to try and recognize where that was and see if he could visit her 'gravesite.'

He pulled into a roadside rest stop west of Amarillo, taking a walk with Mayah to stretch his (and her) legs. Davis had been driving for 12 hours, stopping just to eat and take bathroom breaks. It was late afternoon and Davis found a concrete picnic table for them to get a change of scenery. He sat Mayah on the bench and leaned back against the table, soaking in the sun low on the horizon to the west. He closed his eyes and yup, sure enough, fell asleep. He found himself elevating to an eagle-eye view, searching for Lucy's final resting place. Sure enough, he found it, and there was Lucy, almost completely buried now from years of wind and erosion. Davis was enjoying the feeling of riding the thermals; it was relaxing, peaceful. And yet, there was another voice, a force, that was working against that repose. His slowly developing paternal side was trying to wake him and alert him to the fact that Mayah may need his attention. His head slumped down onto his chest with a jerk, enough to wake him with a start. He looked around immediately to where Mayah had been sitting.

She was gone.

Panicked now, he rose to his feet, scanning 360 degrees for her, calling her name. He looked to see if anyone else was around that might have seen where she went. There was no one. He spun around in the opposite direction, thinking somehow that might make a difference. Nothing. The rest stop was little more than a parking lot with a few picnic tables—no bathrooms she could be hiding in. The landscape was fairly flat but there were some large rocks and small hills that could be hiding her. He ran frantically from area to area. The vegetation was mostly sage with cholla cactus and some mesquite. At just over two years old, she was mobile enough to get around pretty quickly. He kept calling her name, then stopping and listening for a response. The sound of traffic whizzing by not that far away alerted him to the most serious potential danger: playing in traffic. He raced over to the edge of the highway and was relieved to see nothing.

Running back to the parking lot, he began to cover ever larger circles.

Then, he thought he heard the squeak of her voice. Racing over in that direction, he came to a small rise and there she was, in the middle of a tall stand of cholla.

"Pop," which was what they had arrived at as at least a temporary moniker for himself. "Look." In her two tiny hands was a horned toad. The cholla was about six feet tall with limbs and stalks about an inch and a half around, covered, like all cactus with prickly spines. Mayah had gotten into the center of them easily enough, but there was no way for Davis to. He was going to have to coax her out. She didn't appear to be hurt at all, but was West Texas dusty from head to toe.

"Mayah, honey, you have to come out."

"Look. Frog."

Davis laughed, despite the circumstances, although relief at finding her certainly contributed to a sense of lightness. "Yes, honey: not a frog, though, a toad. A horned toad. But you have to leave him here and come out. Come on out to Pop."

"No. Mine."

This was the first indication of any behavior that was anything other than compliant. Unprepared for it and with nerves wearing a bit thin, it irritated Davis. He raised his voice. "Mayah, get out here NOW!"

Her face dropped, her eyes got big and immediately filled with tears, a situation Davis had no experience with and therefore no wherewithal to deal with.

Exhausted, softened by her tears, he dropped to the ground and sat cross-legged, about six very long feet away from her. He stuffed his frustration and considered another strategy. "Mayah, can you show me the toad?"

She stopped her crying briefly, the tears creating mud on her cheeks and held the horned toad out to Davis in her chubby fist.

"He's a beauty. Can you bring him out to me?"

"It's a girl," Mayah said.

OK, thought Davis, letting part of his mind wonder how she came up with that determination. Can you hand her to me and then you come out and we will go back to the car?" Davis had to lie on the dry, rocky ground and reach his hand into Mayah's spiky sanctuary to have any access at all. "Give her to me and I will hold her until you come out, OK?"

Mayah considered this plan and gently placed the horned toad into Davis's waiting palm. He closed his fingers around the scratchy lizard and retracted his arm. His next job was getting Mayah out without her getting ripped apart. "Mayah, how did you get in there?" She looked around for egress and found it, getting snagged slightly a couple of times, but impressing Davis with her agility.

He hugged her tightly, but she was more interested in getting her hands back on the horned toad. Davis had a sense the lizard would be joining them for the rest of their journey.

He was right.

35

Never There

The phone ring came out of nowhere, like most. Becca had tried to stay as close to the phone as possible, not wanting to miss Davis's calls. Expecting his voice, she was surprised when another male voice presented itself: one she had heard that one time before. "Hello, Becca."

"Oh. Hi. I was expecting Davis."

"He should be well on his way."

"Yeah, well, listen..." She paused, not sure exactly what she wanted to say. "Who ARE you? I mean, I know I owe you a debt of gratitude, but for all I know, you are the person who took Mayah to begin with. Who the fuck ARE you?"

"I didn't take her, but I became aware of the abduction and I knew it was wrong. Who I am is not important. Just consider me a benevolent... uncle, who has your and Mayah's best interests at heart. If you feel like you have to refer to me somehow, just think of me as Uncle Jerry."

"But where was she all this time? Who had her? Was she in danger?"

"What has Davis told you?"

"Very little, other than they are on their way back and she seems to be OK."

There was a pause on the line. "He didn't tell you what transpired in New Orleans?"

"No, he said it didn't go as planned, but he would fill me in when he got home. What happened there? What do I not know?"

"I shouldn't be talking to you, and probably shouldn't have made this call and you may not ever hear from me again, but here is what is important for Davis to know: he was NOT in New Orleans. He is to deny having visited that city. Tell him I cleaned up after him as best I could and I am assuming he did too. The story on getting Mayah back is she was left on your doorstep and that is all you know."

"What?"

"Do not contact the authorities for a few days. Lay low. If Davis has any obvious injuries, he is to come up with an appropriate story to explain how they might have happened in New Mexico."

"Wait. Injuries? What happened?"

"I can't talk much longer. Look, Mayah had been taken by a group of white supremacists that were upset with you having a mixed–race baby. She was placed with a black family in New Orleans that had no idea where she came from. When I got involved and explained the circumstances to the mom, she felt like it was wrong for Mayah to be taken from you and agreed to return her."

"So, she knows who I am?"

"Yes, she does."

"And why did you get involved?"

"I know your music and I am a fan. But I am also in law enforcement and was aware of your case and am also an... associate of the person who master-minded this. I wasn't aware of his involvement at first, but once I found out, I knew it was just wrong but it took some time to put a plan into place to make it right."

"So, we are to lie about this going forward? How do we know it won't happen again?"

"That is very unlikely."

"I don't like the sound of this. What happened to Davis? What injuries are you talking about? He didn't say anything."

"I'll let him fill you in on all of that; I wasn't witness to it anyway. Just know sometimes telling the truth is not in your best interest."

Becca let that sink in, but she wasn't drawing any conclusions yet.

"I guess I should thank you."

"I'm just glad Mayah will be back with her real mom, although you should know, she was loved and accepted in her temporary home. I'm sure they will miss her. You will probably not hear from me again. I have some tracks I need to cover. Remember, Davis was never here."

"Right. Davis was never there."

The phone clicked on the other end and Becca was left holding the receiver in her hand until it went to dial tone.

36

Home Again

Davis got Mayah situated back in her car seat, once a suitable container was found for "Pokey." There was a conversation about wandering off like she had, and how that could never happen again, but Davis also had to own his part in the dilemma, not to mention the extenuating circumstances of a tempting spiky reptile that was apparently begging to be adopted.

On a much less important note, Davis's 'meditation' was not for naught. He was able to locate Lucy's grave, taking a few quick moments to pay his respects. She was certainly not the first car in New Mexico to be so interred: one fender peeking out as a surrogate tombstone, rusting innards going back to the earth from whence they came. Davis didn't pause there long, having plenty of time driving to reflect on how far he had come since he had first passed this way. It seemed easily a couple of lifetimes ago.

They stopped in Tucumcari to gas up and grab a bite. Davis took the opportunity to call Becca to tell her they were just a few hours away.

She answered the phone on the first ring. "Hello?"

"Hi Bec. It's us." It occurred to him it was the first time he had used that plural pronoun. "We're in Tucumcari."

"Davis. Jesus. I just got off the phone a short while ago with Uncle Jerry."

"Uncle Jerry..." Davis stretched out the name as a question, not knowing who she was referring to.

"Uncle Jerry is the alias we are using for the man who has found Mayah for us. He filled me in on some of what happened. Davis, baby, are you Ok?"

Davis paused. "What did he tell you?"

"I can fill you in on that later, but I'm more concerned about what he didn't tell me. He said you are never to admit to anyone you have made this trip, that Mayah was returned to our doorstep and you may have been injured somehow. Davis, what happened?"

"There was an altercation. A serious altercation. After the transfer was made, I think it was with someone that had to do with the original abduction."

"Are you hurt?"

"I'm a little sore," and then in an attempt to lighten the mood; "but you should see the other guy."

"Uncle Jerry said we won't have to worry about him anymore. What does that mean?"

"I think that is true, but I don't know who else was involved. What I do know is I have a bright-eyed, lovely young girl sitting in her car seat playing with Pokey and we are less than three hours away and I can't wait to see you. We will figure this all out. And I will tell you one thing; no one is ever going to take this girl away from us again. No one."

The "us" that Davis used was not lost on Becca. She liked the sound of it.

It was about 9 PM when the car pulled up to the casita. Becca ran out and charged Davis. He was bone tired and exhausted but fully engaged in their embrace. Mayah was asleep in her car seat and she got the same warm welcome—a little less passionate but every bit as exuberant. The three of them went into the house as one, Becca being sure to lock the door behind them.

Davis said, "Let's catch up on everything in the morning, OK?"

"Sure, baby. Davis went straight for the bedroom, shedding shoes and clothes along the way. He collapsed on the bed and was asleep in minutes.

Becca spent time with Mayah, undressing her and putting her into some PJs she had bought that very day. She laid her on the bed next to Davis, even though they had a room already set up just for her. She laid down on the bed facing them, running one hand along Mayah's back and the other through Davis's hair.

She had her family back.

37

A Little Peace

As much as Becca was wanting to know the details of what had transpired, she darkened the bedroom and let Davis sleep through most of the morning, busying herself with getting Mayah clean, fed and familiar with her new surroundings. Davis finally staggered into the kitchen just before noon, his hair disheveled, his eyes not used to the bright New Mexico sunlight yet. Becca rushed him with a hug he returned as well as he could. His body was stiff not only from the altercation but sixteen straight hours of driving.

"Pop!" Mayah yelled and rushed to where Pokey was taking up residence, retrieved her, then glommed onto his leg with her free arm.

"There's nothing wrong with that kind of reception," said Davis. Squinting, he looked at the clock and rubbed his face, trying to complete his awakening. After a cup of coffee, they sat on the couch with Mayah sequestered in her room. Davis relayed all the events that happened in New Orleans, leaving nothing out. Becca listened without interruption, maintaining a constant physical contact with him at all times, whether it was a touch or a knee. When he was finished, she repeated the mantra that had been looping in his head ever since the event: "Now what do we do?"

The "we" was not lost on him.

"Well, on the bright side, we have Mayah back, and that feels right. And good. She is a sweetheart," said Davis. "If we go to the authorities with what happened, there is no guarantee we will be able to keep her; I will be tried for killing a federal agent and I don't trust a self-defense defense will hold up. They protect their own."

"I know. I've been thinking along those same lines. At the same time, we will be living a secret—a bad secret—that at least one other person knows about. A stranger, albeit a seemingly benevolent one."

"Yeah. Uncle Jerry. I'd like to believe his motives are as well-meaning as the person who took Mayah's were not. We have no way of knowing. What does your gut say?"

"There are so many layers to this. I have no doubt whatsoever what you did was to protect yourself and Mayah, so if I am judge and jury, you are already exonerated. On the other hand, I don't like lying, and this is a big one."

"If we go to law enforcement, I will be tried for killing one of them. I also think it is important the advice we have been given by another cop is to very specifically not come forward. It makes me wonder how far-reaching any dirt-dealing or corruption might extend in all of this."

"That's putting a lot of eggs in Uncle Jerry's basket."

"Yeah. Uncle Jerry." Davis thought back to the few minutes he spent sitting across from the man in that hotel room. "My take on him is he is sincere. He has everything to lose and nothing to gain by going against the law enforcement brotherhood. He would be totally ostracized if they were to find out he is covering up what happened. And even though he wasn't a direct witness, he knows what happened."

"Assuming he is who he says he is."

"Right. I wasn't in a position to check his credentials. But if he's not actually FBI, this is a really elaborate ruse to make us believe he is. You haven't actually seen him, but you don't think this is someone you know?"

"His voice doesn't sound familiar, and he hasn't given me any reason to believe he knows me outside of my music. He said he's a fan."

"A fan. Let's hope he is not some star-crazed stalker who is looking to gain favor. A fan... it's kinda weird to think about total strangers knowing so much about your life and then being able to insert themselves."

"Yeah, I guess it comes with the territory. It's a part that I don't like, especially now with all of this. Part of me just wishes we could just hole up here—just the three of us—and never have to deal with the outside world again."

"I'm with you. I feel like I have everything I need right here. I am so glad to be back home."

They hugged a long hard one, neither one wanting to release, until Mayah emerged from her room, clutching PoohBear—her link to her short and not distant past—but seemingly rapidly adjusting to her new digs.

"I'm hungry," she said.

Becca bound up. "Hungry? Let's see what we can do about that."

Because it was going to be hard to hide, Davis pulled Gloria aside to tell her Mayah was back and to keep it under her hat for a day or two until they could figure out how they wanted to "handle" the announcement of her return. When pressed for details, Davis just explained t a private party had contacted them and arranged for her return.

In the end, Davis's being gone for a few days barely went noticed, he was that much of a loner. Mayah's reappearance required more of a concoction. Since she was so young, her memory was not fully formed around her experience and no one was going to get close enough to question her anyway. The story they ran with was they received an anonymous phone call (which they had) and an unknown benefactor (which they also had) was going to set up a reunion as long as they agreed no law enforcement was to be involved and no further questions would be asked.

The local cops were not happy they were not brought into the loop. The feds were suspicious but had enough on their plate with unsolved cases to be spending time on one that was. They had found nothing to tie Mayah's abduction to the murder of an agent a thousand miles away; whatever Davis had not cleaned up in New Orleans, it appeared that Uncle Jerry had.

It didn't take long for them to fall into a full domestic routine. Having a toddler around will do that. After two weeks of no drama, no violence, no secret phone calls and not even a whiff of murder, in a late–night discussion over a bottle of wine they decided whatever had happened around getting Mayah back would be buried. The 'x-factor' in that plan was having a stranger being part and parcel to it and trusting he would never have a reason to hold that over their heads. The alternative was just too daunting.

It was an especially hard decision for Davis, seeing as how he didn't really trust anyone. In his quiet moments, he would go back to sitting with Uncle Jerry in the hotel room and try to re-enact the one-sided conversation, but even more than that, to get a sense of who that person was, his motivations for getting involved and what the upsides and downsides were to keeping the secret.

Then in his dark, quiet times he would relive the altercation: the primal rage that had kicked in, his sense of preservation, protecting Mayah and even the bigger questions around issues like the sanctity of life. He had undergone military training and been taught how to kill, and that killing was OK, under certain rules, against certain pre-determined enemies, chosen by others. His proximity to gun violence again and again haunted him and he was determined to remove himself from situations like that should they arise again.

All he wanted now was a little peace.

38

1987

A School for Mayah

For Davis, being a homebody was a perfect fit; he had everything he wanted: security, love, creativity—all without having to mess around with the outside world and all of those, you know—others.

Despite not having been around many kids, Davis found himself to be a natural dad. He appreciated, that, for the most part, children, as long as they were getting their needs met, were guileless. In a decidedly conscious way, he wanted to be more involved than his parents were, without taking it to extremes. Many baby-boomers made the mistake of overindulging their children, giving them ultimate freedom without boundaries, then wondering how they lost control over their households. Because they didn't have typical nine-to-five jobs, Davis and Becca were home a lot and, in many ways, it established a natural, sustainable household hierarchy.

The specter around Mayah's abduction also gave Becca additional motivation to not take motherhood for granted. Her first priority was to catch up with her daughter and reestablish their connection. Mayah seemed to have suffered no ill effects from the abduction and was perfectly fine with slipping into a situation where she was the center of the universe.

As could be expected, once they had Mayah back, for a good long time, there were no occasions when she would be out of direct contact with at least one of them. There were no playdates at the homes of other children; it seemed far too risky, and as a result, Mayah was growing up in an adult world. Both Becca and Davis knew at some point they would have to loosen the apron strings as she got to be ready for school.

Given the sorry state of the local public school system, they experimented with home-schooling, but decided it was important for Mayah to learn coping skills and how to be around others her age. After considering Waldorf and various Montessori alternatives, they found a private school called Reach the Children.

When they visited to see what a typical day was like, they got to see a special morning circle celebrating one of the children's birthdays. The birthday boy sat in the center and got to bask in the limelight as each child voiced what they appreciated about him. Davis found himself having an emotional reaction to the affection and care so openly encouraged. Later, he said to Becca, "This is what all schools should be like."

They enrolled Mayah and she thrived in the diverse environment. It also came with its downside–the socialization part—dealing with kids occasionally being cruel. Fortunately, part of the curriculum at "Reach" was around conflict resolution, even at a pre-school age.

When a five–year–old Mayah parroted "What's a different way we can look at this?" around a situation at home, Davis and Becca could only laugh and feel like their schooling decision went considerably beyond arithmetic and penmanship.

A bit to Becca's dismay, Mayah became a daddy's girl and once she became more independently mobile, he would even occasionally take her with him on his forays into the wilderness to paint. She always found ways to entertain herself, as if she realized the amount of concentration necessary for her dad to create his art.

She enjoyed the physicality of being out in nature. At first, Davis would engage in a fair amount of both literal and figurative hand-holding, but once he realized her capabilities, he would let her run free, jump and climb. Once she got to be seven years old, he had ultimate confidence in her ability to safely negotiate the harsh desert landscape. Still, they had rules around how far she could venture away—within earshot, if not line of sight.

39

July 1992

A Perfect Union

Bedtime for both Davis and Becca was generally reserved for sleep, their passionate interludes notwithstanding. They were both sound sleepers and slept well together. That sounds like an odd way to describe their time together in bed, but they would often refer to it as their "bedded bliss." It was a place of comfort and safety. If one of them tossed or moved, contact with the other was an anchor, a sanctuary.

Davis did wake one windy night. He repositioned himself, assuming he would just go back to sleep, as usual. But he didn't. He found himself staring up at the ceiling until his rods and cones adjusted and was able to see remnants of light. He rolled onto his side and was startled to see what looked like glowing embers on the bed next to him. His tentative reach felt no heat but did create shadow, light being projected from behind the venetian blinds covering the window. He got out of bed, pulling one slat down to discover a brilliant full moon blazing cool white light behind a foreground of leafy trees jitterbugging in the wind.

Looking back behind him, on the bed, he realized what looked like hot coals was the moonlight playing on Becca's hair, splayed behind her, crimson-red. He got back in bed, still warm from where he had recently lain and gently placed his hand underneath her locks, as if scooping up a handful of lava. Bringing his handful of her fire up to his face, he imagined he could feel the heat. What he didn't have to imagine was her smell; as much as he loved looking at her red mop, he always enjoyed being close enough to be able to smell it.

I can feel your fire, he thought. Becca stirred and Davis felt himself respond. He scooted closer to her until his body was touching hers: bedwarm, soft, familiar. Part of him didn't want to wake her and yet another persistent part of him was asserting itself, front and center.

The moonlight behind the trees was dancing slatted on his face. He let the front of his thighs cozy up with the back of hers, just barely, being careful not to prod where that could be an issue. His fingers traced the line of her waist down to her hip, leaving the bony part for the terribly soft skin on her belly He let his touch wander down to where her equally red pubic hair began: fine, not wiry, wavy but not curly and every bit as full as the mane on her head.

Becca inhaled a small gasp when he touched the place where she opened. *Are you awake?* he only thought. She was already wet, his fingers following that slippery dew so lightly they barely felt the skin underneath–that place, HER favorite place–and lingered there for a while. He felt Becca relax and then roll onto her back.

Aroused, but also feeling extremely familiar and content, Davis inched his hand back up to her belly where it came to rest, dead-weight heavy, as he lazily drifted (considering the circumstances)_back into an unlikely slumber.

Meanwhile, Becca WAS wide awake, pretending not to be, waiting for what might be next, but realizing that was a losing strategy. She decided to take matters into her own hands.

Slowly, quietly, she flipped herself around until she was facing him, then gently pushed him onto his back. *Are you really asleep?* it was her turn to think.

She swung her right leg over him, straddling his hips. He was still erect. As she steadied herself with one hand she used the other to coat him with her juice, then, with the least detectable effort possible, slid him inside of her.

She looked at his face, the moonlight casting shadows across his features, then very deliberately raised herself up the full length of him, and back down again, allowing herself to not only feel <u>her</u> pleasure, but because of their graft connection, his ecstasy inside of her. She let those sensations swirl and dance, like they often did between the two of them; it wasn't his or hers; it became theirs.

His eyes were still closed.

Are you awake, baby? She wondered again, partly hoping he thought he was dreaming.

She could feel him getting harder and continued her rhythm, rising, squeezing but not increasing her pace. Becca bent forward so her face was just an inch from his, waiting for his eyes to blink open at any second.

They didn't.

She thought he could see the hint of a smile on Davis's lips, but he couldn't be sure with the light undulating as it was. She could feel the warmth coming off his mouth, letting her lips almost touch his, then felt herself tighten around him, again, again.

And again.

Her orgasm was enough to send him over the edge as well and they released together, his fluid mixing with hers in a way that was completely compatible, as if part of what was comingling was already combined.

And again, because of their graft, that was simply part of what was.

Davis's 'boys' were joyfully ejaculated into Becca's waiting vessel like a releasing of the hounds, the dogs off the leash, those frisky sperm cells free to cavort wildly, willy-nilly in the most primal pursuit known to nature.

On the outside, Becca withdrew from her position as stealthily as she had engaged, not in a spirit of having taken him; quite the contrary, she suspected he had been fully awake and, in more ways than one, 'fucking' with her by pretending to be asleep.

On the inside though, there was a determined agenda, not just on the part of Davis's million minions, but with Becca's sole participant, a pre-arranged agreement that, there will be union!

And there was.

In that split-second moment when fertilization occurred, chromosomes all akimbo, there was a mutual realization that, if it could have been verbalized, would have been,

"Wait... haven't we met before?"

The two of them had discussed and agreed upon the idea of having a child together. In the six months since that discussion, every month, Becca's period has arrived a regularly as it always had.

This time would be different, though.

I, Narrator

On a microscopic level to us as sentient humans, nature's work forges forward, driven by its own set of rules, posthaste, in the perpetuation of the species. Cells merging, multiplying, splitting, specializing, in a wildly random yet pre-determined process to become "One."

It's a fucking miracle, I tell ya, double entendre fully intended.

When did this particular mass of cells become Davis and Becca's offspring, the person? Of course, that is a question for the ages. And the sages (but can we leave the politicians out of it?) Regardless of exactly when, a new being was the ultimate result.

In all of the ways over the years these two have connected, this was perhaps the most profound, in it created not just another bond but another entity, a son–of them, yet apart from them. Grafting was one process, replete with its manifestations, consequences and epiphanies, but this, this was a fusion on a whole 'nother level.

Now their family unit was complete, and together they were determined not to commit the sins of their parents. That's right: the credo of every prospective parent who has suffered a dysfunctional childhood. Because Dylan—we'll talk about the name in a minute—they were going to make sure of, was not "Davis," and Mayah, as she was already presenting herself, was "not Becca." Like so many progeny who had come before them, they were genetic combinations of their parents, but to what end? Being conscious "modern" parents, both Davis and Becca wanted their children to "be their own person," but every father and mother has at the very least a general template they expect their child to fit into and it can lead to disappointment.

There are just too many variables.

Just like the rest of life.

40

1993

Family Life

So, 'Dylan.'

The prospective parents had been tempted to know the gender of their child ahead of the birth, if for no other reason, because now they <u>could</u>, but decided to wait and be surprised. Despite how often it got them in hot water, Davis and Becca were both, at least, occasional fans of the unexpected.

They had names picked out for boys and girls. Davis, despite having suffered somewhat in his growing up with a slightly unusual name, and one with a musical lineage at that, leaned toward the same for his son. His first choice was the King, Elvis.

Becca was not on board.

Of early Elvis, sure. Who wasn't? But her argument against was the decline into Vegas Elvis.

Davis countered with the idea Elvis Costello made the name cool again.

"Yeaahhh... kinda sorta..." was Becca's response.

Anyway, their deal was they had to agree on a name, so lots of others got thrown into the pot. They both wanted something unusual, so 'Bob' and 'Jimmy (and Jimi)' and 'Bruce" and 'Tom' were summarily tossed. When they came around to realizing 'Davis' was actually a surname, 'Dylan' followed fairly quickly and it was a no-brainer. Little did they know they were at the forefront of countless thousands of other 'Dylans" to follow.

Davis was present at the birth, which had also become fashionable. He was surprised at how emotional the birth moment was for him. A miracle, yes, but it still caught him off guard. It was an indicator of how much he had gravitated over to his 'gentler' side, call it what you want: 'yin,' 'feminine,' 'pussy...'" (Whoa, whoa, whoa; what's THAT all about? A bit judgmental in a neo-neanderthal way, don't you think?)

Whatever you want to call it, his swing in that direction was a conscious one. Davis had seen what he felt was more than his share of violence, especially around firearms, and he wanted to move his life, his being, away from that. Even when he took up martial arts, with Mayah, wanting to make sure she would be able to defend herself, it was more for the philosophy and the discipline than the badassery. The first dojo they attended had a decidedly violent thread running through it, despite (or in this case, because of) having a female sensei, so he found an Aikido dojo that was a better fit philosophically.

They kept their surnames after they married since Becca had name recognition around her music. It was agreed Mayah would remain a Lakaris and just to even things out, Dylan would be a Filkins. Yes, Dylan Filkins: it had a 'ring' to it. Because there was a social freedom in Santa Fe unlike most other places in the country (It wasn't called The City Different for nothing), no one batted an eye at their decisions around family structure.

They moved out of the casita once Dylan was born to a small adobe place on the south side of town. It was funky and a bit run down but they were able to get it for a good price and it had some land around it. They created a studio for Becca's music that housed the used upright piano Becca found for Davis at the local Salvation Army. He had a newborn interest in music having what he referred to as "a Rockstar in the house."

They became homebodies, doting on their children, family intact.

Becca had few regrets about leaving LA and the music biz. She did miss the beach and the weather but not the hectic lifestyle. Moving back to New Mexico was a complete paradigm shift; "mañana" was not just a concept, it was a way of life. Time slows down so much there it can appear to not be moving at all, and that suited her just fine.

They settled in.

It took a while, but gradually Davis allowed himself to consider that maybe, just maybe, there was a benevolent soul (read: Uncle Jerry) whose only agenda was to do the right thing. It would take years for that nagging doubt to finally dissipate, but it did lessen, and as it did, a semblance of normalcy enveloped the household.

Sorta.

Becca had made her deal-with-fingers-crossed-behind-her-back with the Dark Entity, and who knew when HE would come knocking (and it <u>was</u> assuredly a masculine energy, of the worst kind–what in later years would be labeled as toxic) but even that had settled into a distant memory.

Mayah embraced the idea of having a baby brother, becoming an instant caregiver and sitter. She was at that stage where kids shoot up inches in a matter of months–especially big for her age, easily the tallest in her class. For most girls, that would be a reason to slouch, but her body was strong and she was comfortable in it, so her head was always held high. It helped she was a gentle soul. It was a common sight for her to be seen with Dylan on her hip. Theirs was a natural, easy alliance, Mayah's dimple flashing whenever they were together and Dylan's boyish laugh filling what little space was ever between them.

Dylan was all boy, constantly on the move. America had been on an exercise kick for years at this point: jogging, gyms, yoga, biking, hiking, but really, all they needed was a Dylan in the house. He was constantly pushing the physical envelope of anyone around him.

Then, every parent's nightmare: once he learned to verbalize, he discovered, embraced and with great regularity, wielded the word "NO."

Whereas Mayah had been all yin: my needs are being met; just give me a horned toad and I'm good, Dylan was all yang, convinced there was more to be had.

Davis and Becca got the parenting books, they discussed, they researched and they fretted. Because this two-year-old was the proverbial "terrible." Mayah was the one that seemed to hold the most sway over him, but she couldn't be around all the time. However, consistent boundaries ("no's") from the three caregivers formed a coalition against the mighty toddler and some semblance of order was reached. As a result, once Dylan gained some more control of his languaging and comprehension skills, while he was still a physical whirlwind, he became manageable.

Two turned into three turned into four and five and it was time to consider school for him. While Rosemary's "Reach" was still available, financial constrictions took private school off the table, especially for two kids. Mayah was finishing high school at Prep, which was expensive, but worth the price for what she was blossoming into. The "upper crust" in Santa Fe had created private school options for those that could afford it to provide educational opportunities that rivaled some of the best in the country and Mayah was thriving in that environment, constantly facing challenges, rising to meet all of them.

Dylan's exposure to "higher" education would just have to wait.

Once public kindergarten started, Dylan seemed to be especially susceptible to peer pressure. He latched onto the idea of old-school masculinity and appeared to be especially drawn to it. This went along with him being a kinesthetic learner. He was firmly IN his body and anything that required movement, large or small, he gravitated towards. Being a boy, he was immediately exposed to the machismo aspect of the Chicano culture, male-dominated, on the surface anyway, aggressive and even violent. His own predilection to being testosterone-driven allowed him to fit in, although it took a few physical dust-ups for him to establish his place and be accepted. Coming home from school more than once bruised and a little bloody gave Davis and Becca second thoughts about their public-school decision. In the interest of considering their perspective of always-turning-the-other-cheek wasn't the only one, they allowed him to remain, wary of their offspring being hurt, but also cognizant of him establishing his place in the social order.

When they spoke to him about it, it was through a six-year-old's sensibilities. "Pecking order" meant nothing. They kept a close eye. Parent-teacher conferences afforded some insight, but from a teacher having to deal with thirty, similar, unequal, disparate students.

Their wherewithal was eventually rewarded, their son returning home, accepted—not bloodied, not shunned, but simply a part of what was, somewhere in the middle, possibly upper-middle if you are want to measure those things. At least they weren't having to wash blood out of his shirts. Davis and Becca accepted they were sending their son out into the world for eight hours a day into, perhaps not an ideal environment, but an acceptable one. They did their best to balance the other sixteen with support and a positive world view.

Their household routine was anything but 9-5 and before Dylan was even considered, there were conscious conversations about lifestyle, household responsibilities and parenting roles. Though the kids were going to be growing up in a musical household, Davis wanted to be sure they were not subject to the grind of music lessons against their will. There was almost always music swirling about, recorded, if not being produced live, and lots of singing.

To the delight of their parents, both kids responded well to the 'hands-off' approach to music instruction. Becca's music inspired Davis to take up the piano again, and Mayah, ever Daddy's girl, asked him to show her some songs. Dylan wasn't going to be left out and his energy just naturally got channeled into banging on things, so, a drum kit was added and became his contribution. He took to it naturally and had what seemed to be muscle memory around where feet, legs, arms and hands were simultaneously supposed to go.

Coming into her adolescence, Mayah wasn't sure where she fit in. With her skin a medium brown color, light enough to let her "Beckles," as they would call them, show through, and her facial features suggesting her dad's contributions: a wide nose, full lips and high cheekbones, she increasingly became curious about her blackness. In many ways, it was said she got the best of both worlds, genetically, as she also inherited her father's body and athleticism. The one trait that couldn't be decided one way or another was her hair; it was like it wanted to be Becca-red, but also kinky-curly. It had a life of its own and was a constant challenge around styling.

Her parents provided her with an education about the birds and bees when she was as young as seven, and she was made aware Davis was not her biological father. Once she expressed an interest in who was, a decision had to be made about disclosure, not only to Mayah, but to her biological dad, who had gone on to be a professional athlete, although not a very high-profile one.

Becca's last contact with Jackson was when he had unknowingly fathered their daughter. Finding him didn't take a serious amount of sleuthing as had gone on to play for the New York Jets for a couple of years as a bench player until an injury ended his career. He had been surprised at the claims of paternity but when he realized Becca had not been looking for a payday and was presented with Mayah's curiosity, he readily accepted his role and expressed a willingness to be involved.

Originally from Alabama, Jackson became enamored with New York City after his stint with the Jets, deciding to stay there and devote his time and energy to developing black businesses in Harlem.

After discussing it with Becca, he wrote Mayah an introductory letter, which she responded to enthusiastically. Eventually, they engaged in an at-first uncomfortable phone call, but Jackson's natural charm eventually won the day.

When Mayah was twelve, she said she wanted to meet him. Davis had a trip planned to the city for some business dealing around the record store, which had now become a small chain and it was decided Mayah would go along.

It was her first time on a plane and her first time in New York. Davis had not met Jackson but they had talked on the phone and so had no trepidation about the meeting other than having a sense of Mayah's nervousness around the first encounter. It was spring and Davis thought Washington Square Park down in the Village would be a good place to meet. Jackson got there first and was sitting on a park bench when they approached. He stood, unfolding his wide 6'6" frame. Knowing his intimidation potential, he stooped slightly and offered his hand. Mayah shook it and they stood just gaping at each other. Then Jackson withdrew his hand and spread his arms wide in a gesture for a hug which Mayah immediately accepted.

Jackson, whose last name was Lewis, had a family of his own: a wife and three children—two girls and a boy. Mayah was intrigued by the thought of having sisters and plans were made to arrange a meeting, which they did the next day, without Davis, who felt completely comfortable with the situation after the initial contact.

When they got back home and were relaying the details of the trip to Becca, her new "family" was all Mayah talked about, which Davis felt a twinge of jealousy about, but also understood.

Later, Davis was standing on the back porch, watching the New Mexico day fade into another showy sunset. He heard steps come up behind him.

"Pop?"

Davis turned to see Mayah coming towards him. She came up next to him and put her arm around his waist, a gesture that had become second nature to them. "It's beautiful, isn't it?" he said.

"Yes, it is." Mayah hesitated a few seconds before continuing. "Pop, thank you for taking me to meet Jackson in New York."

"You're welcome, sweetheart. Your mom and I felt like the time was right, and it all seems to have gone quite well, don't you think?"

"Yes, it did, and I really like him, and I have sisters!" she said, bouncing on her toes when she said that. "But, you know, you will always be my father."

She leaned her head against his shoulder and tightened her grip around his waist.

Davis closed his eyes to blink back his reaction. He buried his face is her hair, which not so long ago would have been at the top of her head, but was now on the side, she being almost as tall.

"Thank you," he whispered.

"His" little girl was growing up just fine.

Mayah kept up a constant communication with her new family. Although her sisters were a few years younger, they were close enough they had plenty in common, and they were just as excited to have a big sister. Plans were made the following summer for Mayah to spend a month with them. She fell in love with the city, despite it being a complete culture shock. By then, she had turned her focus towards dance and away from sports and she was able to take classes and workshops at various studios around the city and then as a surprise Jackson had gotten them tickets to see Alvin Ailey's troupe do a show at the Lincoln Center for the Performing Arts.

A seed had been planted—actually, more than one—Mayah set her sights on studying dance after high school, and she wanted to do it in New York City.

Together, Davis and Becca carved out an income stream that supported their laid-back lifestyle in an area where most working people struggled to make ends meet. They pieced together a comfortable livelihood between Becca's sporadic Too Much royalties and occasional local gigs coupled with Davis's profits from Whirled Records and his paintings that continued to sell at Gloria's gallery.

Becca continued to write songs and would play occasional gigs around town. The music scene there was small but enthusiastic, with not many venues to support serious attendance, but with such a fertile artistic community, an appreciation for what was good. With a population of only about 100,000, Santa Fe was like living on an island. The lack of water in the high desert prevented any major population growth along with the local inhabitants being perfectly fine with not having a lot of out-of-towners moving in and gentrifying their neighborhoods.

Still, Santa Fe style became a 'thing," and 'The City Different' became even more of a tourist destination than before. Impresarios came from elsewhere to try and capitalize on the movement, including the music scene. New venues like The Paramount would pop up from time to time, only to become money pits once the carpetbaggers realized the same rules that applied in most other places didn't work in Santa Fe. It was a desirable destination for artists to visit and play, so places like Club West would book national and regional acts and play to small but enthusiastic crowds. Stevie Ray Vaughn played there before he broke out and became "Stevie Ray Vaughn" and Jesse Colin Young showed up with a drum machine for some odd reason, too long after he had once been "Jesse Colin Young."

National acts would play the Lensic, which was a converted movie house, with its southwest version of rococo ornamentation. Becca opened a gig for Bonnie Raitt, then came out and sang back-up on "Home," a Karla Bonoff song. Bonnie ended up recording one of Becca's songs, citing a rule about "redheads having to stick together."

All in all, Becca was very content to have become a marginally big fish in a fairly small pond.

41

August 1997

On the Road Again...Again

"I got a call from Chad," Becca said.

"Fuck Chad."

"Yeah, I kinda thought that might be your reaction."

"Wasn't it yours?"

"At first, yeah, but you know Chad. He's a persuader."

"Uh-huh. And what is it he is attempting to 'persuade' you to do?"

Becca's countenance scrunched up, her eyebrows raised in an exaggerated questionface: "To go out on tour?"

Davis chuckled, wanting to immediately put his sweetheart at ease. He took her up in his arms, brushed her hair away from her face and kissed her flush on the mouth. It was a good one, too, not just one of those everyday kisses one gets when, well, y'know, you see someone every day.

"I knew it was coming," he said.

"What?"

"That part of you would rear up that needs the attention, the crowd, the affirmation you can't get from me and your babies and the occasional gig at El Farol."

"Oh, Davis. I love our home. I love our family, I love YOU."

"But?"

"Not 'but.' And."

"'And,' what?"

"There is a part of me who loves the safety, the security, of our home, our life, our love. And there is another part of me who wants to have no idea what happens next."

"I know."

Becca pushed him away enough to be able to look into his face. "You know?"

"Yeah. I know. Remember? We grafted, baby. I know every single thought and feeling you have."

"You do?"

"OK, maybe not every single one. And sometimes I just project some of my own shit onto you and wish that was what you were thinking. But aside from those things, yeah, everything else."

Becca didn't respond, but looked at him the way she did when she was truly assessing a situation. Her music had become an integral part of her, like an itch that needed to be scratched, that wouldn't be denied. She had denied that assessment at first—she didn't like the shallowness of it, but when Davis was presenting it in a way so non-judgmental, she realized he was right; she fed off the crowd and also felt the validation of others accepting her music and her wanting to share it.

Davis broke the silence. "So, yeah, I figured this would come at some point."

"And you're OK with it?"

"No, I'm not. I'm jealous. I don't want men in the audience wanting you. I don't want you to be away from us. Ever. And I don't like the idea that your world doesn't revolve around me like mine does around yours." He paused for effect, then said, "But aside from those trivial concerns, sure, go on tour."

Becca was caught in her in-between world where, inside, she knew what was real, what resonated, and that which was outside, on the surface.

"Fuck," she said.

"Ha! I know, right?"

"What do you mean?"

"What do YOU mean?"

Becca slapped him on the shoulder. "I'm having trouble reading you!"

"Huh. After all this time," he said sarcastically.

"I'm serious!"

"I know you are. And I am teasing you and not being entirely transparent, which is why you can't read me. Becca, I want you to be happy. I love your passion for your music. I like to think some of that came from me—from my lineage—my dad, through our graft. Maybe it did, maybe it didn't; it doesn't matter. What matters is what you do going forward. And how you do it. And what I do. And what we do, and our children do. Those doubts and concerns I voiced back there are true. But when I put them up against who you are and how people react to your music, they are inconsequential."

"See? I knew we weren't together just for the sex."

Davis grabbed her ass, since they were still embraced, and pulled her into him. "No, not just. The sex has always just been gravy. Really good gravy. Great fucking gravy. But in a way, I wish we hadn't grafted, because in a way, I feel like we cheated."

"What do you mean?"

"The way we know each other. I wonder if we would have had that anyway. The trust I have for you I don't feel for any other living soul. Not one. You are everything to me and part of my lament is I am not everything to you. But I get it; we're different people and you get fed by the energy of others."

"Yes, that is true, Davis. But nobody feeds me like you do. You are my center, my rock. The strength of our relationship allows me to stretch and take creative risks and also lets me make allowances for the shortcomings of others. It allows them to disappoint me." She paused, then added, "Because YOU never do."

"We are so lucky to have what we have."

"Yes, we are." They hugged one of their long fully-embracing hugs and then Davis said, "But let's get back to the subject at hand; what are you going to do? A "Too Much" oldies tour? Get the band back together?"

"I don't think that's the direction I want to go. Chad suggested an 'unplugged' concept."

"Yeah, but I thought we already decided we were telling Chad to go fuck himself."

"Which can be very satisfying, but he has offered to figure out sponsorship and pay for expenses."

"Yeah, there IS that. It'd be nice, though, if you had some new music to promote as opposed to just rehashing the old stuff."

"It would, wouldn't it?"

"Got any?"

"Sure, there's some of the solo stuff I've been playing. But I'll bet if I put my mind to it, I could come up with some new material. Will you help me?'

"Why not? I could be your muse... Then in addition to a-musing you, I could be 'musing' you."

"Yeah. Good one, Davis," Becca said wryly, though secretly loving his often punny sense of humor.

They discussed some of the logistics of what an actual tour would entail and how it would affect their household. While Becca never reached star status, she had become a critics' darling and had a fervent following in pockets around the country, and Chad felt confident about a tour being a success.

They started working together with Davis on the piano, brainstorming lyrics and song structures. They put some tunes together on a four-track system and after a week they sat down and listened to them.

After listening through a half hour of rudimentary cuts without either of them saying a word, Davis pressed the 'off' button, turned to Becca and said, "OK, then... We suck together."

Becca had the same reaction to the playback and had been dreading how she could gently express those feelings to Davis. "Well, it aint Lennon and McCartney."

"No, it's not. It's not even Sonny and Cher. OK, so now we know. I can play the piano, but I'm not a piano PLAYER, and there's a difference. As for song-writing, it's a whole different perspective to KNOW what's good as opposed to creating something good. That's why the truly creative among us are so valuable. It's a gift. I can maybe do an album cover for you, but you are going to have to be responsible for what's on the inside."

"So now what?"

Davis was quiet for a moment, then said, "I wonder what Bobby's doing."

Becca's reaction was pure "why-didn't–I-think-of-that?" Their collaboration in Too Much had been special. Certain creative types inspire and push each other to new places, and that was what Becca needed. Bobby had sunk into musician oblivion as far as exposure, but was never far away from the music; it was what he WAS.

Becca was able to locate him and he jumped at the chance. It was decided he would come to New Mexico, stay with them and he and Becca would put their heads and hands together and see what came out of it.

Their synergy was instantaneous and easy. Bobby had some material that had been percolating and together they easily came up with more than an album's worth of material. They arranged for the two of them to play one of the local clubs and the new stuff was very well received as well as the stripped-down versions of the Too Much classics.

Discussing the logistics of the tour, they threw around the idea of the two of them barnstorming, taking Davis and the kids along, but the specter of Mayah's abduction as well as the kids' school schedules put a kibosh on that plan. They decided Becca and Bobby would go out on the road and Davis would stay behind and be the solitary stay-at-home parent.

Chad wanted to take advantage of the name recognition for Too Much, but both Becca and Bobby felt like that was a band collaboration and wanted to honor the other band members. Against Chad's protests, he finally relented when he heard their alternative.

They called it the "Just Enough Tour."

42

September 1997

That Thing You Do

Chad set up the itinerary; 25 dates over two months, with a couple of breaks in between for her to come back home and spend some family time. When they got a copy of the dates and venues, Becca saw New Orleans was one of the stops, opening for Willy DeVille. She didn't mention anything to Chad—next to no one knew about what had happened there with Mayah. When she and Davis talked about it, they considered her backing out of that date, but it was after all, The Big Easy, and Becca felt like she wanted to play it at least once, despite the obvious associations. Besides, Mayah would be safe at home with Davis and there had been no contact of any kind, good or bad, since they had gotten Mayah back.

They decided to keep the date.

Brad was able to get the tour started at the Troubador in LA to an enthusiastic response. It gave Becca and Bobby a nice send off for the road. The dates wound through the West, into Texas. By then, Becca was in full concert mode and by the time they got to The Big Easy, any UN-easy thoughts were far back in Becca's mind.

Following an enthusiastic reception to their set, Becca was greeting fans afterward at the merchandise table. Sitting behind a table, signing an album with her head down, she was not prepared to hear a female voice ask, "How's Mayah?"

Becca stopped signing and looked up in the direction of the voice and saw a stately black woman, her hair done up in long extensions. Their eyes met and Becca knew who it was immediately, although they had never met. In a split second, she also sensed the woman's question came from a place of concern and curiosity, without any malice.

She dropped her marker on the table and maintaining eye contact, came out from behind the table and ran to Leticia's open arms, embracing her. They held each other for ten-twenty-who-knows-thirty seconds, then Leticia whispered to her, "I didn't know."

"I know."

Becca broke the embrace and held Leticia at arm's length. "Thank you for caring for her and loving her and for being willing to give her back. And thank you for coming here today."

They both had tears in their eyes, out of a common bond of motherhood.

"To answer your question, she's doing great. Getting tall and strong. And smart as a whip."

"Does she have a good daddy around? That man who came to take her back to you?"

"Yes, Davis is the best father. He's watching her now while I gallivant around the country playing my songs."

"He seemed like a good man, from what I could tell all those years ago. Mayah went right to him."

"Yeah, they are thick as thieves, those two..."

Becca realized she had people lined up wanting her attention. "Can you stay for a while?"

"No, honey, you do what you do. I just wanted to check in. Make sure that girl is doing OK. She was mine for a little while, and y'know how it is..." Her voice trailed off.

Becca hesitated to ask the question, but forged ahead. "Do you have other children?"

"Oh, yeah. There was another man who approached me after—not the same one from the first time—and he got involved with another adoption. I... I can't have no babies myself. I was hesitant at first, but he made sure it was all legal, with papers and all."

"I'm glad. Some women are made to be mamas."

"Aint that the truth?"

Becca hugged her again and returned to the table, absent-mindedly signing autographs for another half hour, her mind now away from "music-mode," back with her family, her tribe. As soon as she was free, she rushed to call Davis and tell him about meeting Leticia. He was worried there might be some regret on Leticia's part, but Becca assured him it didn't feel that way at all. Mayah was already asleep, but Davis assured Becca he would give her a kiss and see her in a week's time.

The lights flashed to let everyone know the second act was to begin. Becca made her way into the theater. She was only peripherally acquainted with Willy's music. He kind of fit into the same category as she did: critic's darling, passionate about his music, flirting with the big time but never quite making it. He had come close in a collaboration with Mark Knopfler of Dire Straits when he penned the theme song for "The Princess Bride," even performing it during the Oscar presentation for Best Original Song.

The meeting with Leticia had stripped away an area of worry for her about being in New Orleans and she let herself open up to the reason she was in this storied city—for the music.

Willy wowed her. His gravelly voice and soulful presentation epitomized the core of rock and roll. Plus, he was just cool as all get out. He smoked onstage and Becca couldn't help thinking, Shit, that's one of the reasons people begin smoking—how fucking BADASS does he look? (Interestingly, that perception would change almost 180 degrees for many once the perils of tobacco were revealed and accepted. Smoking or not, though, there was no denying Willy was cool).

After his show, there was a party backstage she and Bobby attended. Becca wanted to meet Willy and express her appreciation for his work. She was flattered when the compliment was returned. They spoke for about a half hour, in which time Becca told him about their home in New Mexico, how isolated it was from the industry. "It's a blessing and a curse," she said.

"How so?"

"The blessing is the stark beauty of the landscape: how in minutes you can be enveloped in nature. The sky is immense and the sun... the sun shines over 300 days a year. It's very... light."

"And the curse?"

"We humans conjure up our curses, don't we? It's easy to take those blessings for granted and think about what we don't have."

"Like?"

"As crazy as this business, is, I miss the road, the excitement, the immediacy of performing. I play local gigs, but it's always the same people; you know who's going to be there. I like the novelty of playing a new venue with new faces."

"I get that. It's like a challenge to win over a new crowd. Those of us who would put ourselves up there on stage... it's an odd set of needs, but when it's fulfilled, it satisfies a deep longing."

They had an instant bond. Becca invited him to come out and visit, which Willy would do and end up relocating for a number of years. He would get in touch with his Native American roots, but brought a darkness with him that not even the blazing New Mexican sun could overcome and would end in great tragedy.

Their reverie was interrupted by others who wanted their piece. Around them, without them, the party had started and it was destined to be a serious one, which sounds like a contradiction, but this was the music business in the 90's. We're not just talking just booze and pills and pot and cocaine, but off in a corner, some revelers were pulling their kits out. We're talkin' junk. Already buzzed from just the atmosphere, both literally and figuratively, Becca considered for a moment joining in. The peer pressure was intense. She caught Bobby's eye and recognized an almost imperceptible shake of his head. She closed her eyes and took a deep breath, which, considering how many state-altering substances were floating around was probably not the best idea.

The lights in the room were dim, and closing her eyes brought almost complete darkness, when she recognized the presence of that which did bring complete darkness.

Davis had put the kids to sleep and was reading before bed. He had spoken to Becca briefly earlier and she had recounted her experience with Leticia. Having met her just once, Davis had a hard time putting a face to the name, but he certainly had several intense associations with their meeting. He had been a little apprehensive about Becca playing New Orleans but also didn't want to seem the stick-in-the-mud, especially since the threat from back then had been eliminated. Part of him wanted to be there with her to experience the musical soul of the city, but he was also full ensconced in his dadhood, 180 degrees in some ways in the opposite direction.

He read until his eyes began to shut—his nightly ritual. His nighttime reading was always fiction, which set up his dreamworld, and the latest Tom Robbins was certain to send him to wonderfully twisted fantasial places.

He had no idea how long he had been asleep, but became aware of Becca's presence, although different from her usual ebullient energy; this was slow, muddy, syrupy. There were other people around, but no one he knew—men and women, all in a convivial mood. It was a party, that was clear, but with a distinctly sinister air to it.

Where am I? And in that question, what was implied was "in what state?" *Am I dreaming? If I am, something tells me I had better cross over to where this is lucid; I've got a feeling I am going to need my wits about me.*

He approached Becca. She was semi-reclined on a couch, a glass of wine in her hand and seemed surprised, but happy to see him. "Hey hon; what are you doing here?"

"I'm not really sure, but I was asleep and ended up here. Are you OK?"

"Yeah, yeah. We're all just hanging out after the show, but there are some people here who are getting seriously fucked up."

Davis glanced around, and while not personally familiar with all the trappings of serious drug use, the presence of syringes gave him pause. "Looks that way. Are you sure you want to be here?"

"Ohh, sure, why not?"

"I don't know—it's all just smelling a little unsavory to me, that's all. I think a better question might be 'Why?'"

Davis got the sense Becca was a little impaired, probably just from the wine and the second-hand weed smoke in the air. There was a heavy-lidded man sitting next to Becca who then said, "Hey baby; who are you talking to?"

"I'm talking to Davis. My man."

"Davis. Yeah, Ok. That's cool. 'Cept..." and here he leaned over to where he was facing Becca square on and got within a few inches of her face and said, "I don't see anybody else here."

Becca knew when she was being hit on, and was well versed in ways to shut those advances down. Not feeling threatened, but also not wanting to be encouraging, she looked her optimistic suitor in the eye and said, "My man is ALWAYS with me," then turned her attention back to Davis.

"I'm a little tipsy," she said.

"Yeah, I can see that. Let's get you outta here."

Then, out of the corner of his eye, Davis noticed the The Dark lurking in the shadows. "Ah, you again. I should have figured."

The Dark released one of his signature sub-bass emanations.

"Deh-deh-deh-deh-deh-dehh," Davis interrupted, as a way of speaking over his adversary, holding Becca up by her arm. "We're done with your fun and games. You've got plenty of fresh meat here to recruit. How about you just let us depart and you can go about doing what-it-is-you-do?"

The Dark was not used to this type of insouciance. He increased the volume of his growl as well as his physical presence to blot out most of the light in the room.

Davis was undeterred. "Yes, yes, very impressive. But getting bigger and darker is like speaking louder to someone who doesn't speak your language. I KNOW your language. WE know your language, right Bec?"

He turned to Becca, who was barely standing and put his arm around her waist to hoist her up a bit. "OK, maybe right this moment Bec's a little vulnerable, which I suspect is why you are here, but look, you've extracted your pound of flesh from us. Just go away."

Without thinking about it, Davis had expressed absolutely no fear.

The Dark began to retract into its corner and Davis escorted Becca from the dressing room.

"Hey, where you going? The party's just getting started," said the voice from where Becca had been sitting. Without turning, Becca waved over her shoulder as she exited the room alone.

In their daily conversation the next day, no direct reference was made to the incident, but Becca admitted to Davis she was ready to come home.

"Is everything OK?"

"Yeah, I just miss our home, I miss our kiddos and I miss you. And I'm reminded life on the road is not all it's cracked up to be."

"I know what you mean."

"Do you? Your art is different; it's so much more solitary."

"Yes, it is, but I still get a charge out of people appreciating what I create. Granted, it is after the fact. Performance art is in the moment; there's a lot more human involvement."

"A blessing and a curse, that," Becca said, recalling her conversation with Willy from the night before.

"I guess everything has its price, which makes sense when you look at a big enough picture."

There was a silence, then Becca said, "I love you, Davis."

"I love you, too."

"No, I mean, not just our everyday 'Iloveyou,' but a bigger, 'I appreciate who you are, your presence in my life, who you've become and continue to become."

Davis let that sink in, in the way only the two of them could uniquely communicate.

It filled him.

"I like that. Thank you."

"As much as I was ready to get home before, I'm REALLY ready now."

"Yeah? What's going on?"

"I just really miss you. I need to have you in my space."

"'In your space,' huh? That's an interesting euphemism."

Becca laughed. "Not necessarily THAT space, although that's part of it. I just want your presence. I want you AROUND me, both literally and physically."

"I can do that. I WANT to do that."

"It has occurred to me—not that I haven't thought about this before, mind you— there are a LOT of men in the music business. And most of them are assholes."

"Did something happen?"

"No, it's just all of that misplaced testosterone has given me a new appreciation for you. For who you are, for HOW you are, for how you've grown and keep on growing. Just YOU, Davis."

"So, what I am hearing is that you like where I place my testosterone?"

"Becca laughed again, "Exactly. See? Hey, when I get back, will you do that thing you do?"

"'That thing that I do'? Which thing is that? As I recall, there are a number of things you inspire me to do."

"The massage. The one that takes about an hour and you make sure you touch every single square inch of my body, even between my toes."

"And those other hard to reach places?"

"Yeah, and you have me so limp and relaxed."

"And wet?"

"Yeah, and wet. And then you just HAVE me."

"Oh. THAT thing..."

"Yeah, that thing. Will you do that, Davis?"

"Yeah, Becca, I can do that. So... how many more days on the road?"

Becca laughed, feeling the same urge to want to share the same space together. "Too many. But I think it's just another week or so."

"Well, I for one very much look forward to having that week go by quickly. But in the meantime, go out there and kill them onstage. Soak up every minute of it. Make this time apart worth it, OK?"

She did. The rest of the dates took on a special meaning, not just as obligations on an itinerary, but a musical communion.

Chad had actually done a great job in booking the tour; they hit parts of the country where Becca was known and the venue sizes were well chosen for the acoustics and size of crowd. He checked in with Becca and Bobby periodically to see what the response had been and there was talk of compiling tapes from the shows and releasing an 'Unplugged' album. The last date of the tour was in Nashville, which, while known as the home of country music, is a great music town, period. They played a medium sized venue and sold it out. As an homage to the country roots, she and Bobby did a Just Enough version of Patsy Cline's "Crazy" and the crowd ate it up.

There was a mild (not 'serious') wrap-up party at the end of the show Chad had set up as a surprise. He had flown in and shown up in the wings during the show. Despite her mixed feeling for him, she was glad to see him, and both she and Bobby wanted to express their appreciation for what he had done setting up the tour and its subsequent success.

As a promoter, he was sure to have some media types present at the party. Becca thought briefly back to the experience in New Orleans at Willy's after-show scene and how different this was. No drugs, nothing illegal, for that matter.

There were probably thirty to forty people crammed into a fairly tight dressing room, the noise level high with dozens of concurrent conversations going on at the same time. Becca felt a tap on her shoulder. When she turned around, she saw a man she knew was familiar, but it took her a second or two to place. Standing there, in what was now rock and roll glory was Johnny Steele (not his real name), her old friend and almost-lover from her hippie days.

On any given day, not unlike New Orleans, there is music seeping, emanating, oozing, blasting and crashing from every corner of the city. As it turned out, Johnny was going to be playing the Ryman at the Grand Ol' Opry the following night. While she was scheduled to fly back to Albuquerque the following day, and would miss his show, she was thrilled to see him. They had had a celibate, but sexually charged relationship back when she had lived in Taos and was just beginning to find her musical voice. She remembered the first time she had seen him perform when he was first coming up and it had been one of those I-am-in-the-presence-of-genius moments for her. While they had slept together, they had never "slept together" which in the annals of rock and roll was extremely unusual, but Johnny had seen aspects of Becca that went well beyond the usual groupie experience.

And there he was, with a bit of a celebrity halo about him, because he had gone on to major success.

As cool as everyone in the room wanted to appear, a buzz went around and furtive glances and whispers followed his arrival. The energy in the room got bumped up a number of notches.

Johnny said, "I heard you were in town and I just got in. I caught the last part of your set. You really have found your voice from back when you were strumming your guitar on the Taos plaza, haven't you?"

Johnny's voice had gotten raspier, but it was deep and commanding. While his guitar playing was his real genius, his performances were what made him legendary. It's a gift to be able to play an instrument; it's another ball game when your live performances drive people to emote. His shows would affect his fans in different ways, but one thing was certain, they were affected. Becca remembered the first time she had seen him—when he was just coming up—and it had lit more than a small fire in her.

As they stood there, all alone in that crowded room, the same thought went through both of their minds: remind me again why we never had sex...

Becca was aware of her attraction. It had always been there. But this was very specifically NOT a time to be indulging in those kinds of thoughts. Or actions. On the road, she was constantly the object of sexual fantasy: pretty much every guy in the audience, all of the hangers-on, the MEN. They were everywhere, and being men, they naturally wanted to assert their manliness. It came with the territory. What was different now, of course, was her circumstance: Davis and the kids. And she was not inclined to want to jeopardize that arrangement.

Not that it meant she wasn't subject to the pullings of her womanhood. Here was Johnny Steele, in the flesh, and she knew he wanted her.

"I'm so glad you came by," she said.

"Yeah, the timing was perfect. We're playing the Opry tomorrow night and got into town early."

"This is the last date of my tour. This is our wrap party."

"I see that. You will have people wanting to wring their last bit of blood out of you then. I just wanted to come by and see if there was any left for me."

Becca chuckled. "There will always be some left for you," she said and blushed a little, feeling a little embarrassed by her half-intended double entendre.

"Oh, good. You must know now how it is in this business, with the hangers-on and the bloodsuckers. But remember you can always turn off that spigot. Don't let it drain you. Let it fill you."

Becca looked at him, taking a moment to recall their connection and how it had been filled with metaphysical conversations like this one. It had been a big part of his charm.

It still was.

"Can you stay for a while?" she asked.

"Sure."

Chad came over and introduced himself. In the hierarchy of promotion, Chad was a tier or two below managing a talent like Johnny, so he wasn't going to let this opportunity slip by. Becca peeled herself away to make herself available to the rest of the well-wishers, wanting to wish them away and just be able to slip away with Johnny and catch up.

After another round of "thank-you's" and "I-love-your-works" Becca had had enough. The tour had given her what she wanted, what she needed, to fill that adulation cup. She looked around for Johnny and saw him surrounded by his own coterie but sensed he was only sticking around for her. She caught his eye and gave him a tilting of her head towards the door to indicate their exit. He nodded in response.

She came over to him and leaned into his ear. "OK, I'm done. Let's get the fuck out of here. Wait for me at the exit. I'm five minutes behind you." As soon as she had let the "fuck" slip out, she regretted it as suggestive, but there was no taking it back.

Johnny used the bathroom as an excuse to extricate himself and when he came back out, he found Becca, gave her a big hug and said, "Five minutes."

"Yup."

Chad saw Johnny getting ready to leave and made his way in between him and the door. He handed Johnny his card, and started to follow him out the door. Johnny stopped abruptly and held up his hand. "We're cool, man. I'll have my people... you know..."

Chad stopped in his tracks, knowing when he had been dismissed.

Becca used the bathroom diversion to separate herself. When she came out, she found Bobby. "We did good, brother." She hugged him tightly. "I'm taking off for a while. I will see you back at the hotel."

Like everyone else, Bobby had noticed Johnny departing; Becca's subsequent departure was not going to fool anyone. "Do you need a chaperone?" he asked.

"Most assuredly not," Becca laughed. "Johnny and I go way back. We're friends and just have some catching up to do."

While Bobby and Becca had a long musical bond, Bobby had become friends with Davis when he had stayed with them. "You behave yourself. Back home tomorrow, remember."

Becca slapped him lightly on the shoulder. "Bobby, this is me, remember? Take care of our guests, will you?" She turned to exit and then stopped a step away, turned and said, "Thank you again for being my partner in this."

Bobby made a fist and placed it over his heart. "Always," he said.

Becca found Johnny at the door. She hooked her arm in his and dragged him away. "Where to? I don't want to be anywhere where I have to compete for your attention."

"I'm staying just a few blocks from here. Let's just go there."

Becca had no qualms about being alone with Johnny. Their relationship, while close, had never crossed the line into being sexual, although they flirted and had even slept together without taking it over that line. In the back of her mind, Becca heard the vibrating voice of a hummingbird as it whizzed by, saying, "You sure?"

Her tiny hummingbird guides were her most trusted advisors, when she went 'inside' to consult. In the euphoric buzz of the moment, the last night of her freedom, she chose to ignore it.

They went up to Johnny's suite and he broke out a bottle of wine for them. The suite was large with a very comfortable-looking sofa at the far end, overlooking the city. Becca collapsed into it and slumped down, not realizing how exhausted she was.

Johnny brought her a glass, sitting close enough so their knees were touching. "So, catch me up. I've read a few things over the years, but I'm sure there's more."

"Oh, there's more, alright. You may have heard about Mayah being abducted."

"Your daughter, right?"

"Yes. She was just a baby. I had taken her out on tour with me, which seemed like a perfectly normal thing to do, at the time anyway, and she got snatched."

"Wow. Did you know who did it?"

"No..."

"But you got her back, right?"

"Yes, it took a while, and perhaps some negotiation, but there was someone who knew about the circumstances, but not all. When he realized what had happened, he contacted us and we were able to make arrangements to get her back."

"That must have been scary. Did you prosecute the abductor?"

Becca hesitated. She knew she wouldn't tell Johnny the whole story, but wasn't feeling energetic enough to have to conjure up a whole new lie. "No...We were so happy to have her back, we didn't want to relive it. We just let it go."

"Wow, Becca. That's quite a story. Why'd he do it? Did you ever find out?"

"He was some deluded, self-righteous bigot who had a problem with me having a mixed-race baby and took it upon himself to make it right."

"Oh. OK. So your husband is..." He took her left hand in his, fingering her wedding band.

"Uh, no. Not the father. That would be boring and pedestrian. Hardly rock n roll." She smiled and took her hand back. "No, this..." and she held her hand up and twirled the ring around her finger. "This is Davis. Davis and I go back to before you and I met. Our lives have woven in and out of each other's, but it looks like this gypsy has finally found her soulmate. We have a son together, Dylan..."

"Of course..."

Becca smiled. "Yeah, we are a musical family."

Johnny sat silently for a few moments. "Motherhood becomes you."

"Thanks. It feels right. It balances out the urge to do... this." She gestured widely with her arm.

"This? And what is 'this"?"

Becca colored a little, an unusual sensation for her. As close as she and Johnny had been, she was a little "taken" with his celebrity–that she would be here alone in his suite, however innocent, however married, however trusting.

"Oh, you know, The road. Rock n roll. Not soccer mom. You know what it's like, but it's different for you... guys. You're allowed to get away with anything. Am I right?"

"I don't know about 'getting away with anything.' I haven't changed that much from when we were together. It was always about the music for me. She is still my mistress."

Becca laughed. "Uh-huh. I've seen the tabloid stories about your other mistresses."

"My relationships, you mean."

"Whatever. Tell me; I can't imagine some of the names I have seen you associated with would be content with the kind of chaste arrangement you and I had."

"No, you're right. There have been one or two who pulled me out of my shell and enlightened me about the pleasures of the flesh. Taken me to the mountaintop, as it were."

"Huh," said Becca, feigning rejection, "I guess I just wasn't pretty enough. Was that it?"

Johnny put his wine glass down on the coffee table in front of them and positioned himself over Becca, his face just inches from hers. "You couldn't be more wrong. I was intimidated by you. And not just your beauty. Your presence, your strength. Over the years, time and again I've thought about you as the one who got away."

He let his lips brush up against hers.

And she let them.

43

No Call

Davis checked the clock. 11 PM. He knew there would be an after-show wrap party, but figured Becca would call at some point, just to check in—it was their routine. They had purchased flip phones and it made staying in touch much easier when she was on tour. The kids had gone to bed and Davis had settled into his favorite chair, and fell asleep reading.

He shifted his position and his copy of "Half Asleep in Frog Pajamas" clattered to the floor. The reading light was still on. He picked up the flip-phone and saw the time: 4:11AM. He noticed there was not a notification for a voicemail. Hmmm... he thought, half asleep, then went into the bedroom, tossed the phone on the nightstand, got under the covers and fell back asleep.

44

Morning After

Becca woke with a start, disoriented, then realized soon enough where she was; Johnny Steele's suite. She took a moment to recall how she had gotten there. She didn't remember falling asleep, but her cottonmouth and hangover headache were reminders she had drunk more than usual. She found her purse and pulled out her phone to see what time it was. *6:16. Fuck. What city? Oh, yeah: Nashville.* Glancing out the large window overlooking the city, she could see night dissolving into dawn. She checked in on Johnny: sound asleep, snoring. *OK, I gotta go.* She slipped out of the room and took the elevator down to the lobby. At the front desk: "Can you call me a cab?"

"There should be one outside the front door, ma'am."

"OK. Thanks."

She flagged the driver and gave her hotel destination. She pulled out her phone. No messages. Then her realization: *I never called Davis. Call him now? No, it's an hour earlier there; he's still asleep. He's gonna be worried I didn't call. Or mad. Will he be? What time's my flight today? I think it's around noon. What time does Davis usually get up? About 7. With the kids. The kids! I get to go home and see my babies today!*

The cab pulled up at her hotel and there was the usual morning activity of visitors rushing to meet early morning flights. She was glad she had had the sense to not book one of THOSE. She got up to her room and fired up the hotel room coffee maker. *Coffee. Gotta have coffee. And a shower. A shower would be good.*

She decided she would do that and then call Davis. She turned the water up good and hot, the way she liked it and got in, letting the water cascade over her body. *Shampoo? Sure. Why not?* As she was soaping up, she let her thoughts recollect the events of the night before and then jump forward to the day ahead. She felt bad not having called Davis and wondered again what his reaction would be. He wasn't much of a worrier, but this was a break from their normal routine.

When she got out of the shower, she wrapped herself in the hotel robe and wrapped her hair up, turban-style, in one of the towels. She checked her phone and saw there was a message from Davis. Checking the time again, she thought, Hmm... he's up early.

She dialed his number.

He answered on the first ring. "Hi. There you are." Becca noticed a note of what? annoyance? impatience? anger? in his voice.

"Hi Babe. Good morning. I was in the shower and I saw you had called."

"Yeah, well, one of us had to."

Shit, he IS mad. "I know, Davis, I know. The wrap party went longer than I thought and the night got away from me. By the time I thought to call it was late and I didn't want to wake you."

Silence for a few seconds, then Davis said, "I was worried."

"Worried? About what?"

"I don't know. It's a crazy world out there. Shit happens. You always call to just check in. I like that."

"I'm sorry, babe. Like I said, it got late and..."

"Yeah, the 'night got away from you.'"

Another couple of moments of silence and then Davis said, "So, how was the show?"

"It was great. Bobby and I did a couple of more country covers, being here in Nashville and all. The crowd was responsive and it was a nice way to end the tour."

"How about the wrap? How was that?"

"A lot of people stopped by, including Johnny Steele."

"Johnny Steele?"

"Yeah. He has a show in town tonight and saw I was playing and stopped by. He and I go back to when before he was so big. Remember I told you that?"

Davis went back into memory banks and there did seem to be a kernel of that disclosure, but it was interrupted with the more recent information intersection of "Johnny Steele" and "the night got away from me." That confluence swirled, intermingled and then collided into another couple of seconds of dead air.

"Remember? Back in my Taos days?"

Without stopping to measure his words, Davis said, "Is that why the night got away from you?"

Now it was Becca's turn to get triggered.

"What are you suggesting?"

"I'm not suggesting anything," Davis said, feeling a little abashed at his lack of trust but also wanting a little bit of reassurance.

"It sounds like you are."

"No. No, I'm not."

"I thought you trusted me."

"I DO trust you."

"Then, do that. Trust me."

"OK. I will. I do. And I thought we were always open with each other."

"We are."

"Then tell me Johnny wasn't responsible for 'the night getting away from you' and we'll be good."

"What if he WAS responsible for it?"

"What is that supposed to mean?"

"Just what it sounds like; 'What if he was responsible for it?' What if I spent time with him?"

"Did you?"

"Yes, I did. He came to see me. What was I supposed to do? Send him away because my husband might be a little insecure if I engage with him?"

"Engage?"

"Yeah. 'Engage.'"

"I guess it depends on what you mean by 'engage.'"

"I thought you said you trusted me."

"I do."

"It doesn't sound like it."

"Well, if you would have just called..."

"This is not about my 'just calling' or not. This is about you knowing who I am and trusting I won't do anything to betray you. Do you get that?"

"Yeah, I get it. And you could also just say, 'Davis, of course nothing happened' and I would be placated and this conversation would be over."

"Davis, GODDAMN IT!"

"Right. So, what I hear is you being conflicted between just telling me what happened but, instead, having me trust you being more important. Am I getting that right?"

"What? Really? You're going to psychoanalyze me now?"

"No. I'm not. But you might want to concede the point and just give in. You know what? Just get on the fucking plane and come home. Your family's waiting for you."

Becca heard the click as he hung up.

45

Something To Do With Trust

The Albuquerque airport was tastefully decorated with images of Southwest culture, along with a stunning, full-size reconstruction of a Wright Brothers-era plane hanging from the ceiling. Davis brought the kids early to pick Becca up. They were excited at the prospect of having her home. Davis had been too, until the phone call. He did not enjoy conflict. In his heart of hearts, he had not wanted Becca to go back on the road, not that he didn't trust her, but he knew he would miss her. She was the center of his life, and when he thought about their fight on the phone, he knew his position had come from a place of fear—a fear of losing her. He had also done enough personal work to know he had some trust issues. Going over the conversation in his head, which had looped endlessly from the time he had hung up, made him wish he had approached it all differently. Now, on top of everything else, he felt himself pathetic for his part in it.

Having his children with him to pick Becca up would provide a temporary buffer between them. They didn't fight often—hardly at all—but when they did, they always came back to a place of equanimity.

The relatively small airport allowed incoming passengers to be greeted at the gate. Mayah and Dylan were terribly excited to see their mom. Davis had let them pick out a bouquet of flowers for her as a homecoming gift.

Davis somewhat apprehensively awaited Becca's amazing shock of hair to make its way through the portal from the plane. When he saw it, despite his misgivings, his heart leapt a bit. He was glad she was home. Wasn't he?

"Mama!" Dylan had resorted to that moniker for his mom. He rushed to her as soon as he saw her, Mayah not far behind. Davis held his space in the background. Their eyes locked as she approached, each trying to read the other, which they both did so well. This time, however, the information was garbled and confused. They hugged but that too was a mixture of an affectionate squeeze for what they both knew was an icily short duration.

The drive back home was just over an hour. Becca had caught up on some of her sleep on the plane. The tour had sated her, at least that part of her that needed the group validation, but now it felt good to be back home, heading back to her sanctuary, although she knew much of that safety was right here in the car with her.

There was a tacit understanding as soon as the kids were put to bed they would address their misunderstanding. Davis let Becca tuck Dylan in and say her good-night to Mayah and was waiting out on the back porch for her, handing her a glass of wine.

"I'm so exhausted, I think if I drank that wine, I would fall asleep standing up."

Davis had the good sense not to remind her if she hadn't 'let the night... blah-blah-blah" and instead said, "You don't have to drink it, just accept it."

She accepted the glass of wine from him, knowing it was a peace offering.

"Thank you," she said. Then she placed her hand softly on Davis's forearm as her peace offering. "I want to say a few things, OK?"

"Sure."

"First, I apologize for not calling. I should have, but I got caught up in all the merriment."

Davis started to respond and Becca said, "Please let me finish, Okay?"

"Okay."

"You and I are different. We have talked about that. We get our social needs met in dissimilar ways. I'm the gregarious one, you're the introvert. That's what WE are and how we get our needs met. And we go out there in the world and we interact with others, for better or worse." Here she hesitated, wanting to choose her words carefully. "Because of what I do, who I am and also how I look, people want to be around me. Some of them—a lot of them—are men. And many of them have a specific agenda, as you well know. While that used to be fun... even validating, it doesn't have the charge for me it once did. But, it's still flattering and as I get older and wrinkly and my hair turns, if I still get that attention, it will continue to be."

They were sitting on the steps of the back porch. The sun was picking up a few stray New Mexico clouds and painting them, but Davis's attention was on the light it was playing on Becca's face.

Becca continued, "That means, in our social hierarchy, I've had the luxury of being able to choose from a fairly wide selection of men who I might want to couple with. And I have chosen you."

"I'm glad," Davis said, smiling.

"There's more. You're an attractive man—physically. But beyond that, you are creative and intelligent. Empathetic and kind. I KNOW that, in the way only you and I know each other. Are there other people I admire? Sure. Do I like being around some of them? You bet. But you, my love, you are my partner. My one and only partner. And I would like for you to trust that. Can you?"

Davis reached out to her glass, took it from her and set them both of their glasses on the nearby table. Then he came to her, wrapped his arms around her neck and surrounded her with "I-missed-you." Neither of them spoke a word, until after who-knows-how-long Becca said, "Do you FEEL that?"

Davis, already firmly back in Davis-loves-Becca Camp, said, in his best recalcitrant, apologetic, little-boy-admitting-he-was-wrong voice, "Yeah, I guess so..."

It got the intended response, which was a full, body-shaking laugh/sob.

"Do you understand why it was important for me to not have to tell you how I spent my time?" she asked.

"Does it have something to do with me trusting you no matter what, even if it's Johnny Fucking Steele coming after you realizing you're the one who got away?"

One of Becca's inside voices was mouthing, *How the did he know that?* while another was explaining *because that's what the two of you do,* while her outside voice simply said,

"Yeah, something like that."

"OK. Got it."

He took her hand and led her into their bedroom and undressed her slowly.

"Oh yeah, you said you were going to do that thing..."

"Yes. Yes I did."

It was the last major tour that Becca would undertake.

And the last one she would want to.

46

January 1998

Cool Old People

Becca saw an out-of-state number come up on caller ID. "Hello?"

"Hi Becca. It's Willy. Willy DeVille. You may not remember me, but we met in New Orleans after our gig."

"Willy. Of course I remember you; don't be silly."

"What's up?"

"Oh, you know. Back at home, raising the kids. Livin' the dream. What's up with you?"

"Actually, I need some advice." He hesitated. "Let me start over. You... you made an impression on me back in Nawlin's. First of all, I loved your set, your music, but afterwards, at the party... I was watching you, and it's kinda hard not to, but it wasn't like that... y'know, THAT."

"Go on."

"I mean, the rest of us were engaging in what was close to a world class party, but you, you were above it. I was wanting you to join us, but at some point, you just stood up and walked away."

"Well, actually, that night, I had some help."

"I didn't see any help; I watched you get up and just walk away and then wave back to us without looking back."

"Did I do that? Sounds like a very dramatic exit."

"Oh, it was. And that's where the impression came in. I want to do the same thing. I want to walk away."

"From what, Willy?"

"The drugs, that life. It's killing me. How did you do that?"

"I do altered states naturally, so if there is something around that is going to accelerate or exacerbate that, it can send me to bad places, so I've never really indulged in that lifestyle."

"Unfortunately for me, that lifestyle has dictated my very existence, and I don't want it to anymore. Anyway, when we talked and you told me about New Mexico and your life there, it just sounded so idyllic."

"It can be, but it has its downside too."

"Doesn't everything? Which brings me around to why I'm calling. I need a break. I have to get away from this influence. I was thinking of taking a trip to New Mexico with my wife Lisa and seeing if it's a place we could relocate to. And I thought maybe you could introduce me to some places and some people. I have some Native American blood in my lineage and I would like to explore some of that too."

Becca's mind raced with the possibilities. She had been taken with his music and who he was as a person, but she had also seen the intense darkness around him.

Willy continued, "You said you had help that night; what did you mean?"

"My husband and I have this thing: a connection, a bond, and he has this crazy knack of showing up just when I need him."

"Ah, a knight in shining armor..."

"I don't see it that way, and I don't think he does either. It's not that I need saving. He just has a way of directing me to my better angels."

"I could use some of those."

"Willy, come on out and stay with us for a while. Davis has some connections to the Native American community here and more than anything, the land here has a way of..." Her voice trailed off. In the back of her mind, a voice was reminding her to check in with Davis, but she had already extended the invitation.

"I would love that. Thanks, Becca."

Once she relayed her conversation to Davis, he quickly put her fears to rest. "Willy's coming here? To stay with us? Cool!" Davis was a fan, being familiar with his music from the time he had the record store.

Becca explained the circumstances and they agreed there would be no drug use when they were staying there.

Davis introduced Willy and his wife Lisa to Tschuck and some of the other people from the reservation. They went out on some of Davis's favorite trails and Willy took to the landscape immediately. While they only stayed a few days with Becca and Davis, Willy and his wife ended up moving to Cerrillos, a small former turquoise mining town just south of Santa Fe. It was just what he needed.

Willy became part of the local music scene but in a secluded way; he did not play around town, but would do some studio work and jam at private sessions. His focus became his spiritual path.

Unfortunately, as isolated as Cerrillos was, it was just a little less than an hour away from Chimayo, which was a hub for some of the major heroin trafficking throughout the entire US. As a result, where Willy was able to kick his habit, Lisa was not, which led to an extremely divided household. Davis and Becca had been friends with both of them but had started to shy away when Becca could see the darkness returning, especially around Lisa.

Temptation in the music business runs rampant. Musicians and performers are held up as icons and there is always a fan available to fill a void if needs aren't being met. Frustrated with his situation at home, Willy turned to another woman, and it was not terribly secret.

"There IS a lot of temptation, that's for sure," said Davis to Becca, discussing the DeVilles, then he quickly caught himself, lest he risk opening up the Johnny Steele can-o'-worms. "And some people have stronger constitutions about being able to resist them, I guess."

"Well, we all have our demons and our quality of life depends on how we deal with them. It seems like for some people, the demons just won't stay away and maybe they just get worn down having to fight them all the time."

There was silence for a while as each of them went through memory banks of engagements with the dark side, and how it had been a while since they had had that kind of challenge.

And how good that felt.

"Hey, have you ever seen 'Harold and Maude'?" Davis asked. Once-a-week movie night at home was a regular event, sometimes with the kids, sometimes without. They had amassed quite a VHS library, with new (and old) titles constantly being added.

"No, I've heard about it. It's become sort of a cult film, hasn't it?"

"Yeah... but more than that. It's a comedy but also a love story, albeit an unusual one. Harold is a rich, spoiled, 18-year-old who stages fake suicides and meets Maude at funerals. She's 79. It sounds weird, and it is, but they make it believable. It's funny, but makes you think about life and death and the choices we make along the way."

"OK. Let's get it. 'Harold and Maude' movie night!"

Davis knew what to expect (spoiler alert: Maude takes her own life on her 80th birthday), but Becca got blind-sided a bit by the film. They laughed, they cried and they also had long conversations about outside influences and attitudes, perspectives and life choices.

"Would you do what Maude does at the end?" Becca asked.

"I don't know. Maybe I would if I was Maude."

"What do you mean? It seems like she was leading a charmed life."

"I picked up a few things watching it the second time. Did you notice her arm in that sunset scene by the dump?"

"No, I didn't."

"Concentration camp tattoo. She was a Holocaust survivor."

"So, it wasn't always wine and roses for her, I guess, huh?"

"No. That's part of the message. Nobody gets to have everything. That and the sanctity of life, along with questions about balance and attitude and perspective."

Becca was quiet for a while. Then Davis asked, "What are you thinking about?"

"You never went into much detail about that night in New Orleans when you got Mayah back. How close was I to losing both of you?"

Now it was Davis's turn to be quiet. He hadn't thought about that night for quite some time. "I don't know, really. I just know I have never been so scared for my life. But it wasn't just me; it was for Mayah, too. It felt like our lives were truly being threatened. If I had it to do over again..." His voice trailed off and then he continued, "We don't get to do it over again, but let me just say I have no regrets about taking that man's life. In our Judeo-Christian culture, it's drummed into us: 'Thou shalt not kill.' But that commandment gets stepped on continually by those who don't follow the rules."

"What do you think about Maude's decision? To go out the way she did?"

"I think we can get too righteous about suicide. If someone wants to take their own life, who is someone else to say 'No?'"

"Would you do that?"

"Do what? Put an expiration date on my life? I don't know. It's kind of weird to think about half-way through like we are. I guess if my quality of life was such that every day was extremely painful or I knew I was going to die soon anyway. Or... if I felt like I was prolonging my life just 'because' and I was being a burden to someone. To you."

"You would never be a burden to me, Davis. Never."

"Hah! You say that now because you aren't having to wipe my ass every day when I shit."

Becca laughed. "Yeah, well, thanks for that visual, but isn't that what later life should be? Two older people holding each other up until the end?"

"I don't think it's that tidy. People hardly ever die together. Think about the feeling of loss after having been together for thirty, forty, fifty years."

"No. I don't want to. I want to soak up this feeling of being here with you now. With Mayah and Dylan and our life together. I'm thinking our end is going to be like a beautiful love movie where we ride off together into the sunset."

"That's a nice image, but when I think about the distant future, I find it hard to imagine us as old."

"Old. Like how old?"

"I don't know. A hundred. 90. Even 80. Maude figured 80 was enough. Maybe she was onto something. What do YOU think?"

"I think we have a lot of life to live before we even have to start thinking about it. I also think you and I will be the coolest old people ever. Singin' and painting. Playin'. Lovin'. Whaddya think?"

"Yeah, I like that image. Cool old people. Let's do that..."

47

Blood With My Blood

The next year went by as some years tend to: with minimal drama, kids growing up: Mayah coming into her adolescence: tall, beautiful, subtly freckled against her dark skin, smart and every bit her Mama's daughter although her primary bond was with Davis. He was her idol. They would go on long walks, often with their arms around each other's waist, and talk about everything.

Meanwhile, Dylan was turning into full-on boy: testosterone-driven with an always-running motor. Davis indulged his sports obsession which was easy enough considering his own background, but Dylan was taking it to another competitive level; he HATED to lose. Davis tried to temper that somewhat, with his own leanings towards Buddhism and other spiritual practices, but Dylan seemed hell-bent on being first. Davis tried to keep their activities non-competitive, non-scoring but when they were, he found himself being torn between letting Dylan win and wanting to teach him about losing.

But it was all manageable, and beyond. Mayah was old enough her little brother's attempts at dominance were laughable, in a holding-him-at-arm's-length-while-he-flailed-impotently kind of way. Being almost ten years apart, she took on the role of baby-sitter at first and then as Dylan got older, did her best to keep him out of daredevil trouble.

She had shot up in her adolescence but grew into it naturally and constantly having to keep up with her baby brother was like a natural workout. She was encouraged to engage in sports teams—basketball and volleyball in particular. They had a hoop set up in the back yard with the almost concrete-like New Mexican dirt as a surface. Davis used the hoop as a way to stay in shape but it almost meditative at those times when he felt he needed to center himself. A basketball was as much a fixture around the house as a guitar or a canvas.

Mayah would play with him and also play on her school team but volleyball became more of a focus for her. At a time when whatever level of pre-teen angst surfaced, it gave her an independence—an avenue of activity different from everyone else's. Becca often reminded her of how different girls' sports were from when she was Mayah's age—there was basically field hockey, which didn't even exist anymore or cheerleading, which, though physical, had a whole different perspective about a woman's place.

She also became involved in dance and Davis and Becca thought it would be a good way to channel her energy which was moving more towards "girly." Davis and Becca's household was hardly traditional, especially in terms of gender roles, but they also didn't want to put up any barriers in terms of natural predilection.

"We are blessed," said Davis, feeling extremely grateful about life in general.

"Yes, we are. I know we make decisions at choice points throughout our lives, but we don't really know where those choices are going to lead us. So much is based on outside circumstance. Serendipity. And sometimes just plain luck."

"I know, right? Hey, let's celebrate. Have you ever been up to the top of Pedernal?"

Becca flashed on a vision she had once of Davis there. "No, I don't think so."

"Oh, you would remember it if you had. It's like being on top of the world. Let's do a hike up there and do a little ritual, thank God or the gods and the powers-that-be and nature and our ancestors and anybody or anything else for all that we have."

"I like the sound of that. Let's do it."

Pedernal is a mesa situated off by itself in the upper mountain plains of New Mexico. It is visible from hundreds of miles away under the right conditions and is featured in many landscape depictions, most notably Georgia O'Keefe's. Davis had painted it himself, numerous times from various angles but had scaled up to the top only once, as achieving that requires scaling a Class 3 wall that can be intimidating to the uninitiated. Once he got up there, he reveled in the accomplishment; the view was unparalleled and although "only" sitting at 9,862 feet, it truly felt like the top of the world.

Coming down was actually even more dicey and he vowed to never do it alone again.

This time he had his trusty, though equally untrained sidekick Becca in case anything could go wrong. Despite her years in New Mexico, she was still an East Coast city girl at heart but what she lacked in wilderness skills, she made up for in gumption: a trooper and a good sport, physical enough. Really; it was going to be fine...

They drove into the trailhead in Davis's ancient Toyota Landcruiser. It was only about a mile hike to the base of the mesa, after following the forest road winding through pinyon pines and areas of flint rock. Becca was fascinated when Davis pointed the rock out to her. "You mean flint like "flint-you-can-start-a-fire-with?" she said.

"Yeah, watch." And Davis got to show off his Boy Scout skills (never having been one but secretly always wanting to be) by pulling out his trail knife ("You have a knife?") and striking the stones to create a spark. Becca was duly impressed. His efforts at showing her how the Native Americans had chipped edges away to create sharp-edged tools was somewhat less impressive, when he created a small gash in the side of his hand. "See?" he grinned. "Sharp."

"Ah, blood with my blood," Becca said, then took his hand up to her mouth and sucked on it.

Davis smiled. "You are so hot," he said, then grabbed her and kissed her mouth hard.

Becca pushed him away playfully. "OK. Let's get moving. At this rate, we'll never get to the top."

The mesa itself is massive; it could take hours to hike around the base, and there is really only one spot for inexperienced climbers to scale its walls. Over the years, at various times, there had been ropes and even trees or logs positioned to make the ascent easier, which was true when Davis had made his solo attempt. There were remnants of an arrow to mark the spot on the cliff wall a helpful soul had once painted there.

That one really tricky spot to be scaled is about two stories high and while not a straight vertical face with no hand or foot holds, it presents a challenge. When they arrived there, to Davis's lament, there was not the leaning pole that had been there before to aid their climb.

They stood there, staring at the rock face, squinting up into the late morning sun.

"So, this is the hardest part," Davis explained.

"I see," said Becca, in her outside voice, while inside voice is saying "Who's idea was this?"

"There was a pole here before, to help you get up, but it looks like they took that away."

"Yeah, I see the 'no pole' feature, evident in its very absence."

"It's OK. I brought a rope."

In Davis's defense, he had good intentions, but truthfully, he had no idea what to do with the rope he had brought. Was it a good idea to bring a rope? Sure, probably... but either they were going to be able to hand scramble up the side of this cliff or they weren't.

"So. Let's take a few minutes and figure out a plan," Davis said. He took off his backpack, retrieved an apple he had brought, fished out his knife again and cut off a big hunk of apple that he presented to Becca on the blade. She picked the slice off the blade and said, "That is some knife. Crocodile Dundee would be proud."

"I know, right?" Davis said, ignoring her sarcasm.

Davis finished carving up the apple, surveying how he would navigate the climb.

"The trick is to not be afraid—just attack it—just go for it."

"Uh-huh."

"No, really. What is the fear? At worst, you would fall, what? Maybe ten, fifteen feet?"

"Let's not consider that, OK? Especially since there is nothing even remotely soft to land on; quite the contrary."

"Well, how about you go first," Davis said, "and I will stand here underneath you and if you fall, I'll catch you."

Becca looked at him blankly, then batted her eyes at him exaggeratingly and said, "My he-man!"

Then, without another moment's hesitation, she clapped her hands together and said, "OK. Let's do this. Actually, your rope will come in handy. I will climb up first, without my pack. You can toss the rope up, I will pull up the packs, then you can follow."

"Perfect."

Becca planted her left foot in the first foothold and drew herself up. She found handholds and then lifted herself up to the next shelf. She was about halfway up and the next move was going to require her right leg being lifted higher than her knee.

And she froze.

Davis was quiet, watching patiently. And the minutes ticked by. Becca would lift her leg and then put it back down, unsure of her footing.

Davis started to say, "Becca, just..." and Becca cut him off.

"Don't. Say. Another. Word."

He didn't.

For a moment, Becca considered going back down. She looked back over her shoulder and saw Davis vigilantly holding his position as catcher, should she fall. She turned her face back towards the rock wall and said to herself *Really? Really?! Just climb the fucking wall! Other people have done this. You will NOT be one of the ones who didn't.*

She took a deep breath, lifted her leg up high enough to hook her toe into the foothold and pushed. Her leg shook with the exertion but the adrenaline kicked in and lifted her up. She allowed her momentum to push her up onto the next flat area and looked down on Davis.

"Alright, toss me the rope. Let's get the packs up here and then you're next."

She pulled the packs up and Davis began his climb. He got to the same part where Becca had frozen and realized the challenge, although being slightly taller, it was going to be easier for him. Still, he hesitated.

Becca watched him from above. "C'mon," she said, "Don't be a pussy."

Davis placed his forehead against the rock surface, chuckling. "I love you, Becca. I truly do." He had to stop himself from laughing before he continued but was able to lift himself up to the next level. He stood there facing her, put his hand under her chin, lifted it slightly and kissed her. "I truly do."

The rest of the way up to the top, while sketchy in places, presented no real challenges. When they got to the top, they could see twisted junipers that had staked out claims over the years on the flat surface but very little other plant life.

Becca walked over to the edge and extended her arms up to the sky. She turned and face Davis. "OK. I get it. This is a magical place. Thank you for bringing me here."

They found a spot in what seemed like the center and sat facing each other, his legs spread apart with hers over his.

Davis said, "I fell in love with you the moment I first saw you and we had that connection. Then I lost you. When I found you again. I was stupid enough to leave you—not once, but twice. I feel like we have grown so much. I'm smarter now, and I never want to not have you by my side or for you to feel like I am not by yours. I am blessed to have you in my life. Flesh with my flesh. Breath with my breath. Heart with my heart. I love you."

Tears gently made their way down Becca's face. "Oh, my love. I feel the same way. I love our life together. I can't imagine ever being without you, especially when we're old."

"Well. Let's get old together first, then we'll figure out a way to ride off into the sunset together."

"OK. Deal." She reached for his hand to shake it and he winced a little from his recent cut.

"Let me see that," Becca said. She flipped his hand so she could see the cut on the fleshy part of his left hand. "Where's your big old Bowie knife?"

Davis gave her a quizzical look but reached into the pack by his side with his free hand. He handed it to her hilt-first. She took it in her right hand and with no hesitation ran the blade along the same section of her palm as Davis's cut. "Shit, that hurt," she said. "But we might as well do this right."

She took his right hand that had been cut and placed her now bleeding palm over his. "Flesh with my flesh. Breath with my breath. Heart with my heart. And blood with my blood. I love you, too, Davis."

The sun had been obscured by incoming clouds on the last part of the hike up and the sky had turned dark with an approaching monsoon. From their perspective, they could have seen exactly where the local storm would dump, if they had been paying attention, that is.

Which was right over Cerro Pedernal.

The first drops were fat and spaced far apart. They dotted the surface of the stone mesa top and were immediately absorbed by the somewhat porous rock. Subsequent drops could scarcely have qualified as such they were so close together.

"Well, this oughta be cathartic," Davis yelled over the din of the pounding rain and the thunder. A crash of lightning startled the two of them as it struck a tree not far away.

"Yeah, 'cathartic…' that's just what I was thinking," said Becca.

Davis pulled Becca onto his lap and she responded by wrapping her legs tightly around his hips. They bowed their heads, foreheads touching, two wounded hands clutching, the other two behind the other's head, knowing there was no cover there on the top of the mesa. They were drenched in a matter of seconds but hardly noticed.

Their awareness had been drawn completely inside.

They had known physical union before on numerous levels—affection, sex and that other even more cellular fusion through their graft—but something beyond all that was occurring now. Electric, fluid, as if the rain was melting then melding the two of them together. Their heartbeats, their rhythms, their brainwaves had synchronized, completely engaged in one common experience.

Neither wanted to break the bond, but eventually Davis opened his eyes and pulled back from their embrace.

"Whoa..." he said. "That was..."

"I know, right?!"

Davis turned his face up to the sky. The rain was still pelting, cold and strong against his face. "That's a hard rain," he spluttered.

Becca looked at him, his hair plastered on his head like a helmet, his dusty blue eyes mirroring the clouds. She threw her head back, laughing, and sang, "And it's a hard, it's a hard, it's a hard, it's a hard..."

Davis chimed in to finish the chorus, 'It's a hard rain... a gonna fall...'"

"And where have you been, my blue-eyed son?"

"And where have you been, my darling young one?"

"I don't know the words, la-la-la la-la-la"

"I don't know them either la-la-la la-la-la but it's a hard, it's a hard, it's a hard it's a hard..."

"It's a hard rain a gonna fall..."

They didn't move from their spot, secure in the knowledge if they were to be struck and killed by lightning, it could be months before the next intrepid climbers would make their way up to their mesa top and find their bleached and weathered bones intertwined for the rest of eternity after the vultures had picked them clean for the carrion they were.

Or something equally dramatic.

But the storm passed. Drenched, a little bloody but feeling baptized by the gospel of (the other) Dylan, they started making their way back down the mesa, though not without incident. The New Mexican dirt, especially in that area, is largely clay: hard as a rock when dry and slippery as snakeshit when wet. Both of them slipped numerous times on the way down, making the journey much more treacherous than the way up. The first couple of times seemed comical until Davis took a good tumble that put him close to a precipitous fall over the edge. After that, each footfall was more deliberate.

The rain had stopped but every surface was soaked. The clouds overhead were still threatening to open up at any second and while the lightning had tapered off considerably near them, the rumblings of the thunder came from all directions.

Then there was the rockface to deal with, now wet, with the two of them muddy and bloody. After a short deliberation, Davis pulled out his rope. Once again summoning up his ersatz Boy Scout skills, he fashioned a small loop with a series of square knots (one of really only two he actually knew) and then passed the other end of the rope through that to create a lariat. He found a sturdy gnarled pinyon pine that resisted his efforts to pull up as a test of its strength and fastened the free end of the rope around it, again, employing his series of trusty square knots with a clove hitch thrown in. I think that's how it goes...

"Here's the plan. You will go down first. We're going to slip this loop underneath your arms just as a precaution and I will keep some tension on it if you slip, but you will lower yourself down the same way you came up, just in reverse, OK?" said Davis, fairly confident in his strategy.

"Then what about you?" she asked.

"You'll be there to catch me. Y'know, both literally and metaphorically, 'cause isn't that what we just re-upped for?"

Becca gave him The Look. "Only you, Davis, would come up with that in this situation." Davis just grinned. Becca said, "And yes, I would. And yes, we did. But seriously..."

"After you are down, I will pull the rope back up and basically do the same thing. I won't be able to untie the rope from the tree once I'm down, but we can just leave it here for the next couple that's coming up here to renew their vows."

"OK. Sounds doable."

Becca looped the rope around her waist and then let it come up under her arms as she began to make her descent. She lowered herself over the shelf and extended her leg out for purchase, found a foothold and began to work her way down. The rock surface had become slick from the rain but the handholds were substantial enough to easily support her. Davis, meanwhile, took up the slack in the rope, finding whatever leverage he could in the slippery surface above her.

She inched her way down, reaching that tricky part where she had gotten "stuck" on the way up, the foothold being a bit lower than she would have liked. Not being able to see it, she fished around with her boot and thought she had found it when her foot slipped, putting all of her weight on her hands, which then also gave way. This left Davis supporting all of her weight from above and he got pulled forward abruptly, losing his grip on the rope.

The loop around Becca slithered off one of her arms and spun her around so her back was to the rock wall face, tightening with the knot right across her neck. She flailed about, being held in space tied off at the tree above. Davis scrambled to his feet and saw her dangling there, as she tried to reach behind and above her, not being able to get any hold on the rope or the wall.

Peering over the edge, Davis could see if he pulled upwards on the rope it was just going to tighten across Becca's throat but her feet were almost to the bottom of the rock face. She needed about another two feet to give the rope enough slack to take the pressure off her neck. He tried untying the knots on the tree, but the weight on the rope made it too tight.

He decided to climb down the rock face, scrambling as quickly as he could. When he got even with her, he could see the terror in her eyes; the rope was cutting off her windpipe. She was not able to make a sound. He pushed off the rockface backwards, letting himself fall the last ten feet or so. When he hit, he felt his left ankle crumble under him and a pain shot up his leg. Ignoring that, he crouched under Becca's dangling feet so she could stand on his back and take the weight off the rope, which immediately slackened allowing Becca to wriggle away.

He could hear her wheeze in a big breath and then collapse on top of him.

The sound of thunder roared loudly around them.

Davis untangled himself from Becca and propped her up against the face of the mesa.

"Are you OK?" he asked.

Becca's eyes were still wide with fear and she tried to take full breaths, but each intake was labored and raspy. She tried to speak.

But no sound was forthcoming.

Davis said, "Can you breathe?"

Becca again took a labored breath but nodded yes.

"OK, we have to get you to a hospital."

Becca motioned up above them, indicating their packs were still there.

"It's too risky to go back up. We just have to leave them."

Davis tried to stand and his leg gave way underneath him, his ankle broken. Becca stood in an attempt to support him.

"Aren't we a pair?" Davis said. He fought through the pain and stood, the two of them linking arms over each other's shoulders.

It took hours for them to make their way back to the Landcruiser. The sun had set and they had to find their way back to the Landcruiser in the encroaching darkness, the flashlights they had been so proactive in bringing left behind in their packs on the mesa. They collapsed into the hard, torn up seats, that had never felt so comfortable.

Davis had a moment of panic when he considered he may have transferred the key into his backpack, but was relieved when he dug in his left-hand pocket and discovered it was still there. He tried to depress the clutch with his left foot and felt the pain shoot up his leg.

"Fuck!" he screamed. He put the clutch in with his right foot, shifted the 'Cruiser into neutral and got it started. "You don't know how to drive a stick, do you?" he asked. Davis looked over at her, her face barely illuminated by the meager dashboard lights, shaking her head.

"How are you doing? Are you breathing OK?"

Becca rasped in another breath but was still not able to speak.

"OK. Let's switch seats. I am going to teach you how to drive a clutch."

They switched seats and Davis explained the basic procedure of clutching-out while stepping on the gas. Once he got the explanation done, he said looked over at her, her bedraggled hair in ringlets around her face. "Let's not make that an annual event, OK?"

Becca coughed out a chuckle.

"Let's do this. You take care of the clutch, the steering and the gas, I will shift."

There were the to-be-expected number of stalls, but finally, together, they got the Landcruiser to lurch forward heading back down the rutted forest road. Davis was largely able to ignore the pain in his ankle, as long as he didn't put any weight on it. He had turned in the passenger seat, facing Becca, concerned that, at any moment, whatever was preventing her from fully breathing could worsen. He kept his left hand on her shoulder, with his right hand ready to grab the steering wheel if necessary.

He had kept his cell phone in the vehicle knowing they probably weren't going to have service on the mesa anyway and he kept checking it to see if they were getting to any point where he could dial 911, but no luck. When they finally made it back out to Route 287, Davis had to make a decision about whether to head towards Taos or Santa Fe. He chose to go south towards Santa Fe, knowing there was a better chance of finding some help along the way, perhaps in Espanola.

They didn't stop at the stop sign onto the main road, not wanting to stall and Davis was able to coax Becca and the Landcruiser through the gears so they could make some time. The chance of passing a cop while speeding was slim but that would have been best case scenario anyway. As they got close to Abiquiu, Davis finally noticed a bar on his cell service. He pressed the 911 that had already been dialed to send and a voice came over the phone.

"911. What is your emergency?"

48

April 1999

A New Level of Unbelievable

Spring in Santa Fe is completely unpredictable. Sitting at 7000 feet, at the southern end of the Rocky Mountain chain, it can snow all the way until the middle of May. This April, though, the cold weather had held off and the apricot trees had bloomed, promising fruit later in the summer. It had been almost a year since the Mishap at the Mesa, as Davis and Becca jokingly referred to their harrowing experience.

The kids were back at school after break, Mayah now excelling in high school and Dylan finding his way in grade school. It was just past lunch at home with the windows open to let some fresh spring air in. Davis was in the studio, putting some finishing touches on a canvas when Becca came in and tapped him on the shoulder. He turned around to see a concerned look on her face as she motioned for him to come into the family room where the TV was on.

A 'Breaking News' banner displayed on the bottom headlined an ongoing crisis in Colorado, where two students had opened fire on classmates and teachers at their high school.

Davis had a visceral reaction in his gut, after his experiences with those numerous high-profile shootings in the past. With his eyes glued to the screen, he stood as reporters disclosed what information they knew. Davis felt Becca's touch again on his arm and he diverted his eyes from the screen, knowing she had something to communicate.

"My God. This is terrible," she signed.

"Yes, it is," he signed back.

As they watched the tragedy unfold over the next hours, it was brought closer to home, first by having their daughter in a high school, and second, by having one of the perpetrators being named Dylan. The crisis at Columbine would stretch on for hours and the aftereffects for years, as some of the security of everyday life that was taken for granted had been stripped away. For Davis, it put him in a funk for weeks, as he not only revisited his past, but now had a new concern for those his job was to protect. As the immediacy faded, Davis came around to a sense of appreciation for having left so much violence behind, much of which, for him, was symbolized by the bullet that still lay buried in the silt of the Mississippi River off the banks of New Orleans.

Since Davis's uncanny proximity to the Lennon and Reagan shootings, not to mention his involvement at Kent State, he had taken a decidedly anti-gun stance over the years and had been relieved his association to gun-related violence had ended. Having a like-named son was as close as he wanted to be to this one, which was seeming to take America's grisly obsession with guns to a new, horrific level.

49

August 2001

Mayah in the Big City

As Mayah went through her teenage years, she never let go of the idea of attending college in NYC. Davis and Becca supported the idea. After all, both of them had roots there. Davis in particular, as much as he loved the solitude of New Mexico, loved the culture and the hustle and bustle of the East Coast, although more recently, he liked the idea of visiting and calling the Southwest home.

Mayah had stayed in contact with her biological father, and he and Corinne, his wife, were also completely on board. She worked as an administrator in the New York Public school system and had ties with many of the continuing education opportunities in the city, which were almost limitless, including the biggies, like Julliard and Pratt. Mayah was not convinced the performing arts were her final path, and Becca and Davis after discussions with Corrine, felt she might get lost in some of the higher profile programs.

As they winnowed out options, a small college in southern Manhattan kept coming up: Tisch School of the Arts. Nestled in Greenwich Village, it is a small arts-oriented school started in 1965 as part of the NYU network. Their brochure kept going into the pile of keepers. There was some discussion about Mayah staying and living with the Lewises, but Mayah also wanted to have the full 'being away at college' experience, including living in a tinytiny dorm room, grabbing coffee at the local Greek deli on the corner and also having her freedom, a concept both her mom and dad were quite familiar with.

She applied and was accepted in the fall of 2000 and had come back to begin her sophomore year the next year.

The school was located right on Broadway near Washington Square Park, where she had first met her biodad, as she called him. She was able to get a part time clerk position as part of a work/study program at one of the hundreds of companies down in the financial district just a dozen blocks and a bus ride away.

50

September 2001

It Coulda Been Worse

The last few years had been a mixed bag for the Lakaris/Filkinses (as they never, ever, for good reason, referred to themselves). The whole household had to adjust to Becca having lost her voice. Not only could she no longer sing, but they had to adapt to a new way of communicating. Luckily, much of the last tour had been recorded and when news of the accident was made public, it boosted the subsequent CD release sales, much to Chad's delight.

The injury to her vocal cords was rare, and doctors were puzzled over her total loss of voice. At her core, Becca had NEVER been at a loss for words, she ALWAYS had a voice, she STILL had a voice.

She just didn't have an actual voice.

For Davis and Becca, considering what they had engaged in on top of the mesa, and what they had experienced on the way down, they still were on the plus side of the balance sheet. Davis's leg would heal, and although Becca's throat didn't, at least not to the point where it would create sound, they felt fortunate to have come away from their calamity with only the consequences they did.

Somewhat removed from their immediate family but not their community, tragically, Willy DeVille had come home one day to find his wife Lisa having died of suicide by hanging. He had to cut her down; it was devasting to him. Shortly after, in what may have been a suicide path of his own, he got in a car wreck that paralyzed him for years.

He stayed in New Mexico for a while longer but eventually moved to Europe and got back into the music world.

THAT would stay in his veins.

51

Early September

It was late summer.

Davis had been back to New York to finalize paperwork on the sale of his ownership in Whirled Records. Profits over the years had dwindled. CDs had replaced records and although there was a collector's market for vinyl, the availability of all collectibles on the rapidly expanding worldwideweb was causing values to plummet. He felt it was time to get out, and he had a decent offer to sell. He planned to visit with Mayah at school and take another day to visit his Jersey home town to see one of his childhood buddies, Gene, who was still struggling with PTSD from the Vietnam war.

He was due to fly out of Newark to San Francisco and then back home to Albuquerque. It was longer than a direct flight but all of those flights had been booked. He had rented a car and allowed himself what seemed like plenty of time to get to the airport for his early flight. What he hadn't allowed for was how many early commuters there were and the accident on the Garden State Parkway that tied traffic up for an hour and a half.

He returned his rental car and found himself emulating OJ Simpson in the old running-through-the-airport commercials only to get to his gate as the plane was pulling away from the loading area.

Frustrated, he texted Becca to let her know he was going to have to make other plans for getting home.

How did evrythng go? she texted back.

Mayahs doing gr8 Luvs the city   Gt the deal done papers signed $ changed

Im sorry u missed ur flight Hav u chkt 2 c when u can gt on a l8r flt?

Nt yt Im really POd tht I missed this 1 I may have 2 stay ovrnt Anxious 2 gt home IMU

NP IMU2, but Im glad ur OK Hpfly u can gt on a flt 2moro 9/11, 9/12 whts 1 more day rt?

:(TTYL ILU

ILU2 XOXO

Davis made his way over to the ticket counters, only to be told that, for the time being, all flights had been grounded.

"NOW what the fuck?" he muttered under his breath and stormed away from the counter.

He passed by one of the ubiquitous airport bars and saw an unusually large crowd gathered around the TV screen. He moved closer. "What's going on?"

"It's the World Trade Center..."

ABOUT THE AUTHOR

Roman Ramsey is also the author of
"This Glorious Mess:
Creating a New Paradigm for Relationships"

The prequel to this book:
"Within You Without You: a novel."

And the sequel to this book "WITH."

He lives in Boulder, Colorado.

www.romanramsey.com

Made in the USA
Middletown, DE
26 July 2022